Loving Her

Other titles in
The Northeastern Library of Black Literature
edited by Richard Yarborough

LLOYD L. BROWN / *Iron City*
STERLING A. BROWN / *A Son's Return: Selected Essays*
WILLIAM DEMBY / *The Catacombs*
W. E. B. DU BOIS / *The Quest of the Silver Fleece*
JESSIE REDMON FAUSET / *The Chinaberry Tree*
There Is Confusion
GAYL JONES / *White Rat*
ANDREA LEE / *Sarah Phillips*
JULIAN MAYFIELD / *The Hit* and *The Long Night*
CLAUDE MCKAY / *Home to Harlem*
ALBERT MURRAY / *Train Whistle Guitar*
J. SAUNDERS REDDING / *Stranger and Alone*
GEORGE S. SCHUYLER / *Black Empire*
Black No More
Ethiopian Stories
WALLACE THURMAN / *Infants of the Spring*
RICHARD WRIGHT / *Lawd Today!*

Loving Her

ANN ALLEN SHOCKLEY

Northeastern University Press
BOSTON

Copyright 1974 by Ann Allen Shockley

First published in 1974 by Bobbs-Merrill; first paperback printing in 1978 by Avon Books; reprinted in 1987 by Naiad Press. Reprinted in 1997 by Northeastern University Press.

All rights reserved. Except for the quotation of short passages for the purposes of criticism and review, no part of this book may be reproduced in any form or by any means, electronic or mechanical, including photocopying, recording, or any information storage and retrieval system now known or to be invented, without written permission of the publisher.

Library of Congress Cataloging-in-Publication Data

Shockley, Ann Allen.
Loving her / Ann Allen Shockley.
p. cm.—(The Northeastern library of Black literature)
ISBN 1-55553-329-9
1. Lesbians—United States—Fiction. 2. Afro-American lesbians—Fiction. I. Title. II. Series.
[PS3569.H568L68   1997]
813'.54—dc21   97-18233

Printed and bound by Thomson-Shore, Inc., Dexter, Michigan. The paper is Glatfelter Supple Opaque Recycled, an acid-free sheet.

MANUFACTURED IN THE UNITED STATES OF AMERICA
01 00 99 98 97   5 4 3 2 1

FOREWORD

"For Black Lesbians," writes novelist and critic Jewelle Gomez, reading Ann Allen Shockley's first novel, *Loving Her* (1974), "was like reading *The Well of Loneliness* for the first time as teenagers and realizing there were 'others' out there." Gomez's invocation of Radclyffe Hall's novel, published in England in 1928, is apt indeed, for *The Well of Loneliness* was the first novel to engage an explicitly lesbian theme. *Loving Her* is a groundbreaking text as well; not only is it the first African American novel written with an explicitly lesbian theme, but it is the first to feature a black lesbian as its protagonist.

Of course, the operative word here is "explicitly." As critics Deborah McDowell, Gloria T. Hull, Barbara Smith, and others have shown, *Loving Her* does have its forerunners. Nella Larsen's *Quicksand* (1928) and *Passing* (1929); the poetry of Harlem Renaissance writers Angelina Weld Grimké, Alice Dunbar-Nelson, and Georgia Douglass Johnson; the early poetry of Audre Lorde—all of these works are to some degree marked by an unmistakable and yet concealed homoerotics, "lesbian themes" played out, perhaps, in as safe a way as possible. The times in which these authors were writing did not provide the space for them to tell explicitly—if, in fact, they desired to do so—a black lesbian story. The experience of Radclyffe Hall (who was a contemporary of Larsen, Grimké, Dunbar-Nelson, and Johnson) speaks to the politically repressive conditions under which lesbians lived in the first decades of the twentieth century. Hall's work was, upon its release, tried for obscenity in England and subsequently banned in that country; the lower courts of the United States rendered a similar decision on the novel. Only after a successful appeal was *The Well of Loneliness* published here, the fact of which did not, of course, end the controversy surrounding the text and the homophobic diatribes against it.

It took the Civil Rights, Black Power, Women's Liberation, New Left, and Gay Liberation movements of the 1960s and early 1970s—not to mention the groundbreaking Warren Court decisions on obscenity rendered in the late 1950s—to make the space, a very small but important space, for a text such as *Loving Her*. That *Loving Her*'s time had definitely arrived is indicated by the fact that the novel was published in the same year in which black feminists of Boston, calling themselves the Combahee River Collective, organized to fight "racial, sexual, heterosexual, and class oppression"; only months after the National Black Feminist Organization held its first public meeting to address such issues as welfare, sexism within black communities, and lesbian oppression; and a year after *The Black Scholar* dedicated an issue to black feminist concerns.

Loving Her is the story of Renay Lee, a twenty-something musician who, after years of marriage to the abusive, alcoholic Jerome (whom she married because he impregnated her when he raped her after their date at his fraternity dance), leaves him—with their daughter Denise in tow—for Terry, a wealthy white lesbian writer. With Terry, Renay realizes that for all the years she had been with Jerome, she had been simply going through the motions of life. "Now she felt alive again, living to love, loving to live."

Unlike Jerome, Terry encourages Renay's love for music, sends her to school so that she can finish the music degree that she was pursuing before she got pregnant, and provides and cares for Denise, who, in her new environment away from Jerome, "had grown more outgoing." Moreover, Terry helps Renay to face what she knew "had always been there, deep within. Her Lesbianism. Terry had helped her bring it out." In so doing, Terry "helped to kindle the flames" of Renay's "desire. She *enjoyed* sex with Terry. Now she looked forward not only to the nights but to the days. There was life in life now, and love in its moments." Renay, in turn, brings to Terry a sense of family and home. Before Renay, Terry's life had been just a string of endless love affairs in which she gave more than she ever received. With Renay, Terry is now "happier than she had ever been."

But Jerome has no intention of letting Renay go so easily. He soon discovers not only where she and Denise are living, but the

Loving Her

nature of Renay and Terry's relationship. Upon confronting Renay, Jerome threatens to take Denise and beats Renay so badly that she must be hospitalized. Jerome later finds that Denise is staying with Renay's mother, and he promptly apprehends his daughter. Drunk when he takes her away, he consequently has an accident in which Denise is killed and he himself escapes unscathed. Grief-stricken, Renay leaves Terry to deal with her sorrow alone, for she feels somehow that God has punished her for loving Terry. In the end, however, Renay returns to her lover, ready to start life all over again.

Loving Her is not a stylistically successful novel, which is forgivable since it is Shockley's first (she would follow up this work six years later with the publication of *The Black and White of It*, a collection of lesbian short stories, and twelve years later with her second novel, *Say Jesus and Come to Me*). This is not to say that the art of writing was new to Shockley; indeed, her career as a writer dates back to the 1940s, to her undergraduate years at Fisk University, where she wrote for the *Fisk Herald* (Shockley is now the university's Associate Librarian for Special Collections). From then on she contributed articles and short stories to such periodicals as the *Louisville Defender* (published in Louisville, Kentucky, where she was born in 1927), the *Afro-American*, and a host of professional outlets, including *Library Journal*, *College Library Notes*, and *Southeastern Librarian*. Shockley also has edited such works as *Living Black American Authors: A Biographical Directory* and *Handbook of Black Librarianship*. During the 1960s and early 1970s, she contributed work to such journals as *Black World*, *Phylon*, *Umbra*, and *Freedomways*.

Nevertheless, *Loving Her* is marred by a number of formal weaknesses, not the least of which is Shockley's representation of Renay and Terry's relationship as devoid of racial tension. This lack is quite remarkable, given that Terry's "life had been solidly WASP. Before knowing Renay," Shockley writes, Terry "had never been exposed to or closely associated with blacks." Shockley then gives a flimsy rationale for Terry's racial innocence: "In her white-gilded ghetto, she had been totally isolated from" the "ugliness of racism. Besides, her personal burden of invertedness and its stigma had been uppermost in her mind." To believe that such a white person exists is certainly to stretch one's imagination. Granted, Shockley does provide characters who view the couple from a racist perspective. Yet racism is never a *relationship* issue for Renay and Terry; that is, it is never something the couple has to struggle with and fight about from time to time in order to make their relationship work in a racially polarized society.

As the above quotation shows, the novel is also strangely replete with archaic terms such as "invertedness" and "homophile"; thus, it often reads more like a work set in Radclyffe Hall's time than one written not only in the midst of the Gay Liberation movement, but in the same year that the American Psychiatric Association struck homosexuality off its list of mental disorders. Combined with trite language like "he pinned her shoulders down with his weight, trying to shove his male dagger into the secret abyss of her being," and long, ponderous sentences, such terms often make for tough reading.

These and other problems, however, do not take away from the significance of *Loving Her*. As Alice Walker wrote in her 1975 *Ms.* magazine review of the novel, "its exploration of a daring subject boldly shared" makes it a work of "immense value." Moreover, the novel did, as Jewelle Gomez claimed, alert black lesbians to the fact that others were out there, as it also demonstrated that they, too, could write explicitly about their lives.

The consensus among the text's critics, it seems, is that *Loving Her* is valuable only insofar as it is a first and puts black lesbians on the African American literary-historical map. It is also important, I would argue, because it stands among the canon of black women's novels written during the 1970s that, as critic Madhu Dubey argues in *Black Women Novelists and the Nationalist Aesthetic*, "dialogize the ideological discourse" of 1960s and early 1970s black nationalism. *Loving Her*, in other words, conducts a "subtextual dialogue" with black nationalist discourses on a wide range of issues; indeed, the novel often "dislocates" them from their "original context" and reframes them "in an alien fictional context." By so doing, *Loving Her* exposes the sexist contradictions in black nationalist utterances.

Through the character of Jerome, for example, Shockley clearly engages and critiques nationalist rhetoric on the black family and the appropriation of the black matriarchy myth. Asserting that black women not only dominate the black family but are complicit with the "white power structure's" emasculation of black men, many nationalists of the 1960s and early 1970s proposed as a corrective that the black male be reinstated into his rightful role as head of the

Loving Her

black family. In "Will the Real Black Man Please Stand Up?," Nathan Hare, for example, argues:

> Historically, the white oppressor has pitted male against female and, in the analysis of Frantz Fanon, forced and seduced the female to take on his values and through her emasculated and controlled the man.
> This is the day of the black male, when we must take up with ever more resolve the role of liberator, and, in collaboration with the black woman, begin to transcend the role which the black woman heretofore has played as an organizer of the family, our youth, and therefore our future.

Shockley uses Jerome to expose the repressive nature of rhetoric such as Hare's. Having established Jerome as the ruler of his household, she then constructs him as a particularly ruthless and domineering figure. When he is home, for example, Renay is expected to jump to his every command; and if she fails to carry out his wishes, she has to face his brutal beatings. Shockley also makes Jerome ventriloquize nationalist articulations of the matriarchy myth. "You know we black men have a hard enough time as it is making it in the white man's world. . . . All you castrating black bitches want to keep a man down. *Ruin* him. Just like my mama ran my daddy away. Always after him. And *you*. What goddam good are *you* to a man? Not even a good screw!" In having Jerome speak these words, Shockley subtly equates black nationalists' discourse with Jerome's abusive behavior, which is to say that Jerome is, in *Loving Her*, the nationalist discourse incarnate.

Through her characterization of Jerome, then, Shockley argues that the (fundamentally white middle-class) family model that nationalists idealize proposes for black women *not* domestic bliss, but domestic violence. Moreover, it promises for black women a life of enslavement to black men, a point Shockley specifically makes in the scene in which Renay finally decides to leave Jerome:

> She moved her foot tentatively across the bed to assure herself that he wasn't there. No, he really wasn't there. The realization drowned out the rain and caused new life to flow within her. She opened her eyes in relief. He was gone. This meant it had to be today that she would do what she should have done long ago.
> She sprang up, throwing the covers back in disarray. Quickly she

ran across the hall to where the little girl slept curled up with her arms over her head.

If she wouldn't think about it—just *do*. Don't think. Not one second for thought. "Denise—darling—wake up!" Impatiently she shook the child. "We have to go away. Hurry!"

In this powerful scene, Shockley clearly constructs Renay as a runaway slave. Renay doesn't simply leave Jerome; she *escapes*, and under the cover of secrecy. Renay must take advantage of the slavemaster's absence; and since she is never quite sure when he might reappear, she must hurry before he returns. With just a suitcase full of her and Denise's clothes, Renay flees to Terry's apartment—flees, that is, to freedom.

In a particularly radical gesture, Shockley displaces onto Renay and Terry's home the domestic bliss that nationalists imagine will define the black household once it is taken over by men. The relationship between the two women, Shockley writes, "resembled that of a married couple, except that they could not proclaim themselves man and wife." This statement is necessarily ironic, for Renay and Terry's life together hardly resembles Renay and Jerome's marriage, which is the only one that we see in this novel. In fact, the former is based on mutual support and respect. For this reason, Renay's life with Terry is quite liberating. "For the first time in a long while," Renay was "free to do what she wanted when she felt like it, not bound by a routine that had to be followed for someone else. She was free to rest as long as she wanted."

Indeed, the equity in the two women's relationship is part of what makes the sex between Renay and Terry so good; with Terry, sex is "a wonderful feeling, like that of the giver and the gift." Thus, Renay wants it "in the morning, at noon and at night." She could "just lie beside Terry without Terry's touch and feel the stirring spasms of desire." Not so with Jerome. "The bed was his kingdom, the womb his domain, and the penis his mojo hung with black magic." Because Jerome's thoughts had only "been of himself," Renay had never experienced an orgasm with him. After her first time with Terry, with whom she does have an orgasm, Renay proclaims, " 'I didn't know it *could* be like that—' It had never been with him. The hurried mounting of her, the jabbing inside her with the acrid whiskey odor heavy in her nostrils. It had always been over in seconds; then he would turn over and go to sleep."

Loving Her

By displacing onto Renay and Terry's home the domestic bliss that nationalists idealize, Shockley revises their conceptualization of home and family and claims that it must, if it is to be viable, resemble what Renay and Terry have created. Now, this is not to say that Shockley proposes that black women simply give up black men and become lesbians, even though she doesn't think that that would be such a bad idea. At one point, she actually appropriates the black matriarchy myth herself to suggest that becoming lesbians may be the answer: "You know," Renay says to Terry, "it's a wonder all black women aren't in our world. They're the ones who can get the jobs, the ones left alone to bring up the children, the ones who head the families when the man isn't and often times *is* there. Black Amazons whose tallness and strength lie in their hearts and minds and wills." Shockley does argue, however, that black women who choose to be with black men deserve something better than the repressive model of home and family that nationalists offer.

Both Shockley's representations of sex and her decision to develop an interracial lesbian relationship contest yet another nationalist claim: that homosexuality is a "white thing," a product of the decadence of white culture. Shockley absolutely delights in confronting this claim, and nowhere is this clearer than in the moments when she has Renay reflect upon Terry's white body after the two women have made love. "Funny how she could love Terry so deeply that she did not see Terry's white skin—only knew of Terry's heart and the love in it," Shockley writes. And again:

> Tracing the whiteness of Terry's skin with her finger, Renay thought, *It is amazing how I can lie here and see and feel this skin and not think of the awful things others of her color have done to us. And yet, my skin is light-tinged with the sun. Someone, somewhere in the past, must have done and thought and felt like this with another—or hated in a different and helpless way.*
> (italics in original)

And yet again, in a more polemical passage, Shockley asserts, "'Blackopaths' would question her capacity to love a white. She recalled the bull sessions in the dormitory when the girls would wonder how Lena Horne and Pearl Bailey could wake up in the morning to white faces besides them. But now she knew: you can't confine love to color or object."

These moments of reflection become occasions for Shockley to construct desire as exceeding and transcending race or, more precisely, to construct the body as forgetting race in its quest for joy. Renay, for example, doesn't "see Terry's white skin" in the moment of desire; she doesn't "think of the awful thing others of her color have done." Once the body forgets, Shockley implies, then it is capable not only of a vast range of desires, but also of desiring a vast array of objects—which means that race does not truly determine desire. In a sense, the body—Renay's body—frees itself of limiting constructions of race, gender, and sexuality, so that the only thing that is real is how one feels. Homosexuality and homosexual desire, then, are not white, any more than an orgasm is white.

As Shockley realizes, however, race, gender, and sexuality norms can straitjacket the body and its desires. This point she drives home in her polemic on black women's homophobia. Black women, she writes, are

> the most vehement about women loving each other. This kind of love [is] worse to them than the acts of adultery or incest, for it [is] homophile. It [is] worse than being inflicted with an incurable disease. Black women [can] be sympathetic about illegitimacy, raising the children of others, having affairs with married men—but not toward Lesbianism, which many [blame] on white women.

However, she proclaims, black women probably feel this way "because of the fear bred from their deep inward potentiality for Lesbianism." Shockley implies that black women shortchange their potential for experiencing joy (and in this case, the joy of "Lesbianism") and do so by keeping their bodies imprisoned within race, gender, and sexuality norms. Indeed, keeping her own body imprisoned was Renay's downfall, the fact of which Shockley illustrates in the scene with Renay and her college roommate, Marissa. In this passage, Marissa pressures Renay into dating Jerome Lee, who has made his interest in Renay clear:

> "Honey, I just can't see *how* in the hell you can pass up that good-looking hunk of man." Then, angered by Renay's silence, she sneered half-seriously, half-mockingly: "You *do* like *men*, don't you?"
> For some unknown reason, Renay felt the heat rise in her body, flushing her face. Her head swam, blurring the words before her. When

she replied, the voice did not sound like her own. "Of course I do. Whatever gave you the idea that I didn't?"

Marissa gave a short, snorting laugh before turning over to fall asleep. Later, Renay wondered why she had bothered to answer her roommate at all.

To rid herself of Marissa's probing, which was becoming increasingly more persistent, she relented and went with Jerome Lee to a movie. Afterward, there was a steady succession of dances, movies and beer dates.

In exchange for the social legitimacy that heterosexuality accords, Renay gives up her body's potential for joy. "At no time" with Jerome "could she respond or did she feel an answering spark within her . . . During the times of his lovemaking, she would lie there quietly, gritting her teeth, hands gripping the sides of the bed, and wait impatiently for his climax." It is only after she gets together with Terry that she realizes how much "beauty had been wasted in the past." After reflecting on her years with Jerome, Renay realizes that she "could never do that again, for she had found what she wanted and needed most. She was now aware of herself and the part she had tried to deny." Renay, in other words, realizes that she had denied not only her sexuality but pleasure itself.

Unfortunately, Shockley does not always trust her narrative's capacity to undermine effectively the ideological discourses of black nationalism; consequently, she falls back on giving her characters bewildering speeches, such as the one in which Renay wonders why more black women aren't in the life, or she herself interrupts the story to make her own speech. The result is simply weak prose, full of clichés, gross generalizations, and stereotypical constructions of black men and women. The truth is, Shockley is most effective when she is most subtle, when she lets her narrative do the signifying.

Her critical project was, nevertheless, successful enough to incur the wrath of some critics. Frank Lamont Phillips is a case in point. In his notorious review of *Loving Her,* published in *Black World,* it is clear that *what* he takes issue with in *Loving Her* and *how* he does so has everything to do with Shockley's assault on black nationalist discourse. Nowhere is this more clear than in his critique of *Loving Her* as a "shabby example of the novelist's craft. . . . Her short fiction and articles have been published in *Black World* and in various professional journals. She should know better." Phillips is, in coded terms, accusing Shockley of failing to fulfill the criteria for authentic black art. Of course, the issue of *black* art was hotly debated throughout the 1960s and early 1970s by Black Arts Movement artists and critics. Generally speaking, black art, many asserted, should be uplifting, "address and affirm a unified black community" (Dubey), gear black people toward revolutionary struggle, and affirm the beauty of blackness. For Phillips, *Loving Her* fails as black art not only because it depicts a black male in such a negative manner but because it dares to idealize an interracial lesbian relationship. As the critic Rita B. Dandridge remarks, "a staunch supporter of intraracial, heterosexual relationships, Phillips views other sexual unions as unfit material for a black woman novelist to write about."

In *Loving Her*, Shockley confronts directly the repressive implications of the so-called black aesthetics of her day. Indeed, not only does Shockley take issue with black cultural nationalism's narrow definitions of what constitutes *black* art, but she more critically reads black aesthetics as a masculinist, heterosexist discourse, one that constrains black women's creativity. Shockley's critique unfolds through her narrative on Renay's piano. The latter, which Renay's mother sends to her years after she and Jerome are married, is Renay's only respite from the oppression of her household. "Perhaps," Shockley writes, "her mother had sensed from afar the terrible loneliness." Renay had taken piano lessons when she was younger, and her mother worked hard to ensure that Renay could develop her talent. Since Jerome was rarely home and very often did not send her and Denise money to live on, Renay took a job as a pianist at a supper club so that she could pay the bills. Thus, the piano is not only something that makes "her life less lonely in the small, dingy four-room apartment" but also the source of her livelihood.

Jerome is far from supportive of Renay's music, however. "Those times when he would come sulkily home to find her at the piano, he would storm angrily: 'Will you stop that goddam banging! It ain't getting you or me anywhere. Ain't nobody going to listen to that shit. Let me hear some funky music!' " Tired of his criticism and in order "to prove her varied talent," Renay plays "his kind of music to show that she could. But he sneered back at her: 'You just ain't got it. You can't play worth a damn, and it's time you knew it.

I'm your husband, so don't that make me the best critic?'" Eventually Jerome sells the piano when Renay is away from home and declares that it was just "an old piece of junk anyway."

Through this battle between Jerome and Renay, Shockley poignantly dramatizes the debates on black art. Moreover, she uses Jerome to represent the limitations and more repressive elements of black aesthetics—in particular, its condemnation of art and artists that fail to conform to prescribed critical standards. Jerome's selling the piano and proclaiming that it is "junk anyway" signifies the frequency with which black aesthetic theorists have laid waste to so much valuable art by deeming it insufficiently black. And, finally, Jerome's abuse of Renay, his discovery that "deriding her talent" is "the best way to demean and hurt her," critiques black aesthetics as especially repressive for women artists. When subject to male judgment, Shockley argues, black women's work is often denigrated and belittled.

It is only after she escapes Jerome and moves in with Terry, who purchases a piano for her, that Renay's talent once again flourishes. Indeed, Shockley privileges Terry's critical perspective and appreciation of art over Jerome's. That is, through Terry's reaction to Renay's music, we are made to realize not only that Renay is a talented artist, but that her art is both valuable and real: "There were times in the evenings when she played just for Terry, who would lean back, close her eyes and listen appreciatively to the sounds she wove. She would play anything Terry wanted to hear, from Beethoven to Ray Charles."

Ironically, the critic Frank Lamont Phillips ends up occupying the position of Jerome. His patronizing attitude toward Shockley, his condemnation of her art, and his masculinist as well as heterosexist diatribe are precisely what Jerome embodies and what Shockley holds up to ridicule.

Reconsidered as a text that confronts the ideological discourses of black nationalism, *Loving Her* proves to exceed its role as a first and as a feel-good novel for black lesbians. Like its sister texts—*Sula, The Bluest Eye, Corregidora, The Third Life of Grange Copeland*—it must be appreciated for its participation in the critical debates of the 1960s and 1970s on issues that profoundly affected black women's lives.

ALYCEE J. LANE

BIBLIOGRAPHY

"A Black Feminist Statement: Combahee River Collective." In *This Bridge Called My Back: Writings by Radical Women of Color*, pp. 210–218. Ed. Cherríe Moraga and Gloria Anzaldúa. New York: Kitchen Table: Women of Color Press, 1981.

Dandridge, Rita B. "Gathering Pieces: A Selected Bibliography of Ann Allen Shockley." *Black American Literature Forum* 21 (Spring–Summer 1987): 133–146.

———. "Male Critics/Black Women's Novels." *CLA Journal* 23 (Sept. 1979): 1–11.

D'Emilio, John, and Estelle B. Freedman. *Intimate Matters: A History of Sexuality in America*. New York: Harper and Row, 1988.

Dubey, Madhu. *Black Women Novelists and the Nationalist Aesthetic*. Bloomington: Indiana University Press, 1994.

Golden, Bernette. "Black Women's Liberation." *Essence*, Feb. 1974, 36–37, 75–76, 86.

Gomez, Jewelle. "A Cultural Legacy Denied and Discovered: Black Lesbians in Fiction by Women." In *Homegirls: A Black Feminist Anthology*, pp. 110–123. Ed. Barbara Smith. New York: Kitchen Table: Women of Color Press, 1983.

Hare, Nathan. "Will the Real Black Man Please Stand Up?" *Black Scholar* 2 (June 1971): 32–35.

Houston, Helen R. "Ann Allen Shockley." In *Afro-American Fiction Writers after 1955*, pp. 232–236. Ed. Thadious M. Davis and Trudier Harris. *Dictionary of Literary Biography* 33. Detroit: Gale, 1984.

Phillips, Frank Lamont. Review of *Loving Her*, by Ann Allen Shockley. *Black World*, Sept. 1975, 89–90.

Rule, Jane. *Lesbian Images*. Trumansburg, N.Y.: Crossing Press, 1975.

Shockley, Ann Allen. *The Black and White of It*. Tallahassee: Naiad Press, 1980.

———. *Loving Her*. Tallahassee: Naiad Press, 1987.

———. *Say Jesus and Come to Me*. New York: Avon, 1982.

Walker, Alice. "A Daring Subject Boldly Shared." *Ms.*, April 1975, 120, 124.

I could love her with a love so warm
You could not break it with a fairy charm;
I could love her with a love so bold
It would not die, e'en tho' the world grew cold.

—The World Is a Mighty Ogre
by Fenton Johnson

CHAPTER 1

The April rain, insistent in its steady drumming, forced itself like an angry intruder against the narrow apartment windows, awakening her. She lay very still in the bed, not wanting to open her eyes to the grayness she knew was stalking the room. There were no sounds from the tiny alcove across the hall: Denise was still asleep. Despite last night, her daughter could yet sleep the child's rest of quick forgetfulness.

She moved her foot tentatively across the bed to assure herself that he wasn't there. No, he really wasn't there. The realization drowned out the rain and caused new life to flow within her. She opened her eyes in relief. He was gone. This meant it had to be today that she would do what she should have done long ago.

She sprang up, throwing the covers back in wild disarray. Quickly she ran across the hall to where the little girl slept curled up with her arms above her head.

If she wouldn't think about it—just *do*. Don't think. Not one second for thought. "Denise—darling—wake up!" Impatiently she shook the child. "We have to go away. Hurry!"

"Mommy?" The dark eyes, so like his, opened slowly. "Away?"

"Yes. Come. I have to pack our things."

"We going to Aunt Fran's?" Anticipating adventure, a new game, the child sat up quickly.

Opening drawers and flinging the child's clothes into a suitcase, she shook her head. "No, not this time."

"You and Daddy had a fuss again last night, didn't you?"

Had she heard it all? But hadn't she been exposed to the other nights and days of ceaseless argument? The hate spilling out in spiteful memories, the garbage accusations. Marital war more deadly than impersonal group battles. Two people piercing the armor of emotional frailty, crippling the spirit, wounding the heart, making each less human in the other's sight.

"Hurry and get dressed," she urged, moving to her room, where she continued to empty drawers and fill suitcases with the clothes she would need—especially the two black dresses for work. A whiskey bottle on the dresser blocked the path to her lipstick and powder. Reaching behind it, she saw that he had emptied it. Going to the kitchen to pour Denise a glass of milk, she found a half-empty bottle on the kitchen sink. When she handed Denise the milk, she saw a third smaller bottle, unopened, partially hidden near the bathroom.

"What's wrong with your face, Mommy? It's all puffed up." The milk made a light, thin handlebar curving the mouth where dimples garnished each side in deep half-moons. *Born for luck*, they all said, *just like her daddy had spat her out.*

"I must have slept too hard on it," she replied, averting her gaze. Lies, pouring out with ease once the stopper's been released. The back of a large black hand striking out in angry rebuttal against her and all the other black women before and after her.

She dressed quickly, putting on her raincoat and helping Denise into hers. "Let's go," she said, handing Denise the smaller bag and picking up the others.

"Where we going, Mommy?" Uplifted face brimming with excitement.

How to tell a seven-year-old where you were going? Was it even possible she was going there? "To a friend's," she replied quietly, and that was all.

She closed the door, knowing it was for the last time. She would never go back again. Not to that, or to him.

"We going to leave Daddy?"

Had she spoken the words, or were the thoughts that strong? "Yes, we're going to leave Daddy." To go where she wanted to go—the only place she wanted to be.

The rain made sounds like mockery against the cab's windows.

"Renay—you came!" The woman stood framed in the doorway, surprise and happiness brightening her face.

Renay's thoughts went first to the child, holding trustingly to her hand, staring up at a woman whom she had never seen. Had she done what was right? If only the child weren't involved, she thought, looking at the tall, slim woman with the shag-cut auburn hair, breasts small and firm under the white blouse opened low at the neck, hips slim in the blue slacks. The face was not pretty; it was too pale, as if she weren't out in the daylight enough, and the pointed nose was slightly too long over the thin lips. But the countenance showed strength and kindness, and the gray eyes were warm with a concern Renay hadn't seen in eyes for a long time.

"Are you all right?" the woman questioned anxiously, voice low. "Renay—"

Renay swayed, feeling weak from the night and the morning, and from seeing the woman now as she had always seen her, but not as she thought the child saw her. "Yes, Terry, I'm all right—now."

In the large apartment there was a small room just off the den where Terry did her writing. Here they placed Denise. It was a pleasant room with a television set, a studio couch, a large square window overlooking the park across the street, and shelves of books filling the walls.

Then they sat in the kitchen: Terry drinking coffee, and Renay coffee laced with brandy because Terry thought she needed it. She had not known that she needed it, but Terry had known, as always. It seemed to pour strength back into her and to warm her. Even the rain seemed cheerful now.

"He hit you."

It was a statement, not a question. She saw Terry's long fingers tense around the cup.

"Yes," she said quietly, ashamed that Terry should know.

Terry's hand trembled slightly as she reached for a pack of cigarettes. Lighting one, she tossed her head back in the familiar way, blowing wavering smoke trails above her head. "She's a darling—your little girl. I'm glad you brought her."

God, how she can read my mind. The words made her want to reach over, and she did, warming the woman's hand with her own.

"She apparently looks like him, but I think she's like you. Does she play the piano too?"

"A little. I've been giving her lessons." She took a deep breath, her cup making a jarring sound against the fragile saucer as she set it down. "The piano's gone. He sold it."

"What! How *could* he? Music is *you!*"

She shrugged, thinking, how can he do any of the things he does? "Drinking is an expensive habit. He said he needed the money." She gazed reflectively into the bottom of her cup. "Living with an alcoholic is hell—almost unbelievable. What he does, how he thinks and acts—everything is dependent upon how each drink affects him. One can put him in good spirits, two make him sad, and a lot of them, angry and belligerent. Then he just strikes out at everything around him. He starts pitying himself, and each drink helps him more to blame his weakness on someone other than himself—usually me."

"Are you going to work tonight?" Terry asked through tightened lips, deliberately focusing on the cigarette.

"It's Sunday, remember? The club's closed," Renay laughed, not really laughter but a spring of release.

"You don't ever have to go, you know."

"I want to. I'm lost without my music. I have to keep that part of me." Something to take her out of herself, to keep her from wallowing in the mire of self-pity.

"Sunday . . ." Terry savored the word, crushing out the cigarette. "For the first time, we have all day together."

"We have to be careful," Renay reminded her softly, thinking of the child.

"I know. Like married people," Terry smiled, bending to brush her cheek against the hand holding hers. "They wait for night."

Before the night came, they made a game with Denise of unpacking the suitcases and filling drawers. Because they were hungry and Terry didn't like to cook, Renay dug deeply into the kitchen cabinets and huge refrigerator for food. She came up with a dinner of broiled lamb chops, canned peas, instant mashed potatoes, and pear salad. They ate with undisguised delight. It seemed like a banquet.

"I can see that you seldom eat at home," Renay admonished as they did the dishes.

"It's too much trouble. I like your cooking, though. Tomorrow we'll stock up."

That evening they read the *New York Times* while Denise eagerly scanned the mountain of comic books Terry had gone to the drugstore to buy. In between, they worked a puzzle with Denise, listened to records, and said unspoken things to each other with eyes and touches and thoughts.

Finally Denise said: "Mommy, I'm sleepy."

"Off to bed then, darling." Renay took her hand, but the girl drew back.

"Are we going to stay here with her?"

Renay closed her eyes and tried to frame words, but they had already been framed.

"Of course, dear," Terry said gently. "Don't you think you'd like to live here with me?"

"Is Mommy going to be your maid?"

"No. Your mommy's my friend—my very dearest friend."

The girl frowned. "Daddy says the only thing we are to white people are maids and cooks and people who do dirty work. But Daddy's a salesman. He goes to beauty shops and sells stuff for hair."

Terry bent low, bringing her face close to the child. "I'm sure he must be a very good salesman."

The girl looked steadily at her. "I like you. You're not mean and evil like Daddy says white people are."

"There're mean and evil and good people everywhere. And I'm glad you like me."

Suddenly Denise smiled. "Can I call you Aunt Terry, since you're my Mommy's best friend?"

"Please do—"

"Goodnight, Aunt Terry."

"Goodnight, sweetheart."

All the lights were out in the apartment except the one in Terry's room. Terry had made them a nightcap while Renay showered, and now Renay was in the bed, sipping from a tall glass. Terry, still dressed, was sitting in a chair near the bed.

Finishing her drink, Renay set the glass on the nightstand. It seemed as though she had been here many times like this, watching Terry with her head back, eyes half-closed, drink held in her long fingers.

After a while, Terry got up and sat beside her on the edge of the bed. Her fingers traced a feather-light path across the high golden-hued cheekbones, the small nose and full mouth, lingering at the mass of black hair fanned out on the pillow. "Do you think it's all right now? Is she asleep?"

Renay trembled, as she always did when Terry touched her. The contact was electric, causing her body to shudder in a fine, delicate storm. "Yes—," she said almost inaudibly.

Quickly, Terry turned off the light. There was a rustling of clothes and Terry was there inside with her, exactly as she wanted her to be. The familiar smooth nakedness of Terry's skin pressed against hers as the long arms drew her close. It was then, at that moment, that she began to cry.

"Hush, darling. Don't. Everything is all right now. Forget him. You're here with me. You *both* are."

The tears subsided as quickly as they had come. They had been like a summer rain, light, elusive, over in a moment, but bringing with them the relief she so needed.

Terry's lips stroked her forehead, brushed her cheeks to dry the tears, and moved to burn her mouth. It was always like this—evoking the same weakness, draining her, plunging her into a raging sea. It had never been like that with him. Terry's hands were so light, so knowing, like whispers on her breasts, wings on her stomach, so vibrantly alive in the dark mass where love is made. Her fingers probed tenderly, touching, causing Renay to moan slightly in anticipation. Her hips moved gently, urging the perceiving hands, while her own hands smoothed the ivory back poised above her. It had been done like this before, so there was no need for words. Only the slight pressure of her fingers told Terry that she was ready, more than ready, and the fastening together of woman and woman began.

Then the unison of love: the rhythm like a slow mounting blues that grew and grew into a crescendo that left her weak, but still strong enough to make the music and the feeling better. The indefinable pain lifted her to the point where her arms and legs clasped the back that was making the music heighten until the blues ended in a cry of ecstasy—the pain so sweet and yet so sharp that it hurt before subsiding in a low tremor.

"Terry—oh—God, I love you," Renay whispered in weak, spent passion.

Terry placed a kiss smaller than a second on her mouth. "Are you all right?"

"Yes—" The sweat stood out in tiny beads above her lips and her body was damp. The love-smell surrounded them.

"I've made you happy. I'm glad. We have all night—tomorrow—forever, if you want it. Rest now."

Renay turned toward Terry, resting her head in the crook of Terry's arm. For the first time in a long while, she slept soundly.

CHAPTER 2

On Monday, Denise had to go to school. Routines had to be followed again. Terry gave Renay the keys to her car, and she and Denise drove back into the part of town they had left the day before. Here the fringed grayness was encased in crumbling, low-rent apartment houses inhabited by struggling blacks and a few blue-collar white immigrants who had not yet saved enough money to move away. In this part of the city, the streets were narrow and crowded, inflamed with wasted grown-up faces and too-old aggressive children.

As she let Denise out at the large faded brick building, she thought again about transferring her to the modern new school near them as Terry had wanted her to do. Again, she decided against it—the school year was almost over.

On the way back, she stopped at the huge supermarket near Terry's apartment to buy food with the money Terry had carelessly stuffed into her purse. Inside, she took her time wheeling the cart slowly up and down the sparkling aisles, noting the contrasts between this market and the markets where she usually shopped.

There the floors were cracked and dirty, littered with cigarette butts and decaying scraps of produce; the meats were tinged with brown, as were the wilted vegetables marked with exorbitant prices. Here she carefully scanned the cans for the best brands and lingered over the choice meats with their bright red colors temptingly encased in cellophane wrappings. She found herself humming along with the soft music siphoned in from nowhere.

She shopped in careless pleasure, knowing that she did not have to worry about prices or about embarrassment at the checkout counter at having to put back some of the items because she did not have enough money. She surveyed the exotic food section, picking up caviar, terrapin stew, turtle soup and rattlesnake meat like a child marveling over the wonder of it all. It was so different. Even shopping was fun for a change.

Next, she inspected the wine counter with its various cocktail mixes. Knowing that Terry liked to experiment with drinks, she chose a bottle of Bristol Cream and one each of manhattan and martini mix. Moving on to the bakery section, she selected, for Denise, dainty pink and white frosted cupcakes sprinkled with nuts. The cart was soon full, and she felt a twinge of conscience as the clerk handed her the small amount of change.

It was a twenty-minute drive back to the parkway where Terry lived in the expensive high-rise apartment house with its self-service elevator, echoless carpeted halls, and people whom you rarely saw but knew were there.

By the time she had returned with the groceries it was noon. Terry must have been listening, for as soon as Renay set the bundles on the floor to fumble for the key, the door opened.

"Where on earth have you been?" Terry questioned anxiously, helping her with the heavy bags. "I have a surprise for you. Come and see!"

There it was: a shiny new baby grand piano in the corner by the fireplace, just as if it belonged there and had in fact been there all the time. "Like it?"

Renay was so long in answering that a shadow brushed Terry's eyes. "Well—do you?"

"Yes—oh yes!"

It was what she had always wanted but what her mother could

Loving Her

never afford. The one piano in her Kentucky home had been a second-hand, yellow-keyed, scarred upright. To pay for it, her mother had scrubbed white folks' floors and washed their clothes. But she had loved it. She had kept it polished, and she practiced every day.

From sixth grade through high school, she had taken one lesson a week, walking three long blocks through the so-called uppity black residential section, to Miss Pearl Sims's place. Miss Sims taught music at the high school where her father was principal. On Saturdays, she gave piano lessons in her home, mostly to help promising young black musicians. There was no one else in town to teach them.

Renay always marveled at the Sims's house, which seemed a castle compared to hers. A large two-story white frame, it boasted green shutters and a large front porch where a swing and chairs remained both summer and winter. A stone path divided the spacious lawn, and whenever she made her way up the path to the house, it seemed as if someone were following her movements from behind the drawn lace curtains.

She never went to the glass front door. All students had to go around to the side entrance to the little music room. None of the students had ever seen beyond the rose-colored cubicle that housed the well-kept Steinway with its bench top that lifted to expose Miss Sims's stacks of sheet music. The only other furniture in the room were a rolltop desk and two chairs. Because the room was chilly in the winter, there was a small electric heater in the corner.

Renay looked forward to Saturdays and Miss Sims, even though she sometimes heard people making sneering remarks about her teacher. The women would gather around the table in her mother's kitchen, sip her strong hot coffee, and purse their lips as they described Miss Sims as: "Old maid," "spinster," and "too much ed-u-cashon to git a man."

But she liked Miss Sims, who was too thin in the suits she wore and whose tight walnut Indian face wore a perpetual frown of preoccupation. It was only when she directed the school chorus for commencement and special occasions that her face bloomed into a softness that was almost beauty.

She knew Miss Sims liked her. Miss Sims treated her like a star pupil, making her practice harder than the others and chastising her severely when the lesson did not go as she thought it should.

Then she would say, "Renay, you have a wonderful talent. You are going to be a great musician someday." And when Miss Sims spoke with such assurance, Renay just knew that she would indeed be a great musician.

Once—just once—on a Saturday in early spring when the afternoon had a bright, glossy warmth, Miss Sims looked more withdrawn than usual. Her eyes had a sadness about them, and Renay knew that for the first time, Miss Sims had not really heard the prelude she had practiced all week.

Suddenly Miss Sims asked: "Would you like some cake and a glass of iced tea, Renay?"

Of course she would! Shyly she followed Miss Sims's stalklike figure in its nondescript gray skirt and white ruffled blouse. They moved quietly through the large spacious rooms, with their deep carpets, polished oak floors and hardly used heavy furniture, to the kitchen.

"The house is too large now for just my father and me. Before my mother passed away, it was always filled with people," she said, so softly that Renay hardly heard the words.

Miss Sims reached in the cabinet and brought out blue china plates for the cake. Then she placed two tall thin glasses on the table. "Sit down, Renay. Make yourself at home."

The cake was yellow with chocolate icing and was very good. Seated across from her at the square chrome table, Miss Sims only occasionally sipped her tea or bit into the cake. She had a strange, faraway look about her, and as Renay watched her, she wished there were some way she could wipe it away.

It was then with the cake and tea between them that Miss Sims said to her: "Nurture your talent, Renay. Don't let a man turn your head and fill you full of babies and worry. Women can have lives of their own. Talents of their own. There's a lot more to life than simply displaying that you have a man. Too many women of our race think that a man is all that matters. And they bitterly resent those who have independent lives in which there are no men."

She didn't quite understand what Miss Sims was trying to tell her, so she said nothing. Then Miss Sims got up very slowly, as if she were burdened by an invisible weight, and came over to her side of the table, where she bent to brush her lips across her cheek. The kiss was so fragile that at first she wondered if Miss Sims had kissed her at all.

On Sundays, in the Asbury Baptist Church, she put Miss Sims's teachings to work by playing to give pleasure to others while they praised God and dreamed Sunday dreams of a better world.

During the week, she was the student accompanist for the chorus. Because of this, she was called "Miss Sims's pet." She was around Miss Sims so much that sometimes she found herself walking with the brisk leggy strides of Miss Sims and feigning an abstract look when her friends approached her. The two most important things she learned from Miss Sims were a dedication to and a love for music. She soaked these up with a passion and an admiration for her teacher. Sometimes she even dreamed that she was Miss Sims.

"Chile—you going 'round the house like a moonstruck calf," her mother would remark, shaking her head in wonderment. "You in love or something?"

In love? Was she in love with Miss Sims? How *could* she be in love with Miss Sims? But she always wanted to be near her—like a second mother, she rationalized. Too, there was a sadness about Miss Sims that she always longed to brush away.

She wished Miss Sims would kiss her again, but she never did.

Now, as she reflected on her life with Terry, whose gift of the piano had stirred the well of memories, she wondered about Miss Sims. She hadn't thought of her old teacher in years. Yet it was impossible to completely forget some segments of the past, especially when they fit in so neatly with the present.

Renay ran her fingers experimentally up and down the keys of the beautiful new piano, forming arpeggios, chords and brief fragments of songs.

Turning to the other woman watching her in amusement, she asked in awe: "You did this for me?"

"Well, for who else?" Terry laughed, rising from her chair.

"Besides, now you're here, I don't have to spend my nights in the Peacock Supper Club, getting indigestion from that tasteless food, to hear you or *see* you. Why don't you play something?"

"What do you want to hear?" Renay called out, for Terry was busy carrying the bags of food to the kitchen.

"Anything you feel like playing. Want a drink?"

"Yes, a big one" she said. Her hands moved tentatively, getting the feel of the keys, which were too stiff. She played softly at first, adjusting to the keyboard. Then she began developing a theme she had been composing, a melody that nagged her at times for completion—a seed of creativity trying to be born.

"What's that you're playing?" Terry asked, bringing their drinks in frosted glasses, a cherry in one and an olive garnishing the other.

"Something I've been trying to work out."

"I like it," Terry remarked, handing her the glass with the cherry. She slumped into a chair and propped her feet on a hassock.

Renay watched her, thinking that Terry never exactly sat—she collapsed. She sipped the drink. "Ugh! Strong!" she commented, placing the glass on the table beside the piano.

"Ah-h-h," Terry leered pretentiously, "I'm trying to get you drunk to seduce you."

"You don't have to get me drunk for *that*."

"Remember the first time?" Terry asked, her voice low.

Renay's fingers stumbled over the keys as if even now the remembrance were here with them. Does anyone really forget the first time, she wondered—the first meeting with someone who becomes very important in one's life? But in remembering Terry, she had to first remember Jerome Lee.

The bills were mounting and Jerome Lee had been away for a month without a word. With Denise in tow, she had trudged wearily across town to the hair-frying parlors, asking if anyone had seen him. Some of the beauticians had looked at her blankly, others scornfully, over the smoking hot combs, relaxers, dryers, gossip and their patrons' standing hair. All had shaken their heads negatively.

The Apex Beauty Sales Company operated out of Chicago, and Jerome Lee, in an old black Chevrolet, covered his state for them, selling and distributing their products. He filled orders for hair pomades, dyes, hair nets, brushes, combs and other beauty shop supplies. He could have been anywhere. He could even be in the back of one of the shops, looking out at her through the curtains while drinking with the owner.

Finally, when the landlord became more insistent, the refrigerator more empty and she terribly desperate, she answered a want ad asking for a pianist to play from five to eleven o'clock, Thursday through Saturday, at the uptown Peacock Supper Club. The club catered mostly to white diners: Blacks could not afford the prices, and those who could simply lacked the inclination to go. Ruzicka, the owner, tried her out for three days, liked her and kept her on.

This was all she knew, and since she had to work, it was better than the sales clerk jobs she had held. Besides, her training had been in music. The church scholarship committee, along with Miss Sims's strong recommendation to the college, had helped her mother send her to the state college in Frankfort. The church people thought she had promise, and this was their way of showing appreciation for all the Sunday mornings and Sunday evenings when they had raised their voices and tapped their feet to her music.

She had done well at the college, and the head of the music department had wanted her to try for a graduate scholarship at Juilliard. Then, in her junior year, she met Jerome Lee Davis, star football player. He was big and brown and handsome, with stiff curly hair and flashing dark eyes. His ready smile was enhanced by the dimples which he was to pass on to Denise. All the girls were wild about him, and he obviously knew this as he swaggered with a hip-dip walk, hugging and kissing everybody lightly in passing, calling all baby and doll and honey.

Because she did not seek him out, she became a challenge to him. He bombarded the dormitory with telephone calls for her, chased her and cajoled her. He had help from her roommate Marissa, who liked fun and was sexy enough in a kittenish way, with her sloe eyes and secret-filled face.

Marissa had a date almost every night. She called Renay a stick-in-the-mud because she spent all her time in the music department or studying. She just couldn't believe Renay was for real.

When she discovered that Jerome Lee was interested in Renay, she began teasing her, urging her to go out with him. Other girls would give their eyeteeth to date Jerome Lee, she said. After all, he was the best-looking boy on campus. Besides, she ought to date sometimes. Pretty soon they would be whispering things about her like they did about Wylean Smith.

Renay tried to imagine what "they" could be whispering about Wylean Smith. Wylean was a serious student who minded her own business. She played a good game of basketball and had helped spark a winning girls' team the previous year. Wylean had just one close friend—a small, timid, nearsighted girl who was always with Wylean—"her mate," as some of the girls giggled behind their backs.

One night Marissa came into the room reeking of beer more than usual. She fell across the bed, staring glassy-eyed at Renay, who was seated at the desk deeply engrossed in a book. "Saw that handsome Jerome Lee tonight," Marissa began. "He asked about you."

"Oh?" She did not look up from her book.

"Un-huh. Honey, I just can't see *how* in the hell you can pass up that good-looking hunk of man." Then, angered by Renay's silence, she sneered half-seriously, half-mockingly: "You *do* like *men*, don't you?"

For some unknown reason, Renay felt the heat rise in her body, flushing her face. Her head swam, blurring the words before her. When she replied, the voice did not sound like her own. "Of course I do. Whatever gave you the idea that I didn't?"

Marissa gave a short, snorting laugh before turning over to fall asleep. Later, Renay wondered why she had bothered to answer her roommate at all.

To rid herself of Marissa's probing, which was becoming increasingly more persistent, she relented and went with Jerome Lee to a movie. Afterward, there was a steady succession of dances, movies and beer dates. Then one night as she was saying goodnight to him in the shadows of the dorm, he unexpectedly drew her close to his hard, muscular young body and kissed her.

The experience was jarring. For the first time, she felt a man's lips against hers, mashing hard upon her mouth and teeth, prying her lips open to insert a tongue coated with the taste of beer and cigarettes. Shocked, she stood as stone, feeling nothing, knowing nothing, willing nothing. She was a statue in the prison of his arms until he released her. Then, silently, she turned and entered the dormitory's foyer of bright lights and people whom she saw and yet didn't see.

On the way to her room, she thought: I've been kissed by a man and I hated it. The act had been nothing like Marissa's descriptions of flashing lights, headspins, knee-weaknesses and hot excitement.

Mechanically she entered her room, thankful that Marissa wasn't there. She collected her toiletries and went down the hall to the bathroom, grateful that no one was there either. She washed her face and scrubbed her lips. Vigorously, she brushed her teeth and tongue and rinsed out her mouth five times with Listerine.

Afterward, she went out with Jerome Lee just often enough to keep Marissa from worrying her. She learned how to accommodate his goodnight kisses, which seemed to be a social adjunct to dating. All she had to do was close her eyes and mentally detach herself from the act and him.

On the spring night of his fraternity dance, their relationship almost came to an end. By this time it had become a habit for her to will herself to another time and place while in his arms. She could do this with ease. She was only superficially acting out the woman's role she thought she was expected to play in the context of their relationship.

At the dance, she saw that he was drinking more than usual, sneaking out to the cars and bushes where bottles and paper cups were hidden. Each time he returned, he became a little louder, gayer and more flirtatious.

He held her closer than usual during the slow dances. His breath reeked of the cheap bourbon, and whether by accident or design his hand kept brushing that part of her gown strained by the pointed tips of her young breasts. She tried to draw back, but he held her in a barrelhouse hug. Embarrassed, she looked around and saw other couples locked in similar embraces—only the girls' eyes were closed, their heads resting on their partners' shoulders.

The dance over, they walked slowly from the gym down the path hidden by an embroidery of trees. Suddenly he stopped behind a thick cluster of bushes and pulled her roughly to him. His mouth, insistent in its urgency, came down upon hers as his hands roved exploringly over her body.

Frightened, she began to protest, trying to break away from his hot wet kisses. As she strained to escape, she felt the rising spear of his maleness throbbing against her.

"Jerome Lee—let me go! Stop it!" she shrieked, hoping that someone would come by.

He ignored her, holding her tighter, the passion in him making him think only of what he so desperately wanted. He murmured endearments in her ear, telling her that he loved her—that if she really loved him, she would prove it by the only way of proving love.

His kisses rained over her face and neck like hot lava. Suddenly he pushed her to the hard, damp ground. Quickly he shoved up her gown and fumbled to pull down the tight elastic of her panty girdle. He managed to tug it to midway on her thighs, low enough for him to do what he wanted. Impatiently, savagely, he pinned her shoulders down with his weight, trying to shove his male dagger into the secret abyss of her being. He pushed and heaved and grunted against the virginal obstruction of her cavity. She cried out in pain as he finally penetrated her. Now inside, he groaned and plunged until he came in quick, youthful, bungling passion. It was over, and all she knew was the hurt and the stickiness on her legs.

She wanted to cry and vomit and kill him. He rolled onto his back, breathing hard. His passion had drained him. Like a somnambulist, she got up weakly, pulled up her girdle and smoothed out the gown which she knew she would never wear again.

He lay on the ground with his penis limply exposed outside his tuxedo. The sight of it sickened and horrified her even more. There under the night sky she left him, still breathing hard, exhausted. She swore that she would never see him again.

Deliberately she avoided him, not wanting ever again to encounter him who had viciously taken away the part of her that was supposed to be so precious to womanhood. No longer did she care about what Marissa said and thought about her. Wasn't it Marissa who had influenced it all in the first place? Or was it her own weakness in denying what she did not want?

As the days progressed, she realized that she was pregnant. The mornings were filled with fear and nausea, and she could not study or think or absorb any of the lectures. Finally she knew that she had to tell him whom she had shunned and despised and ignored.

He was angry. She should have known what to do. Was it really his? She could have been with anybody after the first time with him. After all, he hadn't seen her since then.

She was frightened when the roundness began to show. The Dean of Women had begun to watch her curiously, commenting on the sudden weight gain. She began to wear very tight girdles.

It was almost time for the summer vacation. She couldn't go home like this, home to her mother struggling alone, going each day on swollen brown legs to the white folks' homes to keep her from having to do the same thing. And back there was the church with its sisters and brothers whose Sunday collections of pennies and dimes had been invested in faith and gratitude for making them happy. And there was Miss Sims who had tried to warn her: *Don't let a man turn your head and fill you full of babies.*

God, she despised him. She pleaded with him to *do* something. But what could he do? He didn't have money for an abortion—he was attending school on a football scholarship. His mother supported six others by working in a laundry. His father had walked out on the family long ago, disappearing into the nameless jungle of other withdrawing black fathers. His conscience reminded him that he had been the first with her: she had been hard to get, and she hadn't encouraged or helped him. Half in youthful fear, half in desperation, he married her before they went home in June. She had managed through physical subterfuge to complete her junior year.

After Denise was born, they left Kentucky for the Midwest. He wanted to be in a city with plenty of action, where they were not surrounded by pitying families and by friends who were still untied and youthfully living it up.

He took odd jobs, rebelling at doing anything which did not require a suit, shirt and tie. He began drinking more to forget his plight of having to marry before he was ready. He brooded over his misfortune, his tarnished dream of finishing college and becoming a famous professional football player. He could have been another Jim Brown if it hadn't been for her. It was much later she discovered that he had been flunking out.

He took the sales job with the black company and became quite good at it. All the beauticians, from chocolate brown to high yellow, liked him. He had personality, a quick wit, and a roué's natural way with women.

With the trips to the beauty shops, he began accepting drinks from bottles hidden in the back room and under the shelves. As black women spoil their men, the women took pleasure in spoiling the good-looking young salesman. Work eventually degenerated into a ceaseless party, morning, noon and night. The nips warming his blood, the quick feels and sly kisses made him feel good. He enjoyed bullshitting both the pretty ones and the bats. He had become king of the turf once again.

For herself, the piano was the only thing that make her life less lonely in the small, dingy four-room apartment. Perhaps her mother had sensed from afar the terrible loneliness, or was determined the daily walks to white town would still not be in vain. She had sent the piano on an empty truck a friend of hers was driving there to pick up a load of furniture. Renay had hired a boy to help the driver get it up the dark smelly stairway and through the too-small door of the combination bed and living room. She had them place it by the window. For three days, she had stared at it before touching the keys. It was like home.

The supper club work combined with the tips she made helped her pay the bills. Fran, an old friend from home, kept Denise for her those evenings, charging little, often nothing. Fran had graduated from the college in Kentucky and had gotten a job as an elementary schoolteacher. She had found Fran when her mother wrote to tell her that Fran was living in the same city, and she had recognized the address as being only three blocks away.

She managed to work, take care of Denise, and live, but without really feeling alive. All the days and nights were of a grave sameness, and there were moments when she wondered if she existed at all.

She picked up the strong drink Terry had prepared for her, trying to shake off the nightmarish memories of Jerome Lee.

Terry had entered her life one warm Saturday night, two weeks after she had started playing at the club. The place was filled with people tired of a too-long winter and stirred by nuances of spring. Ruzicka had asked her to play longer. Requests were stacked high on the silver tray atop the piano, and the tips were growing heavier as the customers ate and drank more.

Ruzicka came up to her little elevated stand with its single soft spotlight and whispered that a lady at the table in the far left corner had a request. He handed her a crisp twenty-dollar bill with the note. The woman must be very important for Ruzicka to be concerned.

"The tall one in the corner. She's quite famous, I hear."

Terry was in the corner, sitting beneath one of the bronze lamps jutting out from the cherry-paneled wall. Her reddish-brown hair was slightly tousled as if her fingers had absently brushed through it. When she saw Renay looking, a slight smile crossed her face.

With Terry was a young woman, a tiny blonde with upswept hair and red pouting lips. A strapless dress exposed a far too ample bosom. The girls' eyes narrowed angrily at Renay.

"She also would like for you to join them later. Please?" Ruzicka's dark Italian eyes pleaded as he nervously smoothed back his black satiny hair. He knew Renay did not mingle with the customers. "She is a writer and brings many friends here. They are very generous."

"Oh, all right." She couldn't refuse him. He had been nice to her, and after all, it *was* a woman and not one of the many men on the make. At least Ruzicka kept *them* away.

She looked down at the note—a request for Debussy. Pains of anger and resentment stabbed her. The woman was making fun of her. A nigger knows nothing but blues and jazz. Should she play for the woman's amusement or feed her superior white smugness by pretending she had never heard of Debussy? But it *was* a twenty-dollar bill: she *had* accepted it, and she certainly needed it.

She paused reflectively, head down for a moment. Then she began *Clair de Lune,* remembering how she used to play it, giving herself fully to the lovely patterns of sound. A stillness enveloped the room as if all were startled by the music coming from the sad black girl in the bargain basement black dress with dime store accessories—the girl who had previously played only popular tunes or requests drawn from the attics of their memories. When she finished, there was a long burst of applause. She felt better than she had in a long while, imbued with the exhilarating sensation of knowing that something was still there—that something could still be done.

She left the stand, making her way among the round tables covered with white linen cloths and peacock shaped lamps in the center, passing the heady, scented, white-shouldered women and shadowlike men. To her surprise, the blonde companion had gone.

The woman smiled from gray eyes which seemed to have endless depth. "Hello, I'm Terrence Bluvard. Everyone calls me Terry." Her voice was low and Renay noticed the smooth, blasé look about her. "Sit down. Renay—isn't it? Would you like a drink?"

She had finished for the night, and Ruzicka had asked her to go over to the table. "A whiskey sour, please."

Terry beckoned for the waiter, gave the order and leaned back. "I love music. It's a relief to come here and just hear a piano instead of those awfully jarring combos with their far-out sounds. You play well."

Renay gazed sullenly at the simple but expensive ice-blue dress—a month's salary to her. Again she felt anger at this white woman languidly smoking and being patronizing because she could play a piano. She was probably amused at her playing Debussy or even being able to read music. If the woman met her walking down the street tomorrow, she wouldn't even glance at her, but instead simply look through her as they all did—unless you had something to offer.

The anger spilled over. "Why did you ask me to play Debussy?"

"Why? Because I like him. Why else? Besides, you seemed as if you could do justice to him. There's a subtlety in his music that demands special sensitivity on the part of the pianist. You sounded like you had it. I wasn't wrong."

Something in the woman's voice was quieting Renay's anger. Was it sincerity, warmth? "I thought you were making fun of me—most white people do make fun of us, you know. We are the clowns in your circus." The words came out in a bitter gush—a child's venom at nothing. She was a little shocked at herself.

The woman's look of surprise disappeared as quickly as it had come.

"I'm sorry," Renay said quietly. "I didn't mean that—" But why apologize to a white person? White people insulted you every day by tolerating your being alive.

The drink came and the woman lit another cigarette with a tiny gold lighter. Renay sipped her drink, confused by her outburst and not knowing why.

After a while, the woman asked: "Are you usually this quiet? Or perhaps you would prefer that I change my skin color?" A faint mocking smile touched the lips slightly tinted with lipstick. "I can't do the latter, but I wish I could, if it would make you feel any better toward me."

It is inborn, Renay thought; when white and colored first meet there is always the consciousness of color before the actual knowing takes place. There was something about the woman—an undercurrent like electricity—a knowing, yet not wanting to know. It was like being drawn by a current. She looked for rings and saw none. The fingers curving around the glass were long and strong, dotted with tiny islands of almost invisible freckles.

"I don't usually go around with a chip on my shoulder."

"I'm glad," the woman said. Then she began to talk in the most natural and knowledgeable way about music and musicians she knew, and before Renay realized it, she had joined in.

How long since she had talked of music with someone? She even forgot the woman was white and obviously important. She only knew the woman had an uncanny way of making her feel comfortable and relaxed. She accepted another drink, then had to leave to pick up Denise.

The next Saturday night she saw the woman at the same table, alone this time. She nodded, played Debussy without a request, and on her break, walked to the corner table, surprised at her boldness and desire to do so.

"Hello—" she said softly, wondering why there was a tremor in a word that should come so easily.

The woman smiled and whispered to a hovering waiter. In a

magical moment, her favorite drink was before her. "I'm glad you came over, Renay. I'm feeling very lonely tonight. Would you like to go for a drive with me when you're finished?"

A drive? A drive would be nice. Away from the people, away from the home worries growing more intense each day. "All right—"

Later, outside, the humid air hinted subtly of rain. But Terry released the top of the white convertible and took a deep breath. "Ah-h-h, fresh air. I love it!"

Terry was a good driver, weaving skillfully through the dense uptown traffic and onto the winding, secluded road following the river. She parked beside the bank and turned slightly toward Renay. A bridge loomed high overhead, suspended in space. They could see the flashing car lights like zooming fireflies, while below, the water made muted sounds of its own.

"You're married, aren't you?" Terry said abruptly, breaking the silence.

"Yes—" One word about which so much could be said.

"Children?"

"A little girl. Denise."

Terry fumbled for the pack of Kools she kept on the dashboard and pushed in the car lighter. She drew on the cigarette, tossing her head and blowing smoke trails that disappeared like shimmering ghosts. "But you don't love him."

Startled, she accepted the cigarette from the pack Terry held out to her in the darkness. Her hand shook slightly as she accidentally touched Terry's hand holding the lighter for her.

"You wouldn't be taking a night drive with me if you did. You would hurry home like a dutiful wife."

Dutiful. In a way, that was what she was. Doing it and playing it by the book because that was what she should do even if he wasn't there. Or perhaps no one had come along to make her want to forget the rules.

Terry's voice became so soft it was almost inaudible over the murmur of the river. "I'm wealthy. I'm used to getting what I want, even if it means buying it. You've probably guessed what I am by now, or else you're terribly naive. I'm one of those women who prefers her own sex and I want you. However, as trite as it may sound, I want you for real. But I won't bother you if you don't want me to. I'll be happy just to have you as a friend, knowing you and enjoying your talent. But if you ever need me—come. I'll be waiting."

Renay drew thoughtfully on her cigarette, conscious of the words, not surprised by them but slightly bewildered. Somewhere within her, a desire to be loved and to love existed, as in everyone. But could it be met in this form? The strangeness of it. For a brief reflective moment, the vision of Miss Sims wavered before her and just as quickly vanished. Then she remembered Wylean Smith and her nearsighted companion. Then the present, the now. Was this actually happening to her? Who had the right to dictate that it had to happen a certain way or not all? A knowingness stirred her like truth itself. Perhaps she had known all along.

"I've startled you. Perhaps you didn't know."

Renay threw out the half-smoked cigarette and squeezed her eyes tightly shut, trying to summon words, thoughts beyond the swimming tightness that was excitement in her head. Finally she said: "I knew."

"How old are you, Renay?"

"Twenty-seven." Terry laughed shortly, taking careful aim to flick her cigarette into the water. "Twenty-seven—" she repeated, as if to be twenty-seven were unimaginable to her at this time in life. "I didn't mean to frighten you. Forgive me. I won't pressure you. Despite what some people say about my kind, we don't deliberately seek to be proselytists."

Renay thought silently: pressure her? Was pressure needed when an obstacle wasn't there?

Terry started the car, pumping the accelerator harshly before pulling out onto the road. During the long drive back, both were silent, each absorbed in her own block of thought.

Jerome Lee came home early the next day, appearing suddenly from his latest extended absence. This time he brought a friend with him, a bartender who worked in a cheap bar down the street.

Stew was of medium height, the color of bronze, and sported a thick beard. He was dressed in a pink knit suit, pink tie and white shirt. His right hand clutched a fifth of scotch.

"I been telling Stew here about how I used to play football back there in Frankfort," Jerome Lee muttered, the words thick.

"This your old lady?" Stew asked, eyes appreciatively measuring Renay, who was busily trying to ease Denise out of the room.

"Yeah. I suppose you can call her that." Jerome Lee laughed loudly, slapping his thigh. "Sit down, man, and let's start on this bottle. After that, there's bound to be more where that came from."

Renay hurriedly left the room and went to the kitchen, where she began to prepare a quick supper for Denise before going to work. She could hear the loud bass sounds of the record player he had just turned on. The music had a rock beat and shook the walls of the small cluttered kitchen. She put a TV dinner in the stove for Denise. Later, she would eat a sandwich at the club.

"What the hell you sticking a TV dinner in there for? Stew and me can't eat that." Jerome Lee glowered at her from the doorway.

"Everything else is frozen," she said, turning to face him. "How did I know you were coming home tonight?"

"Ain't for you to know." He pushed her aside as he opened the refrigerator to get ice cubes. "Now you find something for me and my friend to eat."

His eyes were bloodshot, the skin around them puffed. The white shirt was soiled around the collar and his suit looked as if he hadn't changed it in a week. My God, she thought, why do you do this to yourself?

"What the hell you staring at me for? Go on and get us some supper."

Denise sat quietly at the table as she had learned to do when her father came home.

Halfway out of the kitchen with ice and glasses, he stopped suddenly and turned to Denise. "You been a good girl while I been gone?" The question was routine, the words apparently the only ones he knew to communicate with her.

Denise nodded her head, staring empty-eyed at this stranger who was her father. Stew loomed in the kitchen, eyeing Renay.

"Man, how'd you git such a good-looking woman?"

"Bullshit. Let's drink up this Johnnie Walker."

Renay hurried to the grocery to buy food for dinner. She returned to cook fried chicken, corn and peas. When dinner was ready, Stew had to leave because he had a date, and Jerome Lee was slumped in a drunken stupor on the sofa.

She collected the dishes and glasses and packed an overnight bag for Denise to stay with Fran. She did not want to leave her alone with Jerome Lee—for she knew his pattern. As soon as he awakened, he would be seeking another bottle.

She was late for work for the first time. Luckily the club wasn't crowded, for she played badly that night. All during the evening, she searched the corner hopefully for Terry, but she didn't come.

When the evening was thankfully over, she tiredly gathered her things and went out into the cool night to hail a cab. She hoped Jerome Lee would be gone and not in bed with the whiskey boiling hot inside him, making him toss and turn recklessly as if demons were pursuing him. Frequently, he yelled and moaned, waking Denise. Sometimes he couldn't make it to the bathroom, vomiting on the bed and floor.

"Taxi, lady?" A familiar voice called out to her.

She looked up to see Terry's car, its top lowered, pulling up beside her.

It was just what she wanted: to see and be with Terry. Somebody just nice and comfortable to be with. Somebody to make the world a little less gray.

Gratefully she got in, breathing a long weary sigh. "Thank you."

"For what?"

"Just being here." The car moved off into the lonely night streets. "May I have a cigarette, please?"

"Of course." With one hand on the wheel, Terry lit the cigarette and handed it to her. The cigarette was wet at the tip, and she felt a little shock as her lips closed around it. "Would you like to go home with me for a drink?" Terry asked, not looking at her.

A frozen moment of indecision. Why not? Denise was spending the night with Fran, and she wasn't anxious to go home and face Jerome Lee. That situation was becoming unbearable. Now, sometimes, Denise was frightened at the spectacle that was her Daddy. More than once she had cried out in her sleep—even when he wasn't there.

"Yes, I'd like very much to go home with you," she replied quietly.

The car moved to the edge of the city where the streets were broader and cleaner and well-kept lawns graced the neat houses. Terry parked in front of a fashionable apartment building. The elevator was like a vacuum with nothing but the two of them and the silence tight and heavy between them.

Terry turned on the light in the living room. "I suppose the place is a little large for me, but I like space."

Renay surveyed the room and liked it immediately. The red wall-to-wall carpeting, low black couch and matching chairs, and the stone fireplace surrounded with books gave her a warm, secure feeling. Everything was in good taste, but without the decorative frivolities of the usual feminine touch. A long stereo console filled one corner of the room, and she went to look at the records.

"What do you want to drink?" Terry asked, going into the dining room with its small built-in bar. "The usual?"

"Please." She could see Terry getting out the bottles and glasses. She heard the opening and closing of the refrigerator, the sounds of ice cascading into an ice bucket.

Terry returned with the drinks to sit beside her on the couch. For the first time, Renay noticed the almost invisible star-flecks of gray in the autumn-colored hair. She remembered Terry's words: *how old are you, Renay?* and wondered whether it mattered.

She was silent for so long that Terry asked: "Is something wrong?"

Renay bit her lips to stop the trembling. She wanted to cry out, "Yes! Everything is wrong. Life, people, the world about you. How to set it right?" She downed the drink hurriedly, then reached for the bottle of bourbon Terry had placed on the coffee table.

"You can't solve it like that. I tried it once. It took bottles, running away to far-flung places, and an analyst. In the long run, it's really all up to you." She reached out and gently took the glass away. "Renay, what is it? Can I help?"

Help? Help a drowning, a wish unfulfilled, a death? No, that was impossible. "I *despise* him!" The words poured out, and as though they had weakened her with the weight of their meaning, she swayed, leaning toward the woman whose arms went around her but just as quickly withdrew.

"No, please—keep them there," Renay whispered, surprised at her boldness.

The arms returned, drawing her closer. Terry's long fingers worked gently at the base of her neck and slid underneath the hair to bring her face nearer. "Are you sure—?"

Renay buried her head in the thin shoulders to hide her tears. The woman's hand pulled her head back from the protective arc.

"Please, Renay, look at me."

In doing so she saw deep into the gray eyes that were like quiescent pearls. Mesmerized, she watched as Terry's lips moved slowly towards hers, pausing only words away from her own. "I don't want you to be afraid or ashamed. I don't want it to be like that."

"I'm not—I'm not."

The mouth meeting hers was soft like her own and very, very gentle, unlike the hardness she had been accustomed to feeling. Then it increased its pressure and the tongue went into the cavern of her mouth as if it belonged there, joining hers, and the hands brushed over her face and down to her neck where it stopped. Her eyes were closed, and she felt a warmth consume her—a warmth she had never known before. She didn't want Terry to stop. She wanted the lips and hands to return to her—to where they belonged.

"Renay—come."

She opened her eyes and stood up shakily to follow Terry to the other room. Eyes clouded with passion, she hardly saw the large bed with the dark blue spread that Terry flung back. Then Terry undressed her and left her for a cold instant on the smooth white sheets while she quickly threw off her own clothes.

Immediately Terry was beside her again, and she was no longer alone. She closed her eyes, shuddering at the delicate kisses being showered all over her body like light rain.

"You're so golden brown, so beautiful," Terry murmured in the hollow of her neck. "Relax, darling—relax."

Shyly she put her arms around Terry, exploring the white body that was new to her—the downy hair like peach fuzz on Terry's back, the strength of her limbs, the small firmness of her breasts which nestled against her own like twins.

When Terry's hand began feeling, exploring and kneading, she shut her eyes once more, losing herself in the gloriously strange wonderment of it, lying back and thinking nothing until the pressure of the fingers created a little fire of sensuous pain she hadn't known before. The flower of her made a honey-damp dew between her legs, and she felt Terry quiver as she breathed in her ear: "I've made you ready for me, darling."

Terry's hands spoke a language all their own, touching her legs to insinuate a wider path. She was conscious of lips on her breasts, of the tip of a tongue encircling her taut nipples. Then Terry was above her, moving, and just as she had known and wanted this all her life, she matched the love movements of body against body—movements which increased to such an intensity that Renay cried out, startling even herself.

"Terry—oh, Terry—it's good. It's so good—" The cries were there as a curtain of blackness struck and she sang out in pleasure.

Cradled later in Terry's arms, she said: "It was the first time I've ever had an orgasm."

Terry kissed her lightly, hugging her closer.

"You—you didn't," Renay said fretfully, thinking she had been selfish in her happiness. "You got nothing out of it—"

"Yes, yes I did. Pleasing you. In time, as we begin to know each other, we'll grow together."

"I didn't know it *could* be like that—" It had never been with him. The hurried mounting of her, the jabbing inside her with the acrid whiskey odor heavy in her nostrils. It had always been over in seconds; then he would turn over and go to sleep. Now she knew she could never do that again, for she had found what she wanted and needed most. She was now aware of herself and the part she had tried to deny. So much of beauty had been wasted in the past.

She crushed out her cigarette, wanting to return to Terry. She shifted to face her on her side and stuck out her tongue to make patterns on Terry's face.

"Stop, Renay! You're tickling me!" Terry laughed.

Filled with a happiness she had never known before, she laughed back. "I *want* you. Again and again."

A week later she came home to the bleak apartment to find the old piano gone, a vacant corner where it had once been. She had stood immobile, staring at the space, somehow knowing, but hoping she was wrong. He was sitting on the couch in his T-shirt and

boxer shorts, watching a football game on TV and drinking a can of beer.
  She turned slowly and looked steadily at him. "Where is it?" she asked evenly.
  He glared back at her in stony, defensive silence. "I sold it." Her hands doubled in little hard knots which seemed like weights at her side. "Why?"
  He shrugged indifferently, getting up. "Hell, I needed the money. It wasn't nothing but an old piece of junk anyway."
  Junk! Childhood hopes and adult dreams in one treasured package—*junk!*
  "You ought to be glad I could get something for it. It'll keep us going. Playing that shit in Charlie's club ain't helping *that* much. You know we black men have a hard enough time as it is making it in the white man's world. Be damn glad you could help me. I could have been somebody if it wasn't for you. All you castrating black bitches want to keep a man down. *Ruin* him. Just like my mama ran my daddy away. Always after him. And *you*. What goddam good are *you* to a man? Not even a good screw!"
  Her head was throbbing as she listened to the repeated accusations, the malicious bulwark he erected to justify what he always did.
  "You shouldn't have, Jerome Lee. You shouldn't have! Not the piano— Oh, *Christ!*"
  She was beside him, her little fists pounding the huge towering man who easily waved a big hand like a fly-swatter back and forth, sending blows that sprawled her on the floor. She lay there sobbing, listening to his curses, and thinking how much easier it was to stay down than to get up.

  "Don't remember too much, darling," Terry's voice brought her back from the past. "The thoughts take you too far away from me." Terry was standing behind now, hands light on her shoulders as only Terry's hands could be.
  "I'm so happy you are here, Renay."
  "Are you, darling?" She didn't look back. She couldn't right then.
  Terry squeezed her neck playfully. "I'm going to leave you

with that inanimate object you're bestowing all that love on. I do have an article to finish."

"Terry?" Renay stopped her.

"Yes?" Terry had picked up her drink again and was smiling over the glass.

Renay pushed the glass away from Terry's mouth to reach up and touch Terry's lips with her own. "Thank you."

"Cut it out. I have work to do," Terry chastised lightly.

"Yes, ma'am," Renay laughed, slightly astonished at how easily she could laugh now. "But I can think of much better things to do!"

CHAPTER 3

Renay picked up Denise after school, then stopped to see Fran, leaving Denise in the car to prevent her from childishly blurting out where they were staying.

Fran opened the door, staring at Renay in surprise. "Renay! Where have you been?"

"Hello, Fran," she smiled, feeling a little guilty. She should have let Fran know she was all right.

"Come on in, honey. Let me turn down the stove. I've just started dinner—such as it is."

Renay followed Fran to the kitchen where chops were sizzling loudly over the gas flames. Fran did everything hurriedly, her short plump form always in perpetual motion. An Afro bush, tinted a light red, framed a smooth brown face highlighted by large expressive dark eyes.

"I'm going back to Weight Watchers again next week," Fran laughed, shoving a tray of french fries into the oven. "This week, I thought I'd live it up."

"Your weight looks all right to me," Renay commented, remembering that Fran was always on and off with weight watching.

"Sit down," Fran said, pulling out a chair at the kitchen table for Renay. "Your husband came by last night looking for you."

"Jerome Lee!" She sat down, feeling a little surprised at the mention of Jerome Lee. Why should he look for her? He had never looked before. But she hadn't left him before either. A bird out of the cage—the cat ready to pounce?

"Yes, Jerome Lee, unless you got another stashed away someplace," Fran quipped. "He wasn't exactly the most sober man in the world. He said that you had left him." Fran turned the stove down, poured a little water in the pan, and placed a lid over the simmering chops. "He accused me of having you hidden in the closet or under the bed. I had one hell of a time convincing him I didn't."

Fran reached in her apron pocket for a pack of cigarettes, then sat down. "Have one?" She offered the pack to Renay, who shook her head. "By the way, Renay, just where *are* you staying?" she asked, frowning over a lighted match. "If that's any of my business."

"With a friend," Renay said quietly. It would be best for Fran not to know. Then, she wouldn't have to be involved, nor shocked. Fran's life was men and nothing but men. She had a string beaded with them and she shifted the beads around at will. Men were almost a hobby with her. Fran would never be able to understand her loving a woman as Fran loved a man.

Black women were the most vehement about women loving each other. This kind of love was worse to them than the acts of adultery or incest, for it was homophile. It was worse than being inflicted with an incurable disease. Black women could be sympathetic about illegitimacy, raising the children of others, having affairs with married men—but not toward Lesbianism, which many blamed on white women.

The women of her race loved their men, urged strength in them. And hadn't they for centuries been accused of castrating them? Besides, black women had been made masculine all their lives by forced matriarchy—a role thrust upon them by a racist society. Conversely, she thought, this should soften their outlook on the Lesbian woman, or make more black women Lesbians.

But most black women feared and abhorred Lesbians more

than rape—perhaps because of the fear bred from their deep inward potentiality for Lesbianism. For her to be in love with a woman who was white *and* a Lesbian—Fran would never understand. People never try to understand things they do not want to. Her love for Terry would have to be a secret hidden even from her best friend. She was now heeding the first lesson of her new existence.

"Is this just a scare, or are you leaving him for good?"

"No scare, Fran. I'm leaving him for good."

"Now you're talking!" Fran waved a clenched fist. "I don't blame you one damn bit. Jerome Lee's just no good. I'd have left him long ago." Then she asked, watching Renay narrowly as she put out the cigarette, "Got another guy on the hook?"

"No—no one." Why does there have to be another man for a woman to leave?

"Well, as pretty as you are, it won't be long. Just try not to get another jackass like him. If he comes back here loud-talking me again, I'm going to have him put out."

"I'm sorry, Fran. I hope he doesn't bother you anymore."

Fran opened the oven door and peered in at the potatoes. They were a golden brown. "Why don't you stay for dinner, honey? There's enough."

"No, thanks. I have to go." Denise was still in the car, and Terry was waiting.

"Renay," Fran stopped her, eyes flashing. "I just got a wonderful idea. Why don't you and Denise drive home with me when school's out? You can see your mother. Maybe even decide to stay."

Home. Not home. The small but comfortable frame house filled with pleasant memories, baking smells embedded in the walls, and warm laughter and love suspended from the ceiling. Her childhood had been left there where an adult world would never fit.

"Fran—I can't."

"Just a suggestion," Fran shrugged, walking to the door with her.

"I just stopped by to let you know we're all right."

"I'm glad you did. I was worried as hell after seeing Jerome Lee. Be careful. I wouldn't trust him an inch. You still want me to keep Denise at night?"

Renay shook her head. "Thanks, but it won't be necessary."

Fran glanced reflectively at her and then away. "Let me know if there's anything you want me to do," she said. "Take care of yourself."

Renay kissed her lightly. "Don't worry about us. We're fine. Better than we've ever been. And happier," she added. "I'll stop by again—soon."

Terry had company when they arrived home. The blonde girl, the one who had been in the supper club with Terry that first night, was seated on the couch. The girl did not look surprised to see them. Terry must have told her. A man with thinning long brown hair curled slightly at the ends, wearing cream-colored tight trousers and a red blazer accented at the neck with a blue ascot, came out of the kitchen carrying glasses and a tall, freshly made pitcher of martinis. He smiled when he saw Renay.

"*You* must be Renay! How delightful to meet you. I'm Phil Millard. Terry's best *male* friend." He winked at her from behind square wire-rimmed glasses. "We do a lot of work together. I'm a photographer. Occasionally she adds my pictures to her articles after I plead with her." He spoke in an excited way, talking in a continuous gush and emphasizing words that were important to him while waving his hands in gestures.

"Leave it to Phil to introduce himself," Terry laughed. "Renay, this is Jean Gail."

Renay smiled at the girl, who did not smile back. She was beautiful in a tight-fitting green miniskirt and matching blouse which made her blonde hair brighter and her light emerald eyes sparkle with jaded brittleness. Renay introduced Denise to them and then whispered for her to go to her room.

"What an adorable little girl," Phil said, handing Renay a drink. "I brought some photographs for the article Terry's doing for *Women's Flair* magazine. It's on a small newly formed women's lib group—among of all people—Chicanos! Farewell to machismo." And turning to Renay: "I hear *you* are a musician."

The girl, Jean, smiled. "Aren't *all* colored people musical?"

Renay steadied herself, sipping slowly from the glass. The girl was overdoing the stereotyped white bit. She saw the quick angry glance Terry flung at Jean who crossed her smooth shapely legs to make the skirt rise higher. She retained a condescending smile.

"I have a friend who's not. He's a reporter for the paper I work for and can't sing a note, play a tune, *or* dance a jig." Phil remarked, pouring himself another drink.

Jean extracted a cigarette from a gold monogrammed case and waited, Renay knew, for Terry to light it. Then the long lingering look at Terry over the flame—the look both gave a message and asked a question. Renay felt jealous, envying the girl who had known Terry in the wasted time she wished she had had.

"Darling—play something." Terry got up and went to Renay.

"Blues—I like blues," Jean muttered thickly.

Renay saw that Jean was a little tight, the mouth slack, cigarette held carelessly between her fingers, ashes falling to the rug like gray dust. Renay sat down at the piano.

"Let her play what she wants," Phil interrupted, settling in a chair near the piano.

I wouldn't waste the blues on her, Renay told herself. The blues are for deep inside where they all start and sometimes never end. You don't just listen to the blues. You feel it twisting around inside like a serpentine knife, hurting and sometimes healing.

For sheer bitchiness, she played the *Barcarolle.*

"Lovely!" Phil applauded. "I *adore* Chopin."

"I have to go," Jean murmured suddenly, flattening out the cigarette's end on one crushing twist. She got up a little unsteadily, bracing herself on high thick heels. "You *will* call, won't you, Terry, sweetie?"

Terry did not reply, concentrating on her drink.

"Wait, Jean, I'm going too," Phil called, stopping to kiss Renay's cheek. He smelled heavily of shaving lotion and cologne. "I think Renay's simply a *doll,* don't you? I'd certainly like to photograph her—the fullness of Africa in the sensuous features, sunrise in the coloring, and a dash of the Orient in the eyes. *All* in one face. I still contend that black people are the most exotic for photographing. Don't you agree?"

"Come, Phil, if you're leaving with me," Jean said coldly.

"I'll stop by again, Terry, to bring you the other pictures."

After they had left, Renay felt drained at playing an unexpected scene without a script.

"She still likes you," she said stiffly, thinking of Jean and pecking out a nameless tune with one finger—a bell sound high and shrill as fear.

"Jean? She likes expensive things—not people." Terry began collecting the glasses and stacking them on the tray. "Phil seems fond of you. I can tell."

Oddly enough, she had liked him. At least he was genuine. It was easy for black people to sort out the for-real from the pseudo-real. "He's like—us. Isn't he?" She couldn't yet use the other words.

"Yes. He lives with a boy younger than he—a clerk in a men's store. He's always afraid the boy won't be there when he gets home." Terry emptied the contents of Phil's martini pitcher into her glass. "Maybe like I'm afraid you won't return when you leave and are late getting back. Like today."

"I stopped by to see a friend—Fran Brown. She's the one who kept Denise for me. An old friend from home."

Terry drained the glass, looking into the mirrored bottom. "Did you tell her where you were staying?"

"No."

"Afraid—or ashamed?"

"Neither. I thought it best not to tell her." But hadn't she been a little of both?

Terry knew. "That's the one thing about this life," she sighed. "It's subterranean. An intricate network with its own heart arteries and tear streams and lonely paths for those who have to be careful." She looked gravely at Renay. "I won't keep you here—if someday you want to get out of the life."

"I want to be with you—"

Just as Renay moved to touch Terry, Denise ran into the room. "Mommy, I'm hungry!"

"Yes, so am I. What's on the menu tonight, chef?" Terry rubbed her stomach.

"You people are driving me crazy about food!" Renay hugged Denise playfully. "Tonight we'll have steak."

"Yum-yum! We hardly ever had steak at home!" Denise clapped her hands in childish delight.

"Sounds tempting. Make mine rare, please, ma'am. Come, Denise, and I'll read you a story while Mommy's preparing dinner. It's called *Winnie-the-Pooh* and it's all about a boy named Christopher Robin who named his bear Winnie-the-Pooh," Terry said, taking Denise by the hand.

In the shelter of the bed and the darkness, Renay couldn't sleep. She listened to Terry's quiet breathing and turned to put her arm across her. Terry stirred and moved closer to Renay, lips finding her forehead in the darkness. Terry wasn't asleep either.

"Terry, tell me about yourself." Now was the time for discoveries and reflections—there had never been time in the past.

"Why?"

"I want to know."

"Like what?"

"Why you became a writer."

Terry laughed softly. "Because I like to write. It's a part of me—like breathing. Sometimes there are things I have to get out of me. To say. Like there are things an artist says with his brush and you with your music. I see things, I think things, and I worry about them. I write hoping that others, too, can see and think and worry. Perhaps do something, or at least look at the world and life a little differently."

"Were your parents wealthy?"

"Hmmm. I suppose so. My father was a corporation lawyer. My mother liked to dabble in art—or better still, artists, if they were young and handsome. I was in her way. She sent me to a private school for girls. Later, I found out that I liked to be in an all-girl school—for my own personal reasons, I guess, so I went to a women's college. I'm not going to blame my inclination on the schools or a mother's rejection. I simply like my own sex and that's that. I've come to accept it and learned to live with it, and I've stopped wasting money trying to change myself and conform to what society thinks a female should be and what I don't want to be. Why should I? People aren't made alike, don't all think alike, and aren't pigmented alike. Why should our sex penchants have to be the same?"

"Are they still living—your parents?"

"No. But they left me a trust fund and a house I named Willow Wood, not too far out in the country. It's old, but it's spacious and airy and surrounded by trees that weep on it when it rains. I have a woman who comes in and cleans from time to time. Sometime I'll take you there."

She thought of her house in Kentucky and her mother who wasn't rich like Terry's but who had given her love. "My parents were poor," she began reflectively. "My father was killed in a freak tractor accident while working on a farm when I was a little girl."

Then she told Terry about the old piano and the music lessons, and about the church and the college, but little about Jerome Lee. She didn't want to talk about Jerome Lee while lying here with Terry and feeling like this—the world around but unable to touch them. Someday she would. She thought about how strange it was that lives could span miles to come together and make merging patterns to start all over again.

"You really don't regret being here with me?" Terry asked, and by the muffled sound of the words, Renay knew Terry's face was now toward the wall.

"No." Hadn't she asked that before but in a different way? How could she convince her that she wasn't and never would be regretful, even if it meant losing her identity in Terry's world?

"I'm glad. I'll do all I can to make you happy, to ease some of the pain, and soothe the disappointments. I hope you can stand this life. Sometimes you have to harden yourself to everything and everyone."

"Terry—you forget—I'm black. We're hardened as soon as we come into this world. It's as if our skin's a hard dark shell to hide and protect all the hurts to come." Funny how she could love Terry so deeply that she did not see Terry's white skin—only knew of Terry's heart and the love in it. She felt Terry's hand on her breast, featherlight, warm, warming, and covered it with her own.

Terry's breath quickened as she asked softly in the darkness, "Do you feel like it?"

"Like what?" Renay teased, whispering back.

Terry's laughter was low. "Darling, do you really want me to *say* it?"

"No," Renay said, lips locked in Terry's ear. "*I'll* say it. Yes, I feel like letting you love me, making me cry the way only you can do, and making me so happy that I forget everything but you!"

CHAPTER 4

The first part of the week fled on soaring wings for Renay. Minutes and hours were filled with the intoxication of discovering and learning more about Terry in the framework of their daily living. It was true, she now knew: You really didn't know a person until you lived together.

It was always new and exciting to wake up in the morning with Terry stretched out beside her. Sometimes she would waken early, just as dawn fringed the sky, coloring it mauve, and quietly watch Terry, still asleep. Terry slept either on her side or stomach with her head buried in the pillow. An arm would always be thrown across Renay—somehow. If Renay moved even just a little, Terry awakened quickly, the arm tightening, as if she were afraid Renay would slip away. Then Terry's gray eyes would flood with the presence of her as she would smile and say: "Good-morning, darling—"

Sometimes Renay would lean over and kiss Terry awake, a fleeting wisp of a kiss in the sunken curve of her cheek or just above the arched brow. But that was all she could do in the mornings, for Denise woke up early and Renay had to get her ready for school.

She would prepare a breakfast of fruit, cereal and milk for Denise, and drive her to school while Terry slept. Terry liked to write long into the night at the desk now moved into the living room, or to spread her papers on the dining room table.

Those times when she awakened to find Terry not yet in bed, she tiptoed to the door and opened it to see if Terry was all right. She never bothered her during these times, for she knew Terry wanted to be alone to think, to create without interruptions. Only when Terry fell asleep over the papers and dead cigarettes did she gently arouse her for bed.

The days had a pattern. After dropping Denise at school, she would return to the apartment and prepare Terry's breakfast of grapefruit juice, eggs, toast and the strong black coffee Terry liked. There were so many little things that Terry ignored. She didn't like to make a bed, cook or hang up clothes. These Renay did while Terry read over her night writing with the FM radio station playing in the background.

Frequently she would stop Renay in the middle of her work to get a book from the shelves for Renay to read. Terry loved Edna St. Vincent Millay and Emily Dickinson. And there were some young obscure poets whom she admired and to whom she made casual references—enough for Renay to know they were like Terry.

Now she felt alive again, living to love, loving to live. She worried less about herself and was becoming more sensitive to other people and the world about her. She was even closer to Denise, for now she had the time to get out of herself and her problems. There were flashing moments of pain when Denise's smile would image his, and when her eyes reflected the dancing eyes of her father's eyes that caught and held women's heartstrings and made allies of men. After all, she was a part of him, and this would always be present. But the reflection of him in Denise did not bother her anymore. Love had taught her not to hate.

Denise had changed too. Her smooth round childish face broke more quickly into a smile, the too-quiet somberness was gone, and she spoke more as happy children do. Denise adored Terry, who read to her every night and brought her surprises and took her for drives while Renay cooked dinner.

Their life together resembled that of a married couple, except that they could not proclaim themselves man and wife. But married people have frictions, and their first argument came Thursday when Renay had to go to work.

The day came with Terry silent and brooding. For breakfast, she had only a number of cups of strong black coffee, and instead of lunch, two Bloody Marys. Renay prepared an early dinner, as she had to leave for the club. Terry sparred with the veal chop, prodded meaninglessly at the baked potato and answered Denise's homework questions in monosyllables.

After dinner, while Renay showered, Terry began to drink bourbon and water. When Renay came out of the bathroom, Terry was propped on the bed, smoking and sipping her drink. Wordlessly she watched Renay dress before the mirror, combing up the thick mass of black hair into a sophisticated crown. The black off-shoulder cocktail dress she had put on brought out the creamy glow of her skin. Although the evenings were growing longer, the pale sinking sun still cast faint splintered rays on the blue carpet and yellow walls of the room. The silence was oppressive, thick and heavy between them.

Renay screwed on the pearl earrings that clung like ice globules to the sides of her face. Without a word, she went over to stand with her back to Terry, who reached out and mechanically pulled up the zipper at the back of Renay's dress. The sandpaper sound split into the silence and closed it.

When Terry finally spoke, her edgy voice revealed her uneasiness: "Are you *sure* you want to go to work tonight? I really think you ought to stay home," she said, hoping Renay would change her mind. "You really don't have to work, you know."

Work? Yes, she *did* have to work. To let Denise know she was contributing to their keep, and to preserve her independence, but above all, to keep alive and active that integral part of her—her music.

"Would you like for me to go with you? I can get someone to stay with Denise."

"No."

"Will you stop being so damn noncommittal!" Terry's voice rose in exasperation as she threw her long legs off the side of the bed. "It's just that I'm *worried* about you. Suppose he's angry and looking for you? You said that he drank heavily. God, you never know what people like that might do."

"Terry, I can handle Jerome Lee."

"Like before?" Terry said acidly, stabbing out the cigarette in an ashtray already a burial ground of bent, broken and half-smoked butts. She stood behind Renay, pressing close to her but careful not to wrinkle her dress. Her mouth brushed a nervous path across Renay's neck. "Please—come straight home."

"I will," Renay promised, bending her head back to touch the tip of Terry's chin. As though that weren't enough, she turned around and kissed the spot her head had grazed. Gathering up the coat and pocketbook, she said: "I'll be all right." She smiled in reassurance.

The club was unusually crowded, distended with the aftermath of a college-age wedding party that had just sent the blooming bride and groom away in a snow of rice. The fresh-faced girls, their gleaming teeth showing behind giggling smiles, were dressed in long organdy dresses and matching round saucer-veiled hats. They teased, laughed and flirted with the boys who were trying to look and act older than they were. Flushed with champagne, they gathered around the piano to sing fraternity songs whose tunes Renay easily picked up as they hummed them to her—tunes reminiscent of those on her campus long ago.

When they left, the crowd thinned out, leaving only the middle-aged supper group lingering over their food and drinking more than they ate, their faces drooping heavily with boredom, but staying because it was worse at home. She played their favorites: *Smoke Gets in Your Eyes*, *As Time Goes By*, and *Stardust*. These were the tunes which brightened a memory in their past, or whose melody was familiar. This kind of music made the background comfortable to them.

She had finished for the evening and was preparing to leave the stand when one of the waiters whispered that a man wanted to see her at the second table on the left near the bar. Without looking, she knew it was Jerome Lee.

He was halfway hidden in the shadows, sitting alone. His thick curly hair was neatly trimmed in a medium bush elongated into sideburns. A moustache curved his full top lip like a sickle. He wore a new brown-and-white suit and a white tie that fell neatly against a tan shirt. He almost looked like the Jerome Lee of old. The smell of shaving lotion and cologne wafted around him like a haze.

He had the appearance of a model in *Ebony* magazine advertising a rising young businessman on his way up. All he needed was a briefcase. Only his eyes, puffed and red-streaked, gave him away. A cup of black coffee was before him.

"I figured you'd be here," he began, his mouth carved into a smirking half smile to show how pleased he was with himself and his reasoning. Watching her sit down opposite him, his eyes focused hard upon hers.

"You want something? A drink?"

She knew he had asked so the strangers surrounding them would not think him cheap: he with his coffee, she with her nothing. His pride was motivated by arrogance. She shook her head. She didn't want a thing from him. Only to be left alone. That was all. But it was too something, wasn't it?

"Where you staying? I checked out Fran."

She gazed silently at him. He watched her closely, the smirk still on his face, as if he did not believe she could stay anywhere long without him. Surely he didn't expect her to answer.

"OK, so you don't want to tell," he shrugged, leaning over the table so far that his face almost hid the light from the small round crystal candleholder in the center. "I'll find out anyway. You *know* that, don't you?"

A shiver went down her spine. She would have to be careful, on guard all the time. But she wouldn't worry Terry. Jerome Lee was *her* problem.

Then suddenly he blurted, "When you coming back?" There was an air of confidence about him now.

His male vanity had once again risen to the surface. He just *knew* she was coming back. She *had* to come back. It would have been all right if *he* had left *her*, but he could not believe that *she* had left *him*. That she would not be with him anymore and, above all, that she could go the way of the world without him, was inconceivable to him. She was a commodity to him, something he had bought with a wedding license and, like all possessions, was a part of his army of belongings. To him, losing her was a loss of property.

"I'm not coming back, Jerome Lee. Ever. I'm getting a divorce."

"A divorce? Oh, baby, that's a good one!" he laughed, throwing his head back, uneven strong teeth clashing against the chocolate hardness of his skin. *"You* going to divorce *me!"*

Her eyes followed his shaking hand as he lifted the cup to his mouth. She knew the shaking as a sign of his battle to come off a prolonged drunk. His hands always shook like that—trembling in a sort of Saint Vitus's Dance. Denise used to watch him at the table, her eyes wide, and later ask: *Why do Daddy's hands shake, Mommy?* Renay watched his large hand grip the small white cup.

"We just can't make it together, Jerome Lee." Her voice softened. "Even in the beginning when Denise was on the way, we shouldn't have tried. And now you're sick. You've got to stop all your drinking before you get worse."

His face stiffened, the lips pressing tightly together. "Who the hell are you to tell me what to do? I can stop drinking anytime I want to. I'm not drunk now, am I. *Am I?"*

No, he wasn't drunk now. In a way, she wished he were, for then talking with him would not seem so strange and nebulous, played for cause and effect. But she could tell he wanted a drink. She had seen this in him many times before. He was on edge until he could get out of her sight and stop the hands so flagrantly independent of him—until he could plug up the nausea inside and put life into the ashes to remake a false bright flame which lifted him again into a nubilated world, created by and for him alone. Drinking was a compulsion with him—a chain that needed one drink link to lock the others, continuing on and on until the chain grew bigger and longer and wrapped around and around him to form a mocking prison. He could hardly wait to get out and start linking the chain again.

"You're the one sick, baby, not *me.* You're crazy, going around with your goddam ass stuck up in the air in another world. Paying no attention to me—your husband. I'm just something around the house to be tolerated. You don't even think about my needs. A man needs sex. You never need it. And when you do open your legs, it's like screwing a motherfucking corpse!"

"Sex has to start for women up here, Jerome Lee," she said, tapping her head, "and work down." With him it didn't begin in her mind or thoughts or anywhere. He didn't move her the way Terry did. She would just lie beside Terry without Terry's touch and feel the stirring spasms of desire.

He glared at her, not understanding, not wanting to. "C'mon home," he said brusquely, as if all she had said were meaningless to him.

"Why?" she asked. He had said nothing about being sorry. Why did he want her back? To be his scapegoat? To be the blame for his alcoholic weakness? To be an escape mechanism for the women of whom he wearied, and a safeguard for the ones he wanted for a while? But above all, to be the doormat upon which he could wipe his feet. Wasn't that what most black men wanted their women for? To take their anger at themselves and the world about them, hold their sperm, spew out their babies? This was what made them feel manly: the white man's underdog having an underdog too.

"I'm not coming back, Jerome Lee. We're through."

His voice suddenly grew wheedling, cunning: "Baby, you don't mean that. How you going to make it without me?" His eyes narrowed over the cup between them.

Then he saw the hatred and contempt on her face. His fists hardened into knots as he scowled threateningly at her. Who did she think she was, looking at *him* like that? A woman only looked at a man that way when someone else had taken his place.

"Who's the nigger?" he blurted out. "There's just *got* to be another nigger!"

His sexual narcissism was wounded—the steel armor of black men, the one and only form of manhood the white man had given them in slavery—the myth of their sexual prowess which black males had come to believe and somehow had made black women believe. The black man was the superstud. The bed was his kingdom, the womb his domain, and the penis his mojo hung with black magic.

"I'll kill the son of a bitch if I catch him!" The words were loud, and those nearby looked furtively at their table.

It would be worse if he found out it wasn't a man at all. Most men hated and feared Lesbians. Besides, to them, what could a woman do without a penis that a man couldn't do better with one? Women became Lesbians because of disappointment in a man. All they needed was a good man to put them on the right track again. Most men didn't realize that some women had proclivities for their own sex. To the male sexual ego, it was a serious blow when women chose their own kind.

His voice continued to whip at her. "I wouldn't be surprised if you were cutting out on me all the time I been beating the bushes trying to make a living for us."

"Jerome Lee," she sighed, "I want you to understand, we're *through*. There's no point in blaming it on anybody except ourselves. I've left you and I'm *not* coming back," she said evenly. "Do you understand that?"

He glared back at her in disbelief. "I want my kid back," he said stubbornly. "I love her."

This, he knew, was the only remaining chance he had for making Renay return to him. "You *love* her?" she repeated incredulously. "Love is an easy word to say, but it's much harder to prove." She looked steadily at him. "You love her like you've always loved her, I suppose. Telling her to get out of your way, you were busy. Too busy to read her a story, take her to the zoo, kiss her goodnight." Angrily, she pushed the chair back to get up. "Jerome Lee, don't you come around here bothering me again."

Realizing she meant it and knowing he could not change her mind, he spat out in roaring fury.

"Bitch! Damn yellow cheese-shit bitch!"

Through the maze of embarrassment, she saw Ruzicka frowning across the room at them from the bar stool where he sat. A man at the table behind them glowered at Jerome Lee and whispered to the sleek woman with him. She knew what the words were before they entered her ears: *Damn niggers ought not to be allowed in places like this*—the same people who had applauded her music had now forgotten.

When she stood up to leave him, he rose from the table and in his anger knocked against the table and turned over his cup. The coffee made a muddy stream on the white tablecloth. "I'll get your ass. You just wait. *Just wait!*"

He stalked out, leaving her standing there alone and motionless, gazing at the place where he had been. The image of him made her tremble and want to strike back in frustration.

"Are you all right?" Ruzicka was beside her, dark face anxious.

"Yes—" She reached to set the cup upright in the saucer. The stream was stopped. "That was my husband. I've left him."

Ruzicka's silence flailed her. Was he going to tell her he could not have family arguments in his place? Would she have to find work elsewhere?

"Would you like something to drink? Coffee?" he asked.

"No, thank you." She looked up at him. "It won't happen again. I'm going now."

His dark eyes focused anxiously upon her. "Let me get you a cab."

"Don't bother. I have a way." She had Terry's car parked outside.

"Nevertheless, let me see you to the door," he insisted, following her. "After all, I have to take care of my main attraction."

She smiled gratefully, perceiving him for the first time not as the white man who controlled her job, but as a friend.

As she drove quickly away, she did not see his surprised look as he recognized Terry's car. He stood there for a long thoughtful moment before re-entering the club.

At home, she found Terry still fully clothed, curled on the couch in the living room, waiting for her. The lamp on the end table cast a soft glow where she had been reading. The rest of the room was shaded.

"May I have a drink?" Renay asked tiredly, tossing her light shawl on a chair. Her shoes followed, abandoned behind her.

Terry frowned quizzically. "Of course."

While Terry was in the kitchen, Renay tiptoed to Denise's room and snapped on the Donald Duck bedlamp. Terry had practically remodeled the den into a child's room, adding a toy chest and small desk. The pink draperies printed with animals matched the spread which covered the couch that opened into a bed.

Denise was asleep. It was amazing how deeply children slept, possibly because they were not burdened with the day-to-day worries which plagued adults at night. She slept like Jerome Lee, hugging the pillow. Bending, she watched and heard the calm breathing—peace from a child's mouth. Gently, she kissed her.

Terry had made the two drinks and was waiting for her in the living room. She took the glass and drank deeply from it, letting the liquor spread warm tentacles through her, unhinging the tautness.

"He was there," she said finally.

"I thought he would be."

She slumped wearily on the couch, moving the opened book and the round owl glasses which Terry sometimes used for reading. "He was mean and ugly. I could have killed him!" The vehemence of her words rocked her. She *could* have killed him—with the lone coffee cup. "You don't know how it is to hate a man—" She closed her eyes, trying to relax in the silence that followed.

"Yes, I do—" Terry finally said "I do because of what I am. Some men are our worst enemies."

Renay felt the couch give to the pressure of Terry's weight. "If you don't want to talk about it anymore, don't."

She opened her eyes and placed her drink on the coffee table. "He doesn't know about you and me—and I don't want to know about him."

Terry's fingers absently caressed the nape of Renay's neck. Renay threw her head back, imprisoning the hand between the couch and her head. "That feels good—"

"Does it?"

"I just want him to stay away from me." She picked up her glass and again drank deeply.

"Darling, I can see you've had a night of it. Come, let's go to bed. I've had a hell of a time too, just waiting for you."

Renay fixed her eyes on the rows of books surrounding the fireplace—books which contained worlds of thoughts of other people.

"Come to bed, Renay."

Terry drew her up and led her to the bedroom. In the shadowed mirror reflecting herself, she watched Terry unpin her hair, undress her and lead her tenderly to the bed. Then Terry left the room for what seemed to be a long time. When she returned, she had on red pajamas and smelled of toothpaste. She snuggled closely into the sea of warmth and protectiveness now beside her. Yet Renay could not sleep.

Turning on her side to face Terry, she kissed the hollow in her neck. Her hand moved exploringly over Terry's body, then down to the cleavage separating Terry's legs. Her fingers intercepted the obstacle of Terry's pajamas. Heedless of the hindrance, her hand grazed against the cloth and cupped the spot she sought. Slowly her hand moved up and down in a fanlike caress.

Terry shifted and opened her mouth to say something, but Renay covered her mouth with her hand. She tugged at the elastic of Terry's pajama bottoms and Terry's slim hips lifted slightly to help her slide the legs down. She moved to touch the sunken eye in Terry's stomach with the tip of her tongue.

"The top too—" she whispered in the depth of Terry's stomach. "Take it off. I want nothing between us."

Obediently Terry unbuttoned the pajama top and threw it on the floor. Renay's mouth made a tiny brush-fire spreading all the way to Terry's pointed chin with its slight cleft, then to each corner tucking her mouth, to cheeks, to the tip of her nose and then at rest on her forehead. A heady blaze excited her, surprising her at the passion rising within her, to culminate a worshipful ritual, showing Terry love. This was the first time she had been the aggressor; but even in her aggressiveness she was subservient, trying to please her lover.

Her lips retraced the path to Terry's small firm breasts, lips grazing each globe gently, tongue savoring the round smoothness. Down she continued, pausing to kiss the insides of Terry's thighs.

Terry moaned, hands pushing at her shoulders to make her stop. "No—no, Renay," she protested. "I don't want you to do that."

"I want to—lie still. Can't I show you how much I love you too?"

Terry half sat up in the bed, but the weight of Renay's body pushed her back, holding her crushed against the pillow with lips strong against hers. Renay's fingers sought the route to the other entrance hidden in a brush easily found by instinct. There the fingers spoke of love, belonging and of giving pleasure.

Terry's voice was hoarse. "Please—don't—Renay—"

Her face was now down to where the hand was, and she could hear another heart where a heart wasn't supposed to be. The kneading drawing forth the love mist withdrew as lips took its place. Wine at the temple of Sappho. A magical potion of love's sweetness, the entering of life's origin.

Terry's hands shoved feebly at her shoulders, stopped and fluttered weakly into the strands of Renay's hair. There they sank and stilled. Terry did not cry aloud, but made a strange gurgling sound, convulsing like one killed while surprised.

Renay remained for a stroke of time arrested between life and death before her head rose and sought the small place in Terry's shoulder. "You see—" she murmured softly, "I love you too."

Terry's arms went about her. "You make me very humble."

"Kiss yourself goodnight." Her lips brushed Terry's.

Sleep came out of the darkness and caressed them as one.

CHAPTER 5

Friday morning came, and Renay felt more alive than in a long while, stimulated by the night's new lovemaking and Terry's love. She knew as soon as she awakened that it was a good day to bring out the other part of her that had to be assuaged too—the need to create. Terry had left her early to go out on an assignment, and she had been at the piano all morning working on the composition she was trying to finish. The ideas were coming smoothly, as if they had been waiting a long while to be set free.

The loud shrill of the doorbell interrupted her. Annoyed, she got up to answer it. A short heavyset woman stood in the doorway. She was wrapped in a shabby black lightweight coat and matching floppy hat that shielded both sides of her rough weather-worn face. When she saw Renay, her lips pinched together to form a tight line while the steel-blue eyes darted over Renay in quick analytic movements. Renay could feel the white hostility issuing forth like desert heat.

"Miss Bluvard in?" she asked in a reedy high-pitched voice, clutching a large frayed tote bag protectively to her side.

"No, she isn't."

The woman's bushy gray eyebrows joined in a frown as she peered suspiciously around Renay. "I'm Miss Wilby. I clean up her apartment once every two weeks on Fridays." Then the threadlike lips opened wider to expose a coated tongue flicking against tiny teeth that made the birdlike mouth appear even smaller. *"You doing it now?"*

The question was both an accusation and insult to Renay. Because she was black, she had to be the maid. Holding in her anger, she looked over the mountain peak of the hat to the foyer wall behind Miss Wilby, then back directly into the eyes. "No, I'm not," she replied coldly.

"Well, in that case, I might as well go on in and get started," she announced brusquely, sweeping past Renay.

In a flurry of systematic movements, Miss Wilby quickly donned an apron over her plaid cotton dress, replaced the batwing hat with a dust cap, and took all the cleaning supplies from the pantry closet.

Renay went back to the piano, unable to concentrate now because of the vacuum's hum in Terry's room. She realized the woman's mind was working, wondering who she was. Soon Miss Wilby progressed to the living room, holding the vacuum in front of her like a geiger counter. Renay leaned over her score, pencil in hand, trying to ignore the noise that was scattering her thoughts like broken crystals.

Suddenly the humming stopped, and Miss Wilby's flutelike voice took its place: "Somebody must be staying here now, with all those extra clothes and things in the closets. Looks like a child's in the den. Dolls and comic books all over the place." She began dusting the furniture, which did not need dusting. Her back was to Renay. "I thought I was out of a job when I seen you answer the door. A body sure needs work these days, high as ever'thing is. Went to the grocery store yesterday to buy some hamburger, and it's gone up twenty cents. Used to be the cheapest thing you could buy. Sure takes a mess to live on these days, I'm tellin' you." She paused, as if waiting for Renay to agree. When there was no response, she went on: "I been cleaning up here for Miss Bluvard for 'most two years now. Not too much to do. I clean up other apartments too in this building. I guess she forgot this was my day, 'cause she's usually here waiting for me. You doing any kind of work for her?"

A direct question from an inquisitive white woman who didn't want her day's work taken away, and who was too racist to accept a black's presence here.

"No, I'm *not* doing any kind of work for her," Renay replied curtly, wishing the woman would leave so she could get back to her music.

"I just wondered. You live near?"

Renay decided to say nothing more. She pretended to concentrate on the music, thinking that if she appeared occupied, the woman's questions might cease.

"I ain't seen no colored families out this way, so, I just wondered."

The dust cloth was closer, moving briskly over the glistening piano. "Sure is a pretty piano. Brand new, too. First time I seen it. She must've just gotten it." The dusting motions stopped as she looked slyly at Renay. "I bet *you* can play real good." Apparently not piqued by Renay's reticence, Miss Wilby dragged on tenaciously. "That's what money can do. Get anything you want. Poor folks like me—we got to work and slave for it." She emitted a deep sigh of exasperation as the vacuum's bee hum began once again, receding now into the dining room.

It took her two hours to clean the apartment, which had been clean before she arrived. When she finished, she came back into the living room. Renay hadn't struck a note on the piano the entire time she was there.

"Place wasn't too bad, even if she has got comp'ny. She usually leaves the money in an envelope in the kitchen drawer. You seen it?"

Renay felt hot resentment rise within her at the incriminating question. To think this grubby old petty-minded woman who cleaned other people's houses had the audacity, the supercilious bigotry of the white to hint at theft. She remembered her mother fuming and fussing when she came home from cleaning some of the white folks' houses in Kentucky. She had been upset by the white woman who would sometimes miss things and blame the colored help. It had made her mother madder than hell, and now it was infuriating her. Her mother had to do that kind of work because there was nothing else she could do. But this woman had a white face—the passkey to all gates of opportunity—and yet she was cleaning floors and being vindictive toward her.

She was amazed at the calmness of her voice when she finally managed to speak. "No, Miss Wilby. I have not seen an envelope. I'm certain that if Miss Bluvard left it in the kitchen drawer, it's still there."

The woman sniffed loudly, marching stiffly to the kitchen. Renay gazed out the window, praying that Terry hadn't forgotten to leave the money. The day had started out so nicely. She saw the treetops stretching to the sky from the park across the street. The limbs and their leaves made clasping green necklace patterns against the clear blue horizon.

"It ain't there!" Miss Wilby's voice was an agitated shout behind her. "She usually leaves it in an envelope right in the top drawer of the cabinet where the knives and forks are. And it ain't there!"

Renay felt the accusing eyes burn into her back. Terry had forgotten. She fought the bitter tide of anger, forcing her rage down before turning to face the challenging storm of Miss Wilby.

"She must have forgotten it," she said, trying to keep her words calm.

"Forgotten it? She ain't forgotten it before. All the times I been working for her," Miss Wilby retorted.

"When people get very busy, they sometimes forget," Renay tried to explain patiently. "Now, if you'll just tell me how much she pays you—"

"*You* ought to know!" The woman's tone reached a shrill peak.

The charge hurled by Miss Wilby was stark before her. Staring defiantly back, she searched for her mother's strength and the strength of all of the other black women who had taken such malicious accusations with courage and composure.

Without a word, she got up and stalked like a regal jungle queen to the room she and Terry shared. Returning, she held out two ten-dollar bills—more than enough, she knew, for two hours of work.

"Here—is this right?"

Miss Wilby squinted at the money, fleeting surprise widening her eyes. Just as quickly, they narrowed as she hesitated at taking

Loving Her

the money Renay held out to her. Renay's unfaltering gaze spoke back: *If you don't want to take my black money, go without.*

"Humph!" Miss Wilby snorted, greedily snatching the bills. Then, muttering under her breath, she quickly changed back into her funereal street attire, the old black coat speckled with lint and the wide hat which fell over the sides of her face. Without further ado, she slammed out of the apartment.

"Now, isn't that a bitch?" Renay said to herself, shaking her head in disbelief. That was one for the black books. The phone rang jarringly, taking away her thoughts of Miss Wilby. It was Jean, wanting to speak to Terry. When Renay told her that Terry wasn't home, Jean left a message for Terry to call, saying that it was important that she get in touch with her. She sounded slightly thick-tongued and Renay wondered if she was drunk this time of day.

Terry returned at noon, throwing off her jacket and slumping wearily into a chair. "Whew! I'm bushed! Phil and I finally got the article and pictures off to *Woman's Flair*. I think I just might calm down from all this chasing around and write a novel. I've been putting it off too long." Lighting a cigarette, she asked, "How was *your* morning?"

Renay turned around on the piano bench to face her. "Chaotic. I met Miss Wilby, who couldn't understand for the life of her my being here, and to whom I didn't try to explain. She also thinks I'm a thief who stole her cleaning money."

"Christ, this *is* her day! I forgot all about her. I'm sorry. I should have remembered to leave the money and to warn you. She's quite a busybody. That's why I always leave after she gets here. She was recommended by the apartment manager." Terry picked up an ashtray, knocking off the embers from her cigarette. "What was so strange about your being here?"

"She assumed that I was taking her job."

Terry's gaze concentrated on the silver ashtray. "That's positively ridiculous."

"Uh-huh. Maybe to *you*." Sometimes Terry could be so damn naive. But Terry had never lived in a black world. "It was the part about the money that tore me up—"

"I knew she was a mess, but not quite *that* bad," Terry snapped, grinding out the cigarette. "I'll give her notice. I can get someone else to clean."

"No need, ma'am. Y'all got yo' cleanin' woman right h'yar wif y'all, and sho' nuff!" Renay mocked. One thing about us black folks, she thought, we got a sense of humor, and thank God, for that's what has kept us sane all through the centuries.

"Oh, Renay—" Terry smiled, "I'll find someone. Anything else happen?"

"Yes. Jean called. She wants to speak to you today about something important." Now the message sounded static to her.

Terry drew a deep breath at the mention of Jean's name. "Damn, *what* is so important?"

"She didn't say, and I didn't ask," Renay replied stiffly. Then, because she was curious: "Who, exactly, *is* Jean?"

"Jean is a model—sometimes," Terry explained, avoiding Renay's eyes. "I might as well explain. We had an affair. I met her in one of the magazine offices where I stopped to discuss a story. I forget which one now." Terry's gray eyes leveled with Renay's. "It was just about over when I first saw you that night at the club—" She stopped, reaching for her pocketbook on the coffee table. "Let's forget Jean. Look, I picked up something for you. It's a college catalog from Waterview City College here. They have an excellent music department. I thought perhaps you could start in the June summer session. By this time next year, you should have your degree. They ought to accept the credits from your other school." She handed the catalog and application forms to Renay. "I think it would be good for you. You're young. There's no point in letting talent and mind go to waste."

Renay took the forms. It *was* an excellent idea! It wasn't too late to scrape up fallen pieces and try to put them together again. It would make her feel she was accomplishing something again.

"Think it over," Terry advised. "I know the head of the music department, Dr. Raleigh Larsons. He's a damn nice guy." She got up and crossed the room to Renay, rumpling her hair. "Darling—*feed* me! I'm hungry. What's for lunch?"

"Anything you want."

"Even anything sounds good. How about scrambled eggs with barbecue sauce?"

"Terry—!"

"Well, that's what I feel like eating," Terry reasoned, following Renay to the kitchen. "Do you want to drive over to Jean's with me later on? I'm going to rest first. Knowing Jean, the important is unimportant."

Renay shook her head, taking a carton of eggs out of the refrigerator. "No thanks. I really think Jean wants to see you alone."

"Oh, all right. I'll pick up Denise after school," Terry said quietly, plugging in the coffee pot.

The door to Jean's apartment was slightly ajar, but Terry knocked a warning sound before entering. Jean was sprawled on the curved white sectional sofa, a half-filled martini pitcher beside her on the floor. Clad in black Chinese lounging pajamas, face flushed, she turned languidly on her side to greet Terry.

"Hello, lover—or ex-lover, I should say. I see you'll still come when I call," she giggled, pushing herself up on one elbow.

"And I see you still haven't learned to keep your door locked," Terry said.

"Open for *you*, sweetie. Here, have a drink. Damn good. Made the whole works myself. 'Member? You always said that I could make the best damn pitcher of martinis."

"No, thanks," Terry said, sitting down in a chair opposite her.

"Aw, have *one*—" Jean urged, filling a glass and getting up unsteadily to cross over to her. "Here—" The top buttons of her high-necked tunic were open, exposing the round milky-white braless breasts as she leaned over.

"What did you want with me?" Terry asked cautiously, avoiding Jean's gaze to concentrate on the drink Jean insisted that she have.

"To see you. What else would I want? You've been neglecting me lately," she whined petulantly. Then the red lips curled into a derisive sneer. "Hasn't your appetite for dark meat waned yet?"

Terry's knuckles shone whitely as her fingers tightened around the glass. "That's enough, Jean!" she blazed angrily, setting the untouched drink down hard on the table. "Hurry up, if you *did* have something in mind."

Jean stepped back silently, watching her with a cat's smile of confidence. Her long blonde hair fell over her face in a loose golden shower. "Something in mind—" she repeated huskily. "Why *you*, of course. You're *always* on my mind." She moved closer to Terry, her fingers stroking her hair as she captured Terry's eyes. "You don't think I'd give you up to a nigger bitch, do you?"

The blow wasn't hard, but it came swiftly. Jean, already off balance, sprawled on the floor.

"Don't you ever call her that again!" Terry muttered, teeth clenched in rage.

Jean half rose, shaking her head. "Well! That's the first time you've ever done *that* to me," she said, her head flung back and eyes narrowing as her lips curved in a slow sensuous smile. "Funny, I *liked* it. How does it make *you* feel? Masculine?" Her hands reached out, elusive long pink-tipped spiders spinning an invisible web up and down Terry's legs. "Come on down here with me," she whispered huskily. "I'll make it better than it's ever been with us. Remember how good it used to be? Come on—lover."

Terry stepped back, staring down in contempt. There was a time when she had wanted this girl to desire her with a personal need, not just for the mundane pleasures she could give her. She had found herself praying for more than Jean had returned, with her superficial love making, her artificial words. It had been a money game with Jean for Terry to supplement her needs when she didn't feel like working—which was often. It was safer for her than with men—less bothersome. There had been Jean and others like Jean, along with those who had done it for kicks, for curiosity—and some to allay boredom with sex itself. It was hard to find those completely honest in the life—sometimes the honest were never found. She wasn't going to lose Renay now: This, she felt, was sincere—perhaps bizarre by so-called normal standards, but a relationship in which she was happier than she had ever been. Happier, she supposed, than many in the conventional situations prescribed by society.

"It may surprise you, Jean, to know I'm in love with Renay."

"Love?" Jean got up slowly from the floor, angrily tossing back her yellow mane of hair. "What does a *bulldike* know about *love?*" she scoffed, triumphantly watching Terry recoil at the word she knew she despised. "Love's for men and women. You're afraid of men. You hear me? *Scared* shitless to be with them like a woman should. But *I'm* not. To me—with *them*—is the best. The goddam *best.* Do you hear? Better than it could ever be with *you!*"

She listened to the bitter words being flung at her. Jean's pride was hurt; she had to be defensive. For the first time, Terry realized that Jean, in her anger, was being completely honest with her.

She started for the door, wanting to get out into the air, away from this emotional maelstrom. The shrieks followed her into the hall and down the steps: "Goddam bulldike! Queer! Freak!"

"Hi, Aunt Terry!"

She opened the car door, hearing different shouts around her now. Children yelled and called happily to each other in unbridled release as they poured out of the school. In youthful flight, they darted through the streets, waiting impatiently for the school crossing guard to wave them on.

"What did you learn today?" Terry asked, smiling down at Denise, who was tossing her books on the back seat.

"Our teacher read us a poem called *The Creation*. It was very pretty. It was about how God made the earth. You ever read it, Aunt Terry?"

"No, dear, I haven't," Terry said, maneuvering the big car slowly through the streets crowded with children and cars and yellow school buses.

"A black poet named James Weldon Johnson wrote it. Our teacher said that we ought to learn more about famous blacks since there aren't many in our textbooks."

"I see. Your teacher is absolutely right. I don't think any race of people should lose sight of their history. It is important to learn what they have contributed to the world and who their leaders were."

Denise tucked her feet under her, turning to gaze intently at Terry. "*You* never heard of James Weldon Johnson?" she asked in childish amazement, as if her Aunt Terry, who wrote, ought to know all about other writers.

Terry stopped for a red light. "Honey, I haven't heard of every famous person in the world. I'll go to the library tomorrow and read the poem, OK?"

"Well!" Denise exclaimed brightly. "At last I've taught *you* something!"

Terry laughed, reaching over to hug her. "That's what makes life interesting. People learning from each other."

The traffic had thinned out and Terry drove faster. As she neared the apartment entrance, she slowed to let Denise out. "You wait for me while I find a parking space."

Denise reached for her books and got out, skipping gaily up the steps of the building to wait for Terry.

She found a parking space and locked the car. Walking back to where Denise waited, she glanced across the street in time to see a man sitting on a park bench. He was staring at Denise. The man's eyes took on a puzzled expression as they briefly met hers. Only as they stepped into the elevator did it occur to Terry that the man's features closely resembled those of Denise.

CHAPTER 6

On Monday, Renay went early in the morning to Waterview College to register. The day was sullen with rain falling in a monotonous downpour. Terry stayed home, deciding this day was as good as any to begin work on her novel. She had learned from past experience that to think of writing and to do it were two different matters.

Writing took self-discipline and determination. And at this moment, she was having a difficult time getting started. The paper on the desk was a perfect example of nothingness. Perhaps she was in the wrong mood. Could it be the dulling effect of the rain, or hadn't her ideas materialized strongly enough to bring the characters out of her mind into life on paper? If she could just write one smooth paragraph, she knew that she would be on her way.

In disgust, she flung her pencil down, angry at the futility of it all. Maybe she, like Schiller, needed a rotten apple to inspire her. She looked out the window and saw that the rain had stopped, but the grayness continued to color the sky. The swollen clouds still hung tenaciously above.

Throwing on her old raincoat and hat, she decided to go for a walk in the park. Frequently that helped to stimulate her thoughts.

Just as she stepped from the elevator, she heard someone calling to her. Turning, she saw the manager of the building, Mr. Herald, coming hurriedly out of his office.

"Miss Bluvard—what luck! I was on my way up to your apartment. Could I see you for a minute, please?"

She followed him into his office, a small comfortable den-like room with knotty pine paneling, a wall-length Danish couch and two chairs facing a neat and orderly desk.

"Please have a seat," he smiled graciously, holding out the chair nearest his desk for her. He was a lean, somewhat too immaculately dressed man who looked older than he was because of the dark hair that was receding rapidly, exposing more and more of his large bulbous forehead. He was always dressed in sharply pressed dark business suits and conservative ties, which made him resemble a bank executive instead of an apartment manager.

Politely he offered her one of his long French cigarettes. "Have one?"

"No, thank you," she said, silently hoping he wasn't going to delay her with another of his lengthy interrogations of how the place suited her and if she had any suggestions for improvement.

"Miss Bluvard—" he began, clearing his throat, "I have—ah—a rather important matter to discuss with you. You see, it has been brought to my attention that you have some people staying with you in your apartment—"

Terry stiffened in her chair. What was this all about? "Yes, I do."

"Is the Negress working for you as a sleep-in maid?"

Terry eyed him warily, thinking it was none of his damn business whom she had in her place as long as she paid her rent on time. "No, she is *not* a maid," she answered coldly, voice evenly low. "Miss Davis is a friend of mine who is living with me—and, for your information, Mr. Herald, the word Negress is as objectionable as nigger."

Mr. Herald fidgeted in his swivel chair, crossing and uncrossing his legs in nervous spasmodic jerks. "Forgive me, I didn't realize or mean—"

"If you want more money because two other persons are sharing my apartment with me," Terry continued in her icy tone, "I shall be glad to pay it."

"Oh, no!" he protested quickly, fixing his eyes upon the barely touched burning cigarette held loosely between his carefully manicured fingers. "It's not a question of money. It's—well—" Abruptly he swung his chair around, leveling his eyes on the space beyond her. "Miss Bluvard—this is rather embarrassing to *me*," he began hesitantly. "First, let me assure you that *I* have no objections to—well—*Negroes*. But some of the tenants have seen the woman and child coming and going from your apartment. And they—" he stopped to douse the cigarette, now a long ash. Then, with forced winded constraint, "To be perfectly *frank*, if you've noticed, there are *no* Negroes living in this *particular* section of the city. The unwritten policy of the owners of the building has been *not* to rent to Negroes."

Terry's eyes stung wetly as hot anger welled deep within her. "That's utterly ridiculous!" she heard herself shouting at him. "You rented that apartment to *me*. I don't see whose concern it is who is staying with me or even visiting me. I told you she was a friend of mine. As long as I'm paying the rent and minding my own business—which I'm sorry other people find it hard to do—and not keeping the tenants awake, what damn difference does it make?"

Mr. Herald flushed as he toyed with a world globe paperweight on his desk. "I'm sure she's a *very* good friend of yours, Miss Bluvard," he half smiled, giving her a long knowing look. "But you must understand, the tenants are *complaining*. Only the other day, a woman told me a Negro man was lurking in the hallway reading the names on the mailboxes. He *frightened* her."

She probably was hoping to be raped, Terry thought wryly.

"As much as this *pains* me, I must ask you to either rid yourself of your friends—or move. I had hoped you would understand. We certainly don't want to lose *you*," he added quickly. "But when Negroes move in, there follows a rash of them, and—"

Face livid with anger, she rose, shoving the chair back hard against the wall. "If I had known before I rented this place that it was filled with so many contemptible, sordid and hypocritical people, I'd never once have entertained the thought. Thank you for letting me know what a nice lily-white section of town this is and about the wonderful pure white people who inhabit it. I don't suppose you rent to Jews either, do you?"

Loving Her

"It's not *me*, Miss Bluvard," he protested weakly. "I only follow orders. I don't *set* policies—"

"No," she replied acidly, "but it's perfectly obvious you enjoy carrying them out. Like the Eichmanns and Görings and Himmlers." Her hands dug deeply into her raincoat pockets to keep him from seeing their angry tremor. "You may inform your overly concerned tenants, who want their lives to be one big closed club, that we are leaving!"

She slammed the door, pausing outside it for a moment to suppress the urge to turn and kick it. Fury boiled inside her. It was one son-of-a-bitching world, and she was sorry she had to be the color of those who son-of-a-bitched it up more than others.

She did not go for the walk in the park. Instead, she went back to the apartment and opened a bottle of bourbon to sit down and do some serious drinking and thinking. This was her first intimate encounter with racial prejudice. It seemed so low and compellingly dehumanizing. She had never had any firsthand experience to make her actuely aware of its biting impact. Why should it have been? Her life had been solidly WASP.

Before knowing Renay, she actually had never been exposed to or closely associated with blacks. Her parents had even had white servants. The ugliness of racism had been remote to her; in her white-gilded ghetto, she had been totally isolated from it. Besides, her personal burden of invertedness and its stigma had been uppermost in her mind. For she, too, was a minority and an outcast because of it. Only her burden wasn't as visible, which made it easier to conceal.

She had passed blacks on the streets, her writer's eye noticing their dark tight faces closing against her, but that was all. She remembered the one black girl in the all-girl New England college she had attended. This was before white colleges were actively recruiting black students. Most of the students had shunned the girl, Alice—even though her father was considered well-to-do by any standards and was a diplomat in Africa. She had tried to make friends with Alice, partly because she knew what it meant to be ostracized, but mostly because of her innate feelings of sympathy and understanding, unusually strong in the homophile. The girl, a beautiful brown with pensive dark eyes, had rebuked her overtures of friendliness. She had heard rumors and chose to be engulfed in loneliness rather than have a Lesbian as a friend. Terry reflected on the stupidity of such a choice. Lesbians, too, had preferences, and weren't out to make every female in sight. It was a matter of interest in those who shared mutual feelings and desires.

She refilled her glass, leaving out the ice and soda this time. How many arguments had she had over a drink with others as she upheld the rights of blacks? She had reasoned against those who felt "they" were going too far and getting out of hand with their marches and sit-ins and demands. She had given generously to the movement organizations, and had even read a great deal of W.E.B. DuBois, Martin Luther King, and Malcolm X. She had delved into the recent books focusing on black women. But all of these gestures had been trips into rhetoric, philanthropy, and meanderings into scholarship. If you weren't black you couldn't really know how it felt unless the shit fell loose on you too. Today, it had.

Draining the glass, she was aware of becoming muddled. But what the hell kind of world was this anyway? Anger built aggression within her as she thought about Renay and herself. She would protect her home—her own. Renay wasn't going to be embarrassed and neither would Denise. Her thoughts turned around and around slowly like a creaking rustic wheel until she decided what had to be done. Satisfied at her decision, she smiled. She would tell Renay when she returned.

By the time Renay got home in the afternoon, Terry knew she was high, but it was the subtle tightness where everything had a lucid glow like being both hot and cold and outside oneself looking in.

"Well, I'm registered for the summer term," Renay announced excitedly, bending to kiss her. "I start the second week in June for the summer session."

"Fine—wonderful! Have a drink—" Terry offered, quickly mixing one for Renay.

"All right, but isn't it kind of early?" Renay said, frowning at the bottle and Terry.

"Nope. Not for a *double* celebration it isn't."

"A double celebration?" Renay questioned, pouring more soda to dilute the strong drink Terry had fixed for her.

"Our new beginning. Plus, we're moving. We're going to Willow Wood as soon as we can get the hell out of here."

Renay tentatively sipped the drink. "That's quite a distance from town, isn't it?"

"Not too far. Besides, that's why I'm moving. I'm sick of being near people. I can write better out there. No disturbances. Just think, you can even play the piano in the woods if you like. Besides, I might as well take advantage of my house. Why pay rent? School is almost out, so it won't be too hard on Denise having to get up a little earlier to get there on time."

"I see—" Renay said, as if she didn't see at all.

"I've also been thinking that you'd better go to my lawyer, David Howell, this week and arrange for a divorce."

Renay was silent, gazing questioningly at Terry. "Has Jerome Lee been here?"

"Hmmm. Yes and no. Let's say he's been *near* here—if he looks like Denise." She smiled at her witticism. She had decided that it must have been Jerome Lee searching the names on the mailboxes. "It's best to start your proceedings before he gets warmer. He *could* make it hard for you if he decides to pursue it. He could put up a messy fight, and perhaps even get Denise."

"That's why you want to move?"

"Yes," Terry lied, twisting her glass absently.

"Well, when do we move?"

"Tomorrow."

"Aren't you rushing it?" Renay asked, her eyes questioning.

"Not fast enough."

"Any complaints about *my* being here?"

"What made you ask that?" Terry murmured, unable to conceal her surprise. She avoided looking up—she had never been very good at lying. The liquor tasted sour in her mouth now. She put the glass down.

"I'm black. Been black all my life, and will be for the rest of it. That's how I know. Good old darky instinct. Anyway, I came upon Miss Wilby talking with the manager in the hallway the other day.

They glared at me as if I were a walking communicable disease. Some mornings when I leave to take Denise to school, a few of the others have stared hard too."

"Damn them!" Terry cried out in exasperation. "I'm sorry. God, if only I could exchange my skin for yours to make it less painful for you."

"No, I like my skin the way it is," Renay murmured in the hollow of Terry's ear. "Besides, I wouldn't want to feel as hurt and helpless as you are now inside yours. We have each other. We can learn to bear what each suffers, and even help in that suffering."

Terry closed her eyes, breathing in the warm fragrance of Renay's hair. "I know what it is to be objectionable to people who surmise what I am and hate me for it. But *you*, now you have triple strikes against you of being black, a woman and living with me the way you are."

Renay chuckled softly, kissing Terry's eyelids to make them open. "Terry, darling, it's perfectly obvious the two of us can't change the world. But it's nice to know that in all the world's confused state, we can think like this about one another. If *we* can, then there must be others like us who can feel and love and live together despite everything else, and even in this smallness, make the world a better place."

Terry rubbed her head gently against Renay's breast. "That was very sweet. You've sobered me up. Let's get busy. I'll call a moving company and ask Phil and his Benjie to come over and help us pack. Phil loves excitement. We'll have a party."

"Marvelous!" Renay said, matching Terry's mood. "We'll really leave Miss Wilby something to clean up next time!"

CHAPTER 7

"Do you see the boys?" Terry asked, eyes on the narrow road stretching like an endless gray slab ahead.

Renay shifted slightly to peer over the piles of suitcases and boxes stacked in the rear of the car. "They're coming around the bend now."

The road was narrow and seemed to climb high into the sky. On each side were trees and fields with a sprinkling of houses partially revealed through clustered green foliage. The day was sharply blue and seemed distilled in a glaring sun, making everything alive and clear. There were only the two of them, for Renay had left Denise to spend the night with Fran while they moved.

The convertible's top was down, and Terry's auburn hair rose and fell with the soft rushing movement of the wind. "I'd better let Phil know we're almost there. He drives that Volkswagen like a jet."

Terry slowed and switched on her signals for a right turn. They were now on a winding Indian-like path leading to a two-story Tudor house. It was half stucco with wood posts and brackets and a brick-and-stone chimney. An old-fashioned bay window projected outward. The house was enclosed by the sheltering trees Terry had described. A white birdbath filled with fresh water punctuated the center of the lawn.

"Here it is—Willow Wood!" Terry announced happily, braking to a stop. "I hope Mrs. Levine remembered to see that everything is ready."

The orange Volkswagen drew up noisily behind them, horn beeping merrily. Phil and Benjie jumped out, waving to them. Both were dressed in faded blue jeans and T-shirts. Benjie stood in the middle of the road surveying the house. He was the shape of a reed with straw-blonde hair falling in vermicelli strands over a handsome, boyish, too-smooth face.

"Beautiful, isn't it, Phil?" he exclaimed, his soft blue eyes taking in the scene with delight.

"Definitely *far* away from the madding crowd," Phil commented. "Terry, dear, you never told us about this perfect place."

"Why should I tell you all about my life?" Terry winked, dragging suitcases from the car. "I'm pleased that you like it. Now let's get this stuff inside."

Renay grabbed an armful of boxes and waited while Terry unlocked the heavy wooden door. The moving van had already brought the piano, stereo, TV sets and other items Terry wanted. Since the house was already furnished, some of the apartment furniture had been stored in the rooms above the garage until Terry decided what to do with it. She had given a few of the lamps and chairs to Phil and Benjie for their place. The house had an open, fresh smell, showing that Mrs. Levine hadn't forgotten.

The curved window reaching to the beamed living room ceiling fascinated Renay, with its curved built-in bench to fit. "Oh, Terry, I love it!"

"Glad you do, darling," Terry breathed appreciatively, almost as if she had been a little afraid Renay wouldn't like it. She dumped the suitcases on the highly polished oak floor in the hallway.

"My God! How do people manage who move all the time?" Benjie moaned, bringing in the things from the Volkswagen.

"The way we're doing now," Phil replied, voice muffled over a stack of boxes up to his chin.

Benjie glanced wishfully at Terry. "I could sure use a drink."

"Not another one now. You've had enough for the time being," Phil scolded, shaking his head.

"But, Phil—remember? It's my birthday!"

"And besides, he deserves one," Terry interceded. "Let's see if there are any ice cubes."

The kitchen, separated from the dining room by a latticed swinging door, was large and spacious with a long window matching the length of the sink. Terry opened the refrigerator. "Yes—we have ice," she said, taking out the trays.

"Get the rest of the stuff from the car, Benjie," Phil ordered sharply.

"Oh-o-o, sometimes he can be so disgustingly mean!" Benjie's small lips stuck out in a pout. "And on my birthday, too!"

"How old?" Terry smiled, dropping ice cubes in glasses. The ice made a celebrative sound.

"He's twenty-one and acts sixteen sometimes. Like now. Hurry up, Benjie."

"Mean—mean—mean—" Benjie grumbled, going quickly out the door.

Phil helped Terry put scotch in the glasses. "It'll take you days to get straightened out. What a chore!"

Benjie came back, wiping his forehead with the back of his hand. "Everything's in. Now where's my glass?"

Phil handed him a small drink. "Here, I want you halfway sober for your party tonight. You are coming, aren't you, dears? There'll be just a few friends in for Benjie's birthday celebration."

Terry glanced at Renay. "If she feels like it."

"Of course she feels like it," Phil held up his glass. "Here's to all those under twenty-one and well over like Terry and me!" he laughed.

"Ugh! Tastes like water." Benjie grimaced, gulping at his drink.

"I'd invite you two to stay for dinner," Terry said. "But—" She looked around helplessly.

"Don't fret over it. We'll come another time when you're settled. Anyway, I detest eating in confusion," Phil said, shuddering.

"I just adore this place," Benjie said, draining his glass. "Wish we could afford to buy a house. I'm beginning to simply hate people. Sometimes they look at us like—well—dirt!"

Phil gave Benjie a quick disapproving look. "He always gets like that when he's drinking. Remember, Benjie, I told you that we're not going to let other people ruin it for us. Now, not another drink after this until tonight."

"More?" Terry turned to Renay.

"Later. I'll never get anything done," Renay said, placing her glass on the sink.

"What's upstairs?" Benjie asked, looking around.

"Three bedrooms, two baths and a den where I'll do my writing. Go up and take a look, if you care to."

"If its too-o-o comfortable up there, we might not come down for quite a while!" Benjie leered lasciviously at Phil.

"The liquor's going to his head. C'mon before I take you

home," Phil said, reddening as he pushed Benjie playfully out of the kitchen.

Terry refilled her glass. "I hate to think of all this work. I could call Mrs. Levine to come and help us, but I remembered Miss Wilby and I let her go after she'd seen to opening the house."

"Don't worry, we'll manage. It'll be fun in a way—setting up our very own place."

"Would you like to go out to dinner? There's a unique restaurant near here. A friend of mine owns it."

"If *you* want to—"

Scampering sounds and loud squeals came from upstairs. Suddenly Benjie, laughing breathlessly, rushed into the kitchen. "Phil can't find me!"

"Yes I can too!" Phil shouted, coming in to grab him from behind. "He's still a boy at heart," Phil apologized to them. "Wants to play hide and seek. Let's go home and get ready for the party."

Terry walked to the car with them. "Thanks for everything."

"We'll be back sometime. Don't forget to come tonight." Phil slammed the car door, reaching across to lock Benjie in.

"We won't," Terry assured him, waving goodbye as they drove off.

When she returned to the house, Renay was unpacking the box of china. "Benjie acts so young—"

"He *is* young," Renay said.

"This one's lasted longer than any of the others," Terry observed, bending to help unwrap the plates and put them in the dining room china closet. "Do you really want to go to the party? I suppose after struggling with us for two days, it would be an affront to them if we didn't show up."

"I don't care."

"The few friends Phil referred to usually turn out to be quite a crowd. And sometimes they get—well—rather wild."

"Terry, I've been to wild parties before." With Jerome Lee—to the soul music, chitterlings, pig's feet, rotgut whiskey, pot smoking and writhing black men dry-screwing to a scratchy, never-ending Ray Charles.

"We'll unpack some of the things and then go to dinner."

"Who're our nearest neighbors?" Renay gazed out into the sprawling space framed by the dining room window.

Terry came close to her. "If you look carefully, you'll see a brown frame house almost hidden by the bushes. The house has been vacant a long while. I don't know if anyone's living in it now or not. It looks far away, but it's within walking distance."

"I see it," Renay said. It was a house with a slanted black roof. She was reminded of the storybook gingerbread house.

"I hope you'll like it here." Terry touched her, and Renay felt suddenly warm.

"I'm here with you. Why shouldn't I like it?"

Terry nipped her cheek with quick little harmless bites. "That's why I like you around. You can say the nicest things. Let's hurry so we can go and eat. I want you to meet Vance. She owns a lovely place."

The restaurant was hidden in the woods off the highway and had a picturesque colorful sign in the shape of a bow and arrow—Sherwood Forest Inn. Going inside was like entering a grotto, with walls and ceiling a Lincoln green. A mural of Robin Hood and his merry band drinking ale in a splashingly colorful forest was painted on the entire length of the wall behind the bar. Hidden lights shone effectively down upon it.

They moved toward one of the wooden tables carved like a broad flat tree trunk and sat down on cushioned benches imitative of tree limbs that looked too light to hold them but did. Only a few people were there, for it was early yet, and a waitress was busily spreading yellow linen cloths on the tables.

A short, chunky woman, dressed in a brown pantsuit, with a broad square face capped with black hair streaked in the center by a narrow path of gray, came toward them, smiling widely.

"Terry Bluvard! What a hell of a surprise."

"Hello, Vance. It's good to see you again." Terry greeted her with a hug. "Renay, meet a good friend of mine, Vance Kenton, who owns this stolen scene out of Howard Pyle."

Vance turned inquisitive eyes upon Renay. "Hello—Renay—" The woman's gaze lingered before returning to Terry. "It's been quite a while since I've seen you. Have you finally decided to return to Willow Wood?"

"Yes—" Terry reached for a cigarette.

Vance quickly picked up one of the restaurant's match folders and lighted Terry's cigarette. "I always knew someday you would. We all have to come in out of the rain—sometime," she said softly. "Want something to drink?"

"I'll take a martini. Would you like a manhattan, Renay?"

"Please." Because she felt herself an intrusion between the nuances of their exchange, Renay occupied herself with the menu. The imitation kerosene lamp licked forked shadows over the print.

Vance threw her head back and laughed a deep booming sound. "What, Terry? No straight booze anymore? Times *do* change. OK, I'll mix them myself. The bartender's probably in back anyway flirting with the waitress."

"Vance and I have known each other for a long time," Terry said, over the burning eye of her cigarette.

"I gathered that."

A waitress dressed in a tight green Robin Hood outfit complete with a rakish feather in her hat brought them their drinks. "Miss Kenton said to tell you the drinks are on the house."

"Thank you." Terry lifted her glass in gratitude to Vance behind the bar.

"Do you want to order now or later?" the waitress asked.

"Might as well order now," Terry replied, taking the menu Renay passed to her. "Let's see—I think I'll have the Sherwood Forest special, as Vance calls it. Venison, baked potato and tossed salad. And a big mug of that delicious draft ale!"

"And you, ma'am?"

"I'll have the same," Renay ordered, sliding the ash tray over to Terry, whose cigarette ashes had been forgotten as usual. "This is a very unique place. How did she ever conceive the idea?"

"Vance is full of ideas. She's also an artist. As a matter of fact, she did the mural behind the bar. She paints spasmodically now. Even so, she's given several shows in town. Vance is what I would call a mood artist. She can't work unless she's in the mood. Her moods are motivated by her private life, which she lets consume her. There's her private life now—Lorraine," Terry said, her eyes

Loving Her

watching a slim redheaded girl come uncertainly down the steps in the rear and go over to the bar.

Renay thought that the girl was too thin, and didn't like the way her chalky white face was splotched with rouge. She saw Lorraine lean over the bar and whisper to Vance, who had an angry scowl on her face.

"They've been living together for ten years. Vance met her while teaching at a private college in Ohio. Lorraine was one of her most promising art students."

The waitress brought their food, setting long steaming platters before them. The food looked very appetizing to Renay as she dipped hungrily into the large baked potato.

"Terry, I've been thinking. I'd like Denise to go to Kentucky with Fran when school is out. Mother will enjoy having her for the summer, and I think the trip would be good for her." She thought it would be best, too, since she was going to summer school and Terry wanted to work on her novel.

"Does she want to go?"

"I haven't mentioned it to her yet." Renay said, spreading more butter between the halves of her potato. The butter melted quickly, dispersing a thin yellow film. "I don't think she'd mind. It's been a long time since she's seen her grandmother. I doubt if she even remembers her."

"If you want her to go, I think it would be good for her." Terry pressed out her cigarette. She picked up the wooden mug of cold ale and drank thirstily from it. When she set the mug down, a tiny fleck of foam stuck to her lips. Cutting into her meat, she chewed it tentatively. "Hmmm, delicious. The food's improved!"

"Well, well, Terrence!" The thin girl whom Terry had called Lorraine now stood over their table, smiling down at Terry as she held unsteadily to the back of Terry's chair. "When Vance pointed you out, I couldn't believe my eyes!"

"How are you, Lorraine? I'd like you to meet a friend of mine. This is Miss Davis—Renay."

"Oh?" The girl's eyes flicked over Renay. "Nice—"

"Sit down," Terry invited.

Lorraine sat down beside Terry. "She's peeved with me." Her head jerked toward Vance. "Says I'm tight. Hell, what does she expect me to do all day, keeping me cooped upstairs in the apartment all the time. I've got to get out."

"She's only thinking of your welfare," Terry said patiently.

"I'll bet. Hers, you mean!"

Vance came hurriedly over to join them. "How's the food?"

"Wonderful. You serve the best hamburger for venison I know," Terry joked, holding a piece of meat on her fork in the air.

"Sh-h-h—" Vance winked. "If you stay around here too long, you'll ruin my business. Why don't you two come upstairs for a while when you finish?"

"Thanks, we'd love to, but we have someplace else to go. Another time—" Terry promised.

Lorraine leaned across the table, cupping her chin in both hands as she stared boldly at Renay. Suddenly she began laughing a little girl's laugh of surprise and amusement. "Just think—she's gay! I can't believe it. For the first time in my life, I've met a black Lesbian!"

"Lorraine!" Vance's voice cracked sharply. "That's her biggest fault. You never know what she's going to say or do next." Vance tried to smile, spreading her large hands in exasperation.

A warm flush heated Renay's body. This was the first time she had been called that. The word staggered her as much as if the girl had called her a nigger. She was appalled at herself. How could she equate the two terms? The Lesbian as the nigger of sex? And was it noticeable now? She knew of no visible changes in herself. She still talked, looked and acted the same. Lorraine had concluded that she was a Lesbian simply because she was with Terry. Wrong judgments had been made that way. She felt Lorraine's knee pressing against hers under the table. She knew Lorraine was slightly high.

"Come on, honey," Vance said quickly, getting up. "Since you're down here, you might as well help out." She patted Terry's shoulder. "Stop by again—soon."

"Thanks. We will." Glancing anxiously at Renay, Terry pushed her empty plate aside. "Lorraine's a nice kid—a little impulsive at times."

"Sherwood Forest hides a lot, doesn't it?"

Terry shrugged. "Just like the rest of the world. No difference.

Loving Her

Closets are everywhere. As soon as you've finished, we'll go to Phil's."

It was late when they arrived and the party was in full swing, the lights in the living room low. Hand-printed signs of various designs, reading HAPPY BIRTHDAY BENJIE, were strewn throughout the apartment. A large birthday cake with candles already blown out sat debauched in the center of a long table made of joined card tables and covering them with red plastic cloths. Paper cups and assorted bottles, along with plates of tiny sandwiches, pickles, cheeses, potato chips and nuts, filled the table.

The guests were drinking, milling around, talking and laughing while background music rose above them, sounds which could barely be heard over the caterwaul of voices. Some of the women with extremely short haircuts were dressed in pantsuits or slacks and tailored shirts, standing wide-legged as they talked and gripped their straight whiskies. Most of the men, even those middle-aged, appeared to be boyish, their long hair parted in devious ways to hide the thinness, and diet-exercised bodies encased in tight slacks and colorful shirts. A few of them wore suits and ties.

"You made it!" Phil called jubilantly, rushing toward them. "Renay, you look absolutely *stunning* in that orange dress! Isn't this a beautiful group?" he noted, glancing around approvingly. "A lot of our straight friends are here. The Gay Liberationists are really doing *wonders* at broadening their minds. Benjie and I have been going to some of their meetings. You two should join us sometime. A lot of us are coming out of the closets these days." He laughed. "Go get a drink and play catch up. And *do* see all those gorgeous gifts in the bedroom. Now *where* did Benjie go?" he muttered under his breath, moving back through the knots of people.

As Terry contemplated the array of bottles and food, Renay looked around, believing it was an all-white party until she saw one of the brothers staring at her from across the room. He was young, short and light-complexioned, with a carefully shaped Afro surrounding his face like a wide fan. He wore a black balloon-sleeved Harry Belafonte shirt and snug white slacks that hugged his hips. He stared at her in surprise from behind rimless tinted glasses, and then smiled. She smiled back, thinking it was always good to see a brother or sister in a multitude of white faces.

"What would you like to drink, Renay? Scotch, gin, bourbon—" Terry reached for the bourbon bottle.

"Bourbon's all right."

Two women came to the table to freshen their drinks. The heavyset one in fly-fronted slacks handed a cup to the heavily made-up girl with purple eyeshadow and a bouffant hairdo. "I told you to stop flirting with her," the woman hissed loudly, filling her cup with gin.

The girl saw Terry and Renay and looked away. "I wasn't flirting. I was simply talking—"

"Hah! I know what *your* talking can lead to. I guess it was just talking when you met me—" the older woman snapped, tossing down her drink.

The couple moved away as someone turned the record player louder and the full band sound of *The Stripper* swept the room. Benjie leaped onto a chair and shouted above the clamor: "Have fun, everybody. This is a partie—e—e—ee!"

"How about a striptease, Benjie?" a deep male voice shouted jokingly.

"Phil would kill me!" Benjie yelled back, wiggling his hips coyly.

A man spoke to Terry, and when she turned, Renay felt someone tap her lightly on the shoulder.

"Hello—it's good to see a sister here."

He had a nice voice and a smile to go along with it. His eyes seemed overly bright as they looked at her. "I'm here with my lover. He's white. Most of our friends are white. My friends wouldn't understand it too well—you know—his being white and all." His voice lowered wistfully. "I get lonely sometimes for a black face. I'm the only token nigger on my job." Suddenly he leaned closer to her like a conspirator. "But, hon—ey, let *me* tell *you*, when it gets too goddam unbearable—" his tone half rose as his eyes flashed with mirth, "—Clarence Wigginstone III—that's me—sneaks across town to the Black Bottom Cafe to eat soul food, hear Aretha and listen to that good black ain't-nothing-like-it rhythmic rap!"

Clarence Wigginstone III rocked back on his square patent-leather black medium-heel pumps and laughed softly, his eyes taking in her reaction. "Oh, but I don't do anything else—" he added quickly. "You know. I tried it once—everybody sneaks a little extra piece sometimes—" he appended defensively, as if she were silently censuring him. "Dearie, the guy was as big and ugly-looking as Sonny Liston." He giggled, squeezing her arm. "And treated me like *shit!* I suppose the black superstud image making it these days can't be tarnished." He sipped from his glass. "And because of it, I don't believe there can or ever *will* be gentleness among black men."

Before she could reply, he was taken off by a balding man who looked like a wrestler. The tempo of the music had relaxed, and two women began dancing. Other couples followed, circling the floor. Terry set her cup down and turned to Renay, taking her hand. "You've never danced with me. Would you like to try it?"

Terry's arms went out and Terry's softness blended immediately with hers. She closed her eyes, deadening the thoughts, concentrating on the music, savoring the moment. The music was low and sweet.

She opened her eyes to see a man and woman watching them curiously. The man was one of the few in suits and ties. The woman was very pretty, with a sensuous, sleepy look about her narrowed eyes. When the music stopped, the man approached them, the woman following.

"You two just came, didn't you?" he stated, smiling too broadly.

"Yes—" Terry answered, face wary.

"May I dance with your friend?" he asked, mouth twisted sardonically as he glanced briefly at Renay.

Terry shrugged. "Why don't you ask her?"

Without asking, the man assertively pulled Renay abruptly into his arms and held her tightly to him. Over his shoulder, she could see the woman talking to Terry. Then she saw Terry's arms go around the woman to guide her to the music.

"I'm afraid my wife and I are probably the only straight people here," the man said, laughing in her ear. "How about you? *You* don't really go for that woman-loving stuff now, do you? *I* know what Negro women like. The real thing!"

Angered by his words, Renay tried to push him away, but his

arms were hard about her. He danced in the white man's superior way with black women, believing he was doing her a great favor or honor.

"First time I've ever *danced* with a colored girl. But as the old saying goes, there's a first time for everything!" His hands grazed her breasts.

This time Renay shoved furiously at him. "I'll tell the NAACP how liberal you are!" she retorted, eyes blazing with anger. "Now let go of me!"

"Aw, c'mon, baby. I didn't mean it like that. You colored women *do* things to me!"

Renay could see Terry wasn't dancing now with the woman. "If you only knew what I'd like to do to you," she snapped bitterly, looking spitefully at him before moving away.

"Imagine!" Terry snorted, mixing another drink. "She wanted us to go home with them to have a private party."

"She with you, I suppose, and me with that white bastard of a husband who probably wants to change his luck! The only *straight* people here," Renay mimicked derisively.

Terry tasted her drink. "Don't let them get you down. You meet all kinds at parties."

A man's high giggle rang out behind them. "Now! You just get your hands away from down there—"

Renay watched two men go into a room and close the door. A buxom woman in Levi's and a man's denim shirt muttered: "Damn males'll bugger anyplace." She turned, her freckled face grinning at Terry. "Hi! My name's Stony. Can I dance with your girl here?"

"The belle of the ball," Terry bowed mockingly.

Before Renay could refuse, Stony's well-muscled arms held her in a jailhouse grip. Her dancing didn't include movement except where the hips were. "Like I say, the guys got no morals or character. They'll love it up anyplace—parks, bathhouses, picture shows—me, I like my privacy and not with everybody. You can believe that!" She threw back her head, making the short straight brown hair fall back from her face. "I'd like to see you sometime, kid, when you can slip away. I can show you a good time. I know some way-out tricks others never even heard of before. I'll have you screaming happy all night long."

The fragrance of shaving lotion emanated from the woman's face and Renay wrinkled her nose. *She's like Terry and yet she isn't like her. No one is as sweet and gentle and kind as Terry.*

Stony's hand snaked down her spine to rest on her buttocks, rotating them in a slow circling movement in time with the music. "Jesus, baby, could I go for you!"

An arm came between them. "Renay—" Terry stood there, darkness shadowing her face.

Stony backed off hurriedly. "Nice talking to you, kid. Thanks for the dance."

Benjie ran up to them, his face flushed, his cornsilk hair in disarray. "Terry, Phil's mad at me. On my birthday, too! He thinks I've been with that gorgeous hunk of man over there. See him? He looks like Troy Donohue. Isn't he cute, though?" Benjie tried to cry and bat his long lashes at the same time. "Terry, you'll just *have* to come over and talk to him for me. He'll listen to you."

Terry sighed wearily. "All right—give me time to get another drink."

While Renay waited for Terry to talk to Phil, who was sitting alone brooding in a corner on the floor, she saw Clarence Wigginstone III talking animatedly to a circle of eager male listeners whose eyes conveyed more hunger than interest.

The woman whose husband had danced with her sidled up to her. "I wanted you and your friend to come over later."

"So I heard." Renay did not look at her but at the drink she had been holding all evening. The ice had melted long ago.

"I couldn't ask *her*, but tell me, what on earth do you do?"

Renay stared coldly at her. "What do you mean—*do?*"

The woman's voice lowered intimately: "When you make love—"

The heat of the woman's body and her sweet perfume suffocated Renay. "Go away—please," she whispered harshly, sure that if she didn't, she would throw her drink at her.

"No offense—I—" The woman backed away hurriedly before the storm in Renay's face.

Quickly she drank the warm whiskey. Snatches of liquored conversation pleated in folds around her:

"You're drunk—drunk—*drunk!*"

"If you even *look* at a man, I'll kill you."

"He's got the sweetest little behind—"

Terry crossed the room to Renay; she had apparently made the peace, because Benjie was dancing now with Phil. "Ready to go? We've had a pretty long day."

Renay nodded. "If you are."

They eased around the couple arguing by the door. The woman was shaking her fist at a frightened girl. The sounds of music and the tumult of voices followed them in descending spirals down the steps and into the early morning street.

Terry, silent, drove fast along the dark highway. Thin fingers of dawn began to part the sky in grayish hue. Only when they were home in the bedroom did Renay realize that Terry was angry and slightly drunk.

"Terry, what's wrong?" she asked anxiously, sitting on the edge of the bed in her gown.

"Nothing. Do I look as if something's the matter?" Terry said irritably, buttoning her pajama shirt. A glass was on the bureau and she reached to drink from it.

Suddenly Renay realized. "I *wasn't* enjoying dancing with her."

"If I hadn't stopped you when I did, she'd probably have had you in one of those bedrooms before the record ended."

"Terry—" Renay dropped her arms from around her. Terry's face was flushed, and the strong odor of whiskey singed her breath. "Why don't you stop drinking for tonight?"

"Don't *you* tell *me* what to do!" Terry shouted at her. "I know what *you'll* do one of these days. Disappear with somebody else. After all, I was the first with you. They all end up wanting to try others—"

"You know that's not true. Why should I?"

"Because variety is the spice of life," Terry replied derisively. "I'm going downstairs."

Renay remained quiet in the bed listening to the downstairs sounds of Terry's heavy footsteps to the kitchen, the opening of the refrigerator door, and footsteps back to the living room. After the sounds ceased, she went down to find her sprawled on the couch, a glass on the floor beside her. Daylight was upon them in a dim colorless morning which lighted the room.

"Terry, this is all very silly," Renay said, looking down at her sulking on the couch. Then, surprising even herself, she stamped her foot in disgust. "You're acting like a jealous husband!"

Terry was silent for a moment before she broke into gales of laughter. "That's funny, you know. Real funny. And *me*, the great mediator for the boys!"

Renay knelt on the floor beside the couch. "Come to bed with me—please."

"Why?" Terry teased.

"Because you need the rest and I want you in there with me. This is our first night here. We shouldn't argue—not tonight." Renay rested her head on Terry's shoulder.

Terry groped for her glass. "I have to laugh about that man and woman at the party. What the hell do people think we are? Freaks who live only for kicks? No love, no feeling, no nothing?"

"Darling, didn't you say don't let them get you down? Let's go upstairs," Renay said.

"I don't want to go upstairs," Terry protested stubbornly. "I like it down here." Carefully she set her glass down. Her eyes were bleary and slightly red as they held Renay's. "Birthdays—do you realize I'm ten years older than you?"

"Terry—"

"Soon you'll want somebody more your own age."

"Terry, listen to me. I only want you. I love you." Renay's hand accidentally brushed the soft point of Terry's breast, sending a quiver through her.

Suddenly Terry rolled off the couch onto the floor, pinning Renay to the rug. She began kissing her hard, bruising her lips with her own. "Do you like this? That Stony would love you like this. Don't—don't break away—"

Terry's movements were rough as she jerked Renay's gown above her head, tearing it in her haste. "I'm not going to prepare you. I'm going to be selfish and—"

Her body crushed hard against Renay, and Renay tasted her

own blood as she bit her lips. This wasn't Terry—*her* Terry—doing this. It was more like Jerome Lee, who thought only of a means to an end. Terry's fingers bruised her flesh as she gripped her tightly and used her knee to spread her legs. Then, just as quickly, Terry rolled away.

"I can't—not to you."

Renay was quiet, feeling the deep rug cushioning her back. At that instant she felt Terry's lips meeting hers, as gently this time as the caress of a flower's petal.

"I'm not too drunk to know that I've been acting like a jealous fool. I'm sorry."

Renay lay quiet beneath her, feeling tired but happy. A robin chirped a lone morning song outside the window as it cocked its head to look in at them. The morning light was now full upon the room.

"Let's go upstairs, Terry."

"No, I don't want to go upstairs. I want to stay right here like this and make love to you—*my* way—down here." She seized Renay's face in her hands. "May I?"

"You don't have to ask to make love to me. I'm always ready for you."

"Darling—darling—Renay." Terry's mouth found the smooth roundness of her breast. She kissed and cupped the brown nipples with her mouth, stirring them with the point of her tongue. Renay's hands tangled in the crop of Terry's hair as she buried each finger in the auburn moss.

Renay felt the familiar racing of her heart as Terry's softness blazed into her. She reached out to lock Terry closer, tighter.

"I'll make it good for you, darling," Terry whispered in the softness of her skin. "I'll make it very good for you—"

The robin looked in again to sing his chirping song of happiness—the only sound in a morning still very young.

CHAPTER 8

Renay slept soundly until noon, not hearing Terry slip quietly out of the house. When she awakened, the sun had spread a golden meadow of light and warmth into the room. She saw Terry's note propped against the bedside lamp. Terry had gone back to the apartment to make a last-minute check in case they had forgotten something.

Still slightly tired from the packing and moving of the past two days, Renay stretched her stiff muscles and rolled over into the spot where Terry had slept. A smile pocketed the corners of her mouth as she thought about last night and Terry's jealous anger. To be jealous was a healthy sign. She pressed herself into the indentation on the bed and rested her head where Terry's had been. A small pulsation of desire stirred her where the motions of love begin and end.

Strange—she had never felt this way about Jerome Lee. She could never remember wanting him physically. Not like this—in the morning, at noon and at night. It was a wonderful feeling, like that of the giver and the gift.

She pushed herself up and reached for one of Terry's cigarettes on the night table. For the first time in a long while, she was free to do what she wanted when she felt like it, not bound by a routine that had to be followed for someone else. She was free to rest as long as she wished, and to be completely alone with herself and her thoughts.

Her eyes took in the comfortable room with the fresh spring air blowing through the curtains. Terry had done this for her, given her not only a house but love along with it. She had pleaded again and again with Jerome Lee to move to a better apartment—they could not afford a house. An apartment less dismal, with more windows to let in the daylight, one without the peeling paint, rattling pipes and the splintered floors Denise had played on. But he had always countered that it was another car they needed, not a place to live.

His thoughts had been of himself. Terry's concern was for her happiness. Terry gave her a part of herself and showed Renay what love was. Terry knew that music was an intrinsic part of her, the side of her nature that needed expressing and nurturing, and for that need Terry had given her a piano. Terry understood this because she was interested and cared enough to know.

Jerome Lee had never attempted to understand her or what her music meant to her. Perhaps it was his lack of sensitivity. To him, a flower was just a plant, a bird's chirping just noise, and a pink sunset the end of a metallic day. The music he liked was loud, blaring rock, or rhythm and blues—music which best served his background for drinking and man-lies and woman-tales.

Those times when he would come sulkily home to find her at the piano, he would storm angrily: "Will you stop all that goddam banging! It ain't getting you or me anywhere. Ain't nobody going to listen to that shit. Let me hear some funky music!"

Then, spitefully, he would turn on the record player, the loud sound of a rock group shaking the tissue walls of the apartment with cries and moans of baby, baby, baby-y-y.

One time, to prove her varied talent, she played his kind of music to show that she could. But he had sneered back at her: "You just ain't got it. You can't play worth a damn, and it's time you knew it. I'm your husband, so don't that make me the best critic?"

Those times, the pain of his words cut deeply through her, especially when she needed confidence in herself. His tearing her down made her question her own ability. He had discovered that this was the best way to demean and hurt her—by deriding her talent.

Terry had encouraged her and given her back her self-respect and the confidence she needed. There were times in the evenings when she played just for Terry, who would lean back, close her eyes and listen appreciatively to the sounds she wove. She would play anything Terry wanted to hear, from Beethoven to Ray Charles.

They did other things together and enjoyed doing them. There had been no companionship with Jerome Lee. They had not gone places together, nor had he stayed at home with her for any length of time. On the rare occasions when he stayed in the apartment, he had been riveted to the TV ball games, drinking and reminiscing aloud about his football days back at State.

Worst of all, he had never communicated with Denise. Terry adored her, spoiling her with attention and affection as Jerome Lee never had. He had treated her like a fixture around the house that was created by him. She was simply proof of his reproductive capacities.

She drew heavily on the cigarette, absorbed in her reflections, particularly of Jerome Lee. In the very early days of their marriage, before the bottle and women and his meanness had taken their full toll, he had tried for a brief period to act out the role of a husband. He bought food regularly and saw to her needs as best as he could in preparation for the baby. But even then, she could not respond to him as a wife or a person.

In their sex life, having a woman beside him every night was a novelty to the new young boy-husband who was used to taking girls out on dates and waiting until they finally gave in. Practically every night he wanted her. She was there for that purpose, and that was the way he conveniently used her. Wasn't that what a wife was for: to screw whenever you pleased and to take care of a husband's needs of washing, ironing, cooking and making him comfortable?

She hated the nights when he came to bed in his T-shirt and shorts, the appendage she thought grotesque either hanging out flabbily or making a tent in his underwear. No matter what time of night or morning he woke up to find her there, he would immediately roll over upon her, asleep or awake, and enter her. Sometimes she thought he did it not because he wanted her, but simply because she was there and available.

At no time could she respond or did she feel an answering spark within her. She began to wonder whether the failure was in her or him. Black men believed that the duration of an erection was the criterion of their sexual potency. The proof of the pudding was how long they could continue to pound a woman through the bedsprings. Few indulged in the outré sexual activities which were considered white folks' nastiness.

During the times of his lovemaking, she would lie there quietly, gritting her teeth, hands gripping the sides of the bed, and wait impatiently for his climax. At those moments, only the monotonous rhythm of the bedsprings penetrated her thoughts.

When he had finished, he would grunt, "Ugh! Like screwing a dead woman!"

She *was* like a dead woman with Jerome Lee. Just going through the motions of living, not caring about anything except Denise. After a while, he stopped his lovemaking and began to stay away more and more and longer and longer. She cherished these times because he wasn't there to nag and belittle her, or mock her sexuality. Even the night she had Denise, he wasn't there. Her mother had gone to the hospital with her. Two days later, Jerome Lee finally came to see her.

She put out the cigarette and settled back on Terry's pillow. Now, looking at herself in the light of her present existence, she realized that even if Jerome Lee hadn't been such a son-of-a-bitch, she could never have made it with him. She was aware of what she was. It had always been there, deep within: her Lesbianism. Terry had helped her bring it out. She remembered Miss Sims, whom she had tried to emulate, whose sadness she had wanted to kiss away. Miss Sims, who they said couldn't get a man, really didn't want one. Miss Sims had preferred to hide or ignore her sexual inclination, suffering in isolation, silence and loneliness.

She was facing what she was and learning to live with it. Wasn't it Popeye who used to sing, "I am what I am and that's all that I am."

This was the part Terry had discovered. Gentle, loving Terry with her thoughtfulness and ability to share had made her realize her self-importance. All of this helped to kindle the flames of her desire. She *enjoyed* sex with Terry. Now she looked forward not only to the nights but to the days. There was life in life now, and love in its moments.

"Blackopaths" would question her capacity to love a white. She recalled the bull sessions in the dormitory when the girls would wonder how Lena Horne and Pearl Bailey could wake up in the morning to white faces beside them. But now she knew: you can't confine love to color or object. Love is what you see, like and admire in a person, how you feel and respond to that person. Look at her own color and the various colors of the black race. Somewhere

Loving Her

down the line, through rape or consent, body chemistry and mind attraction weren't controlled by society's norms or by the system.

Her thoughts reverted to Denise. Someday, when the girl was older, she would have to tell her in a gentle, patient way about Terry. That would be the hardest part, seeking the understanding of her daughter.

She gazed down at the cheap gold wedding band Jerome Lee's mother had helped him buy. The ring suddenly became an inanimate symbol of mockery. Plagued by the thoughts of her past, she threw the covers back and jumped out of bed. Twisting off the ring, she ran to the bathroom. In a gesture of finality, she quickly flushed the ring down the toilet.

A new life had begun for her—a new existence. She wanted nothing to remind her of her past with Jerome Lee. Life was too short to dwell over the dregs of what had gone by.

Terry came back later in the evening with a box of phonograph records, Denise's old one-eared Easter bunny and a bottle of champagne she had picked up on the way home.

"Thought we ought to christen the house!" she announced happily to Renay, who was in the kitchen cooking dinner.

"A beautiful idea," Renay said, taking the bottle and putting it in the refrigerator.

"Sorry I'm so late, but I stopped by the office. You want to pick up Denise now?"

The evening was turning into a faint plum pink, and shadows were beginning to splay the room. "Let's give ourselves one more night. I still have a few more things to unpack and put away. Besides, I want everything to be just right when she gets here. This will be the first time she'll remember living in a house. I'm sure Fran won't mind keeping her a little longer. I'll call her."

"Well—OK—" Terry said hesitantly, starting to warm the coffee left over in the pot. "I'm really beat. Trying to get through a busy day with a hangover isn't the easiest thing in the world. But, if you have something that has to be done, you manage somehow."

"Nobody told you to try to drink everything in sight," Renay laughed.

"What's that I smell?" Terry asked, wrinkling her nose.

"I'm introducing you tonight to what is commonly referred to as soul food. That there what y'all is smelling is known as black folks' delight—chitterlings, hog nuts, or Kentucky oysters. Depends on where you are from and what you want to call them. We're also having turnip greens, potato salad and cold-water cornbread like my mother used to make."

"Sounds good," Terry said, peering skeptically into the large pot of boiling chitterlings. "Whew! They *do* have a distinctive odor, don't they?"

"They sho' do!" Renay laughed, noticing Terry's perplexed look.

"Well, I'm going to take my coffee to the living room and read the paper."

"I'll call you when dinner's ready," Renay said.

The two of them ate by candlelight in the dining room, where Renay had set the table with a linen cloth and silver. Watching Terry slowly working the cork out of the champagne bottle, she remarked cryptically: "First time I've ever had chitterlings and champagne."

"And first time I've had chitterlings," Terry said. The cork made a festive popping sound as she expertly pulled it out.

Renay began filling Terry's plate with the tangled mass. "I hope you'll like them. You know, there's really an art to cooking chitterlings."

"I'm sure there is," Terry agreed, taking the full plate Renay passed to her.

"You have to cook them slowly with onions, celery stalks and a dash of lemon—" She watched Terry gingerly taste and frown. "Here, put some mustard, vinegar and hot sauce on them. They help to bring out the flavor."

Obediently Terry spread mustard and vinegar on the food, then reached for the hot sauce. This time she chewed quickly, reaching for her glass of champagne to wash it down.

"Like it better?" Renay asked anxiously.

"Hmmm. A unique taste." Then hurriedly: "Your cornbread is delicious."

"You don't like chitterlings," Renay observed, seeing Terry hungrily eating the vegetables.

"I'll learn— Maybe it's the thought of what they are."

"Don't feel bad. Some of *us* don't like them either!" Renay laughed. "Next soul night, I'll introduce you to pig's feet, rice and black-eyed peas."

"Whatever you say. You're the boss." She refilled their glasses with the last of the champagne. "Honey, I'm bushed, and I think this champagne has awakened all the stuff I poured in me last night. Mind if I leave you with the dishes?"

"Of course not. After all, I slept until noon."

Terry's eyes held hers across the table. "Wake me when you come to bed."

Without saying, they knew they could go to bed early since Denise wasn't there.

There was no need to awaken Terry, for she was already awake and waiting. She smelled of a fresh shower, lavender soap and mint toothpaste.

"Hangover disappeared?" Renay asked, moving naturally into Terry's waiting arms.

"Just about. Rest is the best thing I've found to cure one."

"Would you like the radio on?" Sometimes they went to sleep by music.

"If you want it."

Renay reached across Terry to dial an FM station that played soft music all night. When she got it, she heard a female singer's clear, bell-like voice singing:

> After years of lone—li—ness
> There is love
> There is our-r-r love

"That song—" Terry murmured sleepily, arms tightening around Renay.

"What about it?" Renay asked.

"It used to be called the national anthem of the gay life. At parties, couples used to stand up whenever it was played."

"Shall we stand?" Renay teased, the tip of her finger tenderly exploring a newly found mole as if it were silver dust.

Terry looked down. "What are you doing?"

"Discovering you."

It was then that Terry noticed. "What did you do with your ring?"

"I flushed it away. It should be floating down the river by now."

Terry took her hand, kissing each finger. The kisses left rings of warmth. "I'll buy you another tomorrow. You belong to me now."

The softness of Terry's body burned into hers. She stayed very still, listening to the music:

> Now I know-w-w
> What kisses can mean
> For those before
> Were ne-ver ne-ver like these

The closeness of Terry and the music spread a warm current through her body. A familiar exquisite pain began to course warmly through her like a flooding, sweeping tide, gripping her in its throes. Her mind became numb as the core of her began to respond to the flowing sensation. She began to tremble, feeling the tempest raging within. "My God," she thought, "it can't be!"

But it was. Her arms squeezed hard around Terry, holding to that which was unknowingly causing the crescendo now weakening and about to capture her. Her mouth half-opened, gasping air as the ache surged hotly through her loins. She moaned, drawing up her knees. Her body began to writhe convulsively and she clasped her thighs tightly together as the pulsating emotion ended in a tremendous shudder.

"Oh-o-o—" she groaned as the sky's pit fell in and stars burst about her in a maddening frenzy. When it was over, she couldn't speak.

"Renay—are you all right?" Terry asked, leaning over her worriedly.

She couldn't believe it, but it was true. It had happened, just lying here quietly beside Terry, without a movement or word from her.

"Witch—" she breathed softly. "My great white witch—damn you!"

"Hmmm," Terry murmured, pleased, knowing now. "Wish I weren't so tired—" Then, smiling, she drifted off to sleep.

CHAPTER 9

"Hello, Mommy!" Denise threw her arms around Renay, hugging her tightly. "I got very good in spelling today!"

"Good for you! Your mommy's real proud of you."

Fran smiled, watching them. "Did you get all moved?"

"Finally. How did you two make out?" Renay asked, kissing the top of Denise's head. She seemed to have grown taller during the two days and nights.

"Fine. We're old boarding pals by now. Here, sit down, if you can find a place." Fran began clearing papers off the couch and stacking them on the desk. "These are all test papers I have to grade. Thank goodness the year is almost over. The kids are about to drive me wild. Nobody can tell me that schoolteachers don't earn their money. Want a cup of coffee? I just made a fresh pot. I thought it would help me to stay awake and finish these papers."

"All right."

In the kitchen, Fran poured two cups of steaming black coffee and set them on the table. "Here's something for you, little one," she called to Denise in the living room. "A cup of cocoa."

"Thanks, Aunt Fran," Denise said, coming in to get the cup handed to her.

"Careful now and don't spill it on you," Fran cautioned.

"I won't. I'm going back to watch Lassie."

Renay put two teaspoonfuls of sugar in her cup and a tiny bit of the powdered cream Fran passed to her. The coffee was hot and strong. Fran's coffee was always hot and strong.

"Are you finally settled?" Fran asked, lighting a cigarette.

"Almost. When do you plan to leave for home?"

"As soon as school's out, and you can believe it! I'm saving up enough money now to get the old buggy tuned up for the trip." She sat down, drawing heavily on the cigarette. "It'll be good to get back to the country air again. No pollution, traffic jams, city noises. I can hardly wait."

Renay stirred her coffee for a long thoughtful moment. "Fran, could Denise ride home with you? I'd like for her to spend the summer with mother. She hasn't seen her since she was a baby."

"Why, sure! You know it'll be all right. She can help keep me awake on the road. Have you written to your mother?"

It had been a long time since she had written. So much to say, and so much that shouldn't be said. "Not yet. I thought I'd ask you first."

"Why don't you come along too?"

"I'm going to summer school at Waterview."

"Renay! How wonderful!" Fran's large eyes expressed approval. "I'm so glad. You with all that musical talent. It's a shame to let it go to waste. Wish I could play the piano or do something exciting like that. Teaching's for the birds. But hell, it's a living."

Denise came back into the kitchen, placing her empty cup in the sink. "Mommy, you ready? I want to see where we're living now."

"In a minute—" Hurriedly she finished her coffee, feeling it warm her.

"Is Aunt Terry there too?"

"Yes—she is."

"Who is Aunt Terry?" Fran's eyebrows raised above the whitish smoke whorls screening her mouth.

"I'm living with her." Renay fixed her eyes upon the dull gray tenements flatly entombed beneath the fading sky. The window was open and a fly rested near a hole in the corner of the screen. She wondered if her voice sounded as tense as she felt inside.

"She's white, isn't she?" Fran said slowly. "I saw her waiting for you in the car the other day when you left Denise."

Renay nodded. "She's my friend." This time her eyes leveled with Fran's. Had she guessed by the reply? She wanted so badly for

Fran to know and understand, but deep within her, knowing Fran, she knew how Fran would feel. At this moment, Fran was probably thinking it a betrayal for her to be living with a white person, let alone calling her a friend.

"And she's my Mommy's *very best friend*. Just like you!" Denise chimed in, spinning around in a make-believe fantasy dance, skirt whirling above her little brown legs.

"She must be." Fran put out her cigarette, eyes hard on Renay. "Where have you been keeping her all this time? Your white friend? I'd like very much to meet her."

"Of course," Renay said quickly, scribbling her telephone number on a piece of paper torn from a writing pad in her purse. "You can reach me at this number."

Fran took the number, not looking at it but studying Renay. "There's something different about you. You look—well—happy."

"I *am* happy." Renay's lips curved in a smile.

Fran stood by the door as they prepared to leave. Denise clutched her small weekend bag and was already in the hall waiting impatiently for her mother.

"Renay, please be careful. I don't want to see you get hurt anymore."

"I know you don't. Thanks for everything." She squeezed Fran affectionately.

Denise curled her hand in her mother's as they walked to the car. Twilight had set in and people were rushing past them in busy streams, hurrying home. A middle-aged brown woman in a cheap cotton dress and sweater, carrying a greasy brown shopping bag with the evening's meal left over from her white folks' table, brushed against Renay. Her eyes met the woman's listless, tired gaze, and she was reminded of home and the flow of other brown women returning to colored town from the day's work on other streets. She thought of her mother, who also trudged that worn path.

"Denise, would you like to visit your grandmother this summer? You were so tiny the last time she saw you."

"Are you going?"

Denise looked up at her with eyes squinting narrowly, as

Jerome Lee's eyes had done when he asked her a question. *You are never completely free if there is a child involved. The reminder—in looks and actions—is always there to keep you from forgetting.*

They came to where the car was parked, and Renay slid behind the wheel, pausing to lock them in. "Not this time. Mommy's going back to college to finish getting her degree. That way, I'll get a better job and be more able to get the things we want. You'll ride home with Aunt Fran."

"Oh." Denise looked at the telephone poles fleeing against the movement of the car. "We aren't going to live with Daddy ever again, are we?"

The question was unexpected, and Renay's hands tightened on the wheel. A car passed her and blew a warning sound. "No. Sometimes people who live together don't get along for a lot of reasons. Even mommies and daddies. So, it's best that they live apart. But even though I'm divorcing your daddy, he's still your father and always will be." Denise was quiet.

"We're in the country!" Denise marveled suddenly, seeing the trees and rolling spacious lawns, her mood changing with the fascinating rapidity so typical of children's moods.

"Not exactly," Renay laughed. "We're in the suburbs. And we're almost home."

Renay wrote to her mother about Denise, saying just enough about Jerome Lee to let her know she was divorcing him. In a few days her mother's reply came, written in her large painstaking hand on lined paper. She would be very happy to see Denise, she was glad to know Renay was going back to school, and she was sorry about the marriage—nothing more. Her mother had never cared for Jerome Lee.

Since Denise was going to be away from them all summer, they centered the remaining weeks around her. On weekends they took her to the zoo, where the monkeys fascinated her with their show-off antics and intelligent, mischievous eyes. Sometimes, when the evenings were warm and still bright, they barbecued in the backyard and ate picnic-style on the new redwood table and chairs Terry had bought. Those times, they dined on hot dogs, hamburgers and baked beans because that was what Denise always ordered.

They were both aware that Denise needed friends her age. They hoped the summer months at home with Renay's mother, where the streets were filled with the shrieks of children at play, would atone for what they could not give now.

"This fall I'll make contacts," Terry said. "That way she can have some playmates her own age. I know some people—"

Meanwhile, they scanned the newspapers for children's movies, shows and recreational places to take her. Denise seemed happier than ever seeing the new sights with them. Sometimes people stared perplexedly—as people do who are usually mystified by those things outside of their sphere of comprehension—at the little brown girl hand-in-hand with the pretty young black woman and the tall, handsome white woman gaily absorbed in the things around them.

Almost before they realized it, the day had come for Renay to take Denise into town to leave for home with Fran. After she had gone, the house was quieter, no longer filled with the sounds of childish chatter and play. Terry commented on the quiet, missing the noisy activity. Denise had grown more outgoing away from Jerome Lee.

The summer came early in hot intensity, and Renay found herself busy with the daily trips to the college. Her studies, combined with the supper club work she still refused to give up, enveloped her in feverish activity.

Terry wrote from morning until late afternoon when Renay came home. Then they had supper and talked. While Renay studied, Terry often went for an evening stroll before dark. The walks helped unwind the tension of writing.

One pink-orange sunset evening, Terry walked farther than usual and came upon a little brook at the end of a hidden grove. Pleased, she sat down on the ground to watch the myriad moving reflections and listen to the unseen babbling sounds of the water. Then, in the mulberry dusk, a woman appeared, walking toward her with a cane. As she drew closer, Terry saw the stately, erect posture of an elderly woman whose straight shoulders were without the rounded stoop of many women her age. The steps nearing her were firm and assured, the hickory cane serving only as a walking stick. A large jet-black mongrel dog panted by her side. Seeing Terry, the dog began to bark furiously.

"Terrence Bluvard—" the woman said, squinting at her face in the twilight. "I have admired your work for a long time. I'm Edith Stilling, your closest neighbor. And this is Walden." She bent to silence the barking dog. I found him abandoned at this very spot—when he was a puppy."

Terry scrambled hastily to her feet, shaking the outstretched hand. "How do you do, and hello, Walden." Hearing his name, the dog's tail wagged as he brushed against Terry's legs.

The woman peered intently at her. She was reminded of a winter sky without the frost. "Stilling—" Terry said thoughtfully. "I remember a Stilling some time ago. He was a professor at the state college and one of my father's friends."

"My late husband. Friends, yes, but not completely in agreement about life," Edith Stilling chuckled, brushing back a piece of white hair that had strayed loose from the bun at the nape of her neck. "Your father was interested in the mundane things in life. My husband was somewhat of an idealist or romantic. He passed away two years ago. He wanted so much to retire and get away to his Walden, as he called it. To a place like this to rest and write." She sighed, absently caressing the dog with the tip of her cane. "I like to think that I'm living out his days the way *he* wanted to. He was a great admirer of Thoreau. Now I even find myself thinking 'My life is like a stroll upon the beach, as near the ocean's edge as I can go.'"

"Your husband was a well-known scholar," Terry noted quietly.

"Everyone thought so but him. Are you living here permanently or just for the summer?"

"I've come home to stay." The words did not sound strange to her. It *was* home now, more than ever before. She had someone to share it with her.

They began walking slowly back with Walden scampering ahead, barking at elusive birds and imaginary squirrels.

"You must come and visit me sometime." Mrs. Stilling paused in front of the house she and Renay could see from their window. "I get so depressed from reading the daily papers with all the horrible news and people hating one another. I like to feel that there are still intelligent and rational people left in the world."

"I shall be happy to. I'll stop by real soon," Terry said, leaving her at the cobbled path leading to the unique and charming brown house.

A white Jaguar was parked outside the door when Terry got back to the house. Renay was entertaining Lorraine and Vance. An array of bottles and glasses covered the living room coffee table. The room was saturated with the heavy odor of Vance's strong cigarettes.

"Hi, there!" Vance greeted her in a booming voice, rising from the couch. "Lorraine and I thought we'd drop by for a while. I brought the bottles. Didn't know how you were stocked. Besides," she added, going over to the coffee table, where she began to mix a drink for Terry, carefully measuring vermouth in the rocket-shaped silver cocktail shaker, "I'm the best damn bartender around."

"It's nice to have the best damn bartender around." Terry grinned sitting on the floor beside Renay's chair. "Since you're doing the honors, I'll sit back and observe."

"Renay was going to play something for us," Lorraine said, kicking off her sandals and curling her legs under her on the couch.

"Don't let me stop her." Terry took the drink Vance handed her.

"Taste that."

Terry tested the drink, savoring it before swallowing. "Delicious!"

"Damn right it is!" Vance passed a second round to Lorraine and Renay. "OK, chicken, play us some sweet soothing sounds. After working all day, that's all I want to hear at this point."

Softly, Renay began *Moon River*. The music enveloped the room in muted gossamer tones, quieting them for a long, thoughtful moment.

"Doesn't Lorraine look better?" Vance said proudly, putting her arm behind Lorraine. "She's even getting some meat on her bones since the last time you saw her."

Lorraine's blue nylon slacks curved her hips tightly, showing the rounded firmness Vance was pointing out to them. Her cheeks had a natural brightness without the thick rouge she had worn before.

"Yes, she does," Terry conceded.

Renay drifted into a medley of Duke Ellington tunes, and Lorraine crossed the room to stand beside the piano, humming off-key along with *Solitude*. "Wish I could play the piano like that. Isn't Terry lucky to have someone around who can play music?"

"I think we're both lucky!" Vance boasted, blowing out a cloudy stream of acrid smoke. "Want another drink, anybody?" Without waiting for an answer, she began refilling the glasses. "Now that I have Lorraine in good shape again, maybe she'll start painting some more."

"Give her time," Terry said softly, turning on the lamps to break the late twilight dimness. "I'm going to find something for us to nibble on. Your drinks are stronger than they look."

Vance followed her to the kitchen. "Mind if I go to the refrigerator and get some ice?"

"Help yourself. I'm leaving the drink department to you." Terry took out a box of Ritz crackers and opened a jar of cheese spread.

"I have to hand it to you, Terry. You must be awfully strong," Vance said gravely over the tray of ice she was breaking into the ice bucket.

"Strong? How do you mean?" Terry began, spreading the cheese on the crackers and arranging them on a square glass plate.

"You really must care for each other or I don't see how it could have gotten *this* far. She seems to be a nice person. It's just that this life is hard enough without additional problems—if you get what I mean."

"What *do* you mean?" Terry asked testily.

"Well—her being—you know—black and all. Some of us in the life aren't so liberal as we seem when it comes to this kind of acceptance. And don't you think someday she might get lonesome for her own?"

"Her own?"

"Er-r-r, people."
"Aren't we her people?" Terry said coldly. "Besides, there *are* such things as interracial marriages. Or hadn't you heard?"
"Uh-huh. But if you've noticed, either for comfort or necessity, the whites usually enter the *black* world."
"So—she's entered *my* world. *Her* choice."
"Hmmm, maybe because there is no black Lesbian world —such as ours—" Vance said speculatively.
"Don't worry about me, Vance. I'm a big girl now."
"Yeah—is *she?*"
Terry looked down at the plate, which appeared unfilled. As an afterthought, she reached for sweet pickles and olives. Picking up the filled plate and a handful of paper napkins, she said, "I haven't heard her crying yet."
As they entered the living room, Lorraine was engaged in animated conversation with Renay. Turning to Vance, she said excitedly: "We must go to the Peacock Supper Club sometime to hear Renay. We could go tonight, but Renay says it's closed for some minor repairs."
"All right, sweetie. We'll go sometime. Meanwhile, I'll let the cashier rob me blind while I'm squiring you around."
Lorraine threw her an affectionate look. "Just so you're not squiring anyone else around."
"Oh, crap! Pass me some crackers, Terry. The lady has an evil mind." Looking at Renay, she asked, "Where're you from, chicken? 'Round here?"
"No, Kentucky. A small town called Tilltown." Renay swung around on the piano bench to face her. "That's where my daughter is this summer. Visiting my mother."
Vance was silent, trying to hide her surprise. "Oh—you've got a daughter? How old is she?"
"Seven—"
Vance cast a quick meaningful look at Terry. "Her name is Denise and she lives here with us," Terry said.
"How nice it must be to have a daughter," Lorraine said wishfully. "Perhaps someday, if I can convince Vance, we can adopt one. She seems to think I'm enough."

Vance's face became a mask as she changed the subject. "Kentucky, huh? I've never been in the South. From what I've heard, I don't ever want to go, either."

"One of these days, it could become one of the best places for my race to live. At least you know where you stand there," Renay said.

"Were you ever in one of those demonstrations down there?" Lorraine asked, eyes inquisitively on Renay.

"No." She had been too busy trying to make a life with Jerome Lee.

"I read someplace where they're going to have a demonstration in town soon for open housing," Lorraine continued.

"*I'll* join *that* one," Terry said bitterly. "You never know what others go through unless you've experienced it yourself. You can sympathize and fret over conditions, but to be hit personally by demon prejudice can make you bleed real hard."

Renay glanced quickly at her. "I've still got a little blood left," she quipped, breaking the tension. "Thanks to people who've shared some of the bleeding with me."

"It's a damn rotten thing, prejudice—in any form," Vance scowled. "People disliking and looking down on other people for one reason or another. Even us, because of the way we are. But maybe that's human nature. If our kind ever got in the majority, it'd probably be the same way. I just don't believe people will ever stop being biased. So, the best thing to hope for is that they'll at least learn to become more tolerant."

"What was it Gibran said?" Terry asked, running her thumbnail around the edge of her glass. "Something about having learned tolerance from the intolerant, yet being ungrateful to the teacher?"

"Well, we have to go," Vance said, looking at her watch. "I can see my money disappearing into somebody's pockets now. We'll have to get together more often."

Lorraine took Renay's hand. "Yes—I'm glad you two are here. It gets kind of lonely out here. It's good to know there are others so near who are—like us. When you're alone for long, you begin to wonder."

"Come on, let's go, Lorraine." Vance said brusquely. "What she really means is she wants me to cart her into town more, to places like Margo's Corner. You know the kind, Terry. See you around."

After they had gone Renay carried out the glasses and bottles. "Lorraine *does* look better," Terry reflected, throwing away the soiled paper napkins and emptying ashtrays. "She's kind of highstrung. Anyway, she has more art talent than Vance gives her credit for."

"Are you coming to bed now?" Renay asked, turning off the lights.

"Later. I have some characters I have to get back to for a while."

"You and your old characters."

"They're like real people to writers, you know. And a little piece of you goes into each one. Either the you who you are, or sometimes the way you would like or wouldn't like to be."

Renay kissed her lightly. "Spend the night with them, then."

Terry grabbed her, kissing her back long and deeply. "Not *all* night. I'll be up to bed soon."

CHAPTER 10

Renay awakened to the bright, gilded sun streaming through the window. It was going to be another beautiful day. Outside, the inquisitive birds chirped their treble song at the window. The blinds were halfway up and she could see the green-decked trees, limbs heavy with their mantle of leaves.

"Hmmm," Terry groaned sleepily. "What's today?"

"Saturday," Renay said, thankful for no classes. She had the whole day to do what she wanted.

"Good. I have you all day. Let's start with the morning—" Terry's arm moved to draw her closer.

"Fresh!" Renay laughed, burying her head in the hollow of Terry's neck. "What do you want for breakfast?" The words were almost muffled in Terry's throat, and she could taste the faint acridness of salt.

"Nothing right now." Terry pressed Renay closely against her, palms flat on her hips. "Young lady, do you realize every morning we're rush, rush, rushing and I haven't had a chance to hold you at leisure like this for a long time—not even at night when we're both too tired?"

Renay stayed still, feeling the warmth of Terry's body. Terry's reddish brown hair was in complete disarray on the pillow. Her fingers tangled in it, curling and hiding in the copper jungle, then moved down to caress the nape of her neck. They were quiet for a timeless moment. The world had stopped. Only their thoughts went on.

Tracing the whiteness of Terry's skin with her finger, Renay thought, *It is amazing how I can lie here and see and feel this skin and not think of the awful things others of her color have done to us. And yet, my skin is light—tinged with the sun. Someone, somewhere in the past, must have done and thought and felt like this with another—or hated in a different and helpless way.*

"What are you thinking?" Terry asked, shifting to look directly into Renay's eyes.

"Oh, about us—and life—and people in general. About how we're made and how life affects us. And above all, how unbelievable *this* is."

"What is so unbelievable?"

"Being able to love you like this."

"Why?" Terry asked gently.

"Because you're white."

"Oh?" Terry was quietly thoughtful for a long moment before she seized Renay's face in her hand and said gently: "Darling, love knows no color." Then laughingly: "You're thinking too much this morning. Education is going to your head. I'll have to put a stop to that, right now!"

She felt Terry's lips press against hers, and she opened her mouth. The tip of her tongue met Terry's and slid beyond to search the cave of her mouth; then she gently drew Terry's tongue into her mouth and held it there in a suctionlike vise.

Terry murmured something as her skilled hands became live, free-wheeling, manipulating tentacles, drawn to their destination as instinctively as ugliness is drawn to beauty, sadness to joy, life to death. When it reached the throbbing, aching brush, Renay knew no sight, no sound, no thought. Then, the tactile movement was in the moist tunnel of her and she grasped the thin sheltering shoulders poised above her to meet the oncoming wind of desire.

Her lips caught at Terry's throat, and teeth clamped Terry's flesh, making a blue love mark. Just as quickly, her tongue sought to kiss and heal the wound.

Now Terry's mouth moved, burning trails in criss-crossed patterns over her body, pausing at the little ring in the center of her stomach to continue like spirals of flame down the inner columns of her thighs, then back to the forest wherein lies the cradle of love.

Renay felt a rampaging sea draw a deafening roar into her ears, drowning her with sweet, fierce passion. If she ceased to live, she wanted it to be like this, with Terry loving her forever into death. When Terry rose above her, her body movements began to gyrate in tune with the rhythm of the bow as she cried out to the maker of the song:

"Terry—*now!*"

"Slower—darling. Stay with me—" Terry breathed, voice from beyond. "Let's make it last awhile."

"I'm sorry—I—can't," she moaned, feeling herself soaring beyond the clouds to find the limitless well of the sky. "Oh, God, *Terry!*" The shriek was wrenched from the depths of her, escaping into flight to become a gasp, stilled in the smoldering harbor of others that had come before.

But this time Terry did not stop. Renay looked up to see the gray eyes cloudy with her and the mouth filled with the taste and smell of her, and the feeling began all over again. In fitful spasms her hands began to explore the tapering spine of Terry's back, stopping at Terry's hips, where they too moved back and forth with the surging tide of her body.

"You're with me again—" Terry whispered.

It had never happened like this with them before, and she closed her eyes to lock in the wonderful newness and feeling of it. But she couldn't close out the heat rising high in her until once again she felt the flames reach to her mouth. She seized Terry hard, feeling Terry's body quiver, hearing Terry's breath catch on a word that sounded like her name, as Terry collapsed against her and as one they reached the peak of the mountain of love and cried out in joy together.

When they awakened, it was noon and the sun was high in the throne of the sky. The inquisitive birds at the window had deserted them for the coolness and shade of the trees. The sheet beneath them was damp with the dew of their bodies and the imprint of their love. The day was half over, yet just beginning for them.

"We didn't eat breakfast," Renay reminded, sitting up to stretch. Her golden arms pointed to the ceiling, making a shouting reflection to the sky.

"I did." Terry ogled her wickedly, getting up. "All right, shall we have breakfast or lunch?"

"Both, with tall glasses of iced tea. I'm starved!"

"OK, but I have to have coffee to begin my day. We'll take a shower, eat and do whatever you feel like doing before you go to work."

They showered together and dressed in shorts and sleeveless sheer blouses left half-open at the top because of the heat. Renay prepared a meal of fried country ham slices, sunny-side-up eggs, round German fried potatoes and tomato salad. As they finished washing the dishes a dog barked outside. Edith Stilling and Walden were waiting at the screen door.

"Hello, my dear. Walden and I were out for a walk, so I thought I'd stop by."

"Do come in," Terry invited, holding the door open for her.

"Walden, you stay there until I come out," Mrs. Stilling cautioned the dog, who stretched out lazily in the shade of the steps.

"Would you like a glass of iced tea?" Terry asked.

"Thank you. I believe I would. It is rather warm today. Usually it's cooler out here than in the city," the woman said, smiling. The smile suddenly changed to a questioning look as she saw Renay coming in from the kitchen.

Terry introduced them, telling Renay that Mrs. Stilling lived in the brown house she admired so much.

"I didn't know you had company," Mrs. Stilling murmured apologetically, "or I would have picked another time."

"Renay lives with me. I'll get your tea."

Mrs. Stilling sat down and focused on Renay. "Are you a writer too?"

"No, I'm not."

"She's a musician," Terry supplied, coming back into the room with a tall frosted glass tipped at the side with a lemon slice.

"Oh? I love music. Are you a singer?"

"She's a pianist," Terry answered, handing her the glass.

"How stupid of me—assuming that she sings." Mrs. Stilling took the glass, propping her cane against the couch.

"We don't *all* sing," Renay said edgily.

"No, of course not. And we don't *all* like fried chicken and watermelon!" Mrs. Stilling added, a twinkle lighting her eyes.

Suddenly Renay laughed. For some reason, she liked the aristocratic-looking woman with the snowcapped head who sipped her tea as if she were drinking champagne.

"I'm not totally archaic and out of touch with the world. You see, my late husband had a number of Negro—or in today's vernacular—black students in his classes at the university. For some reason, they seemed to take more of a liking to him than to many of the other white faculty members. He used to have them over to our house on campus, and sometimes the sessions went on far into the night. As a result, I became more than a little interested in the movement—the militant as well as the so-called more conservative groups such as the NAACP and Urban League. Are you a member of any of the organizations?"

Renay shook her head. "No, but my color gives me a lifetime membership in all of them. Each, no matter how radical or moderate, has something to offer and inroads to make. There are those of us who don't participate in marches or go to jail for the cause and bear intolerable hate. We are the ones who try to live and keep an air of saneness to show something still remaining when the fires burn down."

"Mr. Stilling used to like to quote Langston Hughes's 'Life for me ain't been no crystal stair.' "

"True. For us it hasn't. But the present is what is important. We'll have to use the past *not* as a measuring stick for bitterness, but to illuminate the present."

"It's going to take a long, long time to end this abominable treatment of man toward man because of race. I'm afraid that I won't be around to see it—if it ever happens," Mrs. Stilling said pensively, setting down her empty glass with a sigh.

"Some of us have already ended it," Terry said, "in our own individual way. It's the hate-shouters who put the fog over many gardens."

"How right you are. Now, don't let me keep you two from doing whatever you were doing." Mrs. Stilling got up, reaching for her cane. "You must come over and play Schubert for me, my dear, on my old spinet. It has considerable age on it, but still possesses a truly wonderful sound."

"I'd love to play Schubert for you," Renay said.

Terry walked to the door with Mrs. Stilling. Seeing his mistress, Walden jumped up happily, wagging his tail at the prospect of a wild run into the woods. "I'd like for you to browse through my husband's library, Miss Bluvard. Some great minds are housed there."

Walden sniffed delicately at Terry, who bent to pat his black wolf's head. "We'll come over very soon," Terry said, bidding her goodbye. Returning to Renay, she asked cheerfully: "Well, how do you want to spend the rest of the afternoon?"

Renay glanced at the clock over the fireplace. It was an old-fashioned wooden clock with hands like stiff arms. "There really isn't much time left now to do anything. You took up all of my time this morning before I could even get out of bed."

"Who? Me?" Terry's eyes rounded in surprised innocence. "Doing what?"

"What comes naturally." Renay smiled teasingly. "So, how about driving to the club with me tonight?"

"Good. I can court you all over again."

"Ruzicka doesn't permit flirting with his main attraction."

"I wish I could keep his main attraction at home." Terry squeezed her tightly, and Renay reached up to brush away a speck of soot on Terry's nose.

"I had something to give you this morning, but you kept me so occupied—" Terry laughed. "Wait a minute, I'll get it." Terry went upstairs and came back with a small box. "I hope to hell it fits."

The ring slipped easily on her finger, and for the first time, Renay felt as if she really belonged to someone.

"See—I didn't forget. It's just that it took me a while to decide what I thought suited you." Then anxiously: "Do you like it?"

Renay hugged Terry close to her, not wanting her to see the tears. The ring was a small gold band with two diamonds in the center. "I love it!"

"Good! Now I've branded you." Terry's arms closed around her.

"I have a sort of surprise for you too, tonight," Renay said finally, when the knot in her throat had gone.

"And, I have another for you—later—where surprises mean the most!"

"Oh, Terry!" Renay drew a weary breath in mock exasperation. "What *am* I going to do with you?"

"Just keep me happy, darling," she said, kissing her below the ear. "That's all."

CHAPTER 11

Terry sat alone in the corner shadows of the Peacock Supper Club, lingering over her third drink and waiting for Renay. She knew that she was slightly high, feeling relaxed and ethereal to the point where nothing mattered except the drink and Renay's music. One or two people she hardly recognized nodded and spoke to her; she waved casually to them, not wanting to encourage a visit or long conversation. She didn't feel like talking. Talk would intrude upon the little world in which she wanted to be alone until Renay entered it.

The lights were soft and the voices surrounding her were muted vibrations from somewhere far beyond her. She was an island alone with herself as her thoughts skirted the reflections of other times when she had come here just to see and hear Renay. The first time, her image of Renay had been that of a sad, unhappy girl, but one whose talent showed promise. She had enough knowledge of music to sense the girl's natural talent and sensitivity to music. Those evenings, she had sat and listened and observed her to the point where Renay had become a permanent fixture in her mind. She had wondered why the girl didn't smile more, look at the audience, or hold her head up from the protective fence of the piano keys. There was an untouched youthfulness about her that was captivating. Later, she often wondered in surprise how Renay had managed to retain this aura of freshness.

It came as a small shock to her when one night she realized that she was coming here for more than music. Perhaps, in her writer's mind, she was searching for a narrative thread as she watched, wondered and submerged herself in the object of her attention until Renay had unconsciously become a part of her. She began to recognize the new stirring of interest which lasted long after she had gone home and tried to sleep.

It was Jean who perceived what she really felt the night she had taken her to the club for dinner. When she had invited Renay to their table for a drink, Jean became angry.

"I can see by the way you've been staring at her all evening why you're inviting her over," Jean had hissed at her over the candlelight. "You don't hide your feelings very well." Then, getting up abruptly before she had finished her meal, she snapped heatedly, "I don't like drinking with niggers!" With that, she flounced out the door, leaving Terry there in a state of amazement. She hadn't known Jean was prejudiced—but there had never before been a circumstance in which she could have known.

Oddly enough, she hadn't thought about Renay's color, except for the sun-glow beauty of her skin. Jean's outburst had enraged her, and had brought out personal feelings that she had tried to ignore. She had not only a sexual yearning for this melancholy black girl, but also a desire to know her better, to fathom her thoughts, to wipe away the sadness.

The scenes of the past eclipsed into the now. Slowly she lifted her glass and sipped the drink, letting the liquid roll around her mouth before gradually coursing down her throat to make a warm, cottony bed in the pit of her stomach. A hard tightening began to invade her senses, a warning sign that the drink was acting too fast. The volatile atmosphere spun a cocoon around her, enclosing her in a heady, lighthearted vacuum. Soon, before she realized it, Renay was seated beside her.

"Where's my surprise?" she asked, wrinkling her nose over the round well of the glass.

"It's coming up next." Renay's eyes examined her closely. "Are you all right?"

"What do you mean, am I all right? Don't I look all right?" Terry bounced back with feigned indignation.

"You look red around the nose and your eyes have an extra shine. Frankly, you look like you're feeling *too* all right!" Renay retorted in amusement.

"True, I *am* feeling good." Terry grinned, winking mischievously. "I haven't felt so happy since the first time I walked in and saw you at the piano. Now! How do you like *that?*"

"I think you have some Irish in you." Renay laughed, covering her hand with her own.

"Miss Bluvard! How nice to have you here. I haven't seen you for quite some time." Ruzicka stood above their table, bowing low. The white of his dinner jacket gleamed in contrast with his swarthy skin and midnight hair.

"So you haven't," Terry said, taking out a cigarette and bending to the quick professional flick of his lighter.

His dark eyes narrowed, glancing at Terry and then settling on Renay. "You used to enjoy Renay's music so much."

"I still do," Terry answered cautiously. Her light mood vanished, captured by an insinuation.

"I must get back." Renay excused herself, leaving them.

Ruzicka followed her with his eyes. "You are now good friends. I notice she drives your car to work all the time."

Terry emptied her glass, setting it down sharply. The drink tasted sour. "What else have you noticed?"

"That her husband has seen it too—only without her knowledge. He doesn't appear to me to be quite—shall I say—a rational young man." He shrugged, reaching for her glass. "Please don't misunderstand me. It's just that I like you both. I'll get you another drink, Miss Bluvard. This one is on the house."

Renay was playing again, and Terry heard the familiar theme, recognizing it as the composition she had been working on for a long while. The music was nostalgic and melancholy, yet with an intensity that touched the beauty and terror of fear. Apparently the others in the room felt as she, for when Renay finished on an ascending chord, the applause was loud and appreciative with questioning murmurs of approval heard all around. It was to Terry a very nice surprise. She saw Renay looking at her and she mouthed the word 'beautiful.'

Picking up her glass, she turned her thoughts to what Ruzicka had said about Jerome Lee. Renay had told her bits and pieces about him—his selfishness, the nagging demeaning of her, the drink-sickness—enough to make her hate this nonentity who had given Renay what she could not give—a name and a child. But she had given her that which he was unable to give—love.

She thought too of Denise and the childish letter she had dictated to her grandmother last week. She was having a good time and had met lots of new friends. Children could adapt easily.

"You liked it!" Renay startled her, looking down expectantly at her, a florid excitement about her.

Terry smiled and blew her a kiss. "I liked it very much. What are you going to call it?"

"I don't know. It's just a mood piece—a slice of life, I suppose. Just something for special and not-too-special people."

"In that case, let's call it "Song for Souls." I know a music publisher who might be interested."

"It's not *that* good, Terry," Renay protested.

"The creator is not always the best judge. Anyway, we can try." Terry looked at her watch. "All through now?"

Renay nodded. Terry got up and was surprised at her unsteadiness as the room dipped and swayed. That was the penalty for drinking so much while sitting down. You never knew how hard it had hit you until you stood up. But her mind was still clear, and she braced herself stiffly to walk out the door.

The summer-night air upheld her balance. The street was alive with strolling couples, people sitting outside to escape the inside, and restless roving cars trying to make the night less long.

"You drive," Terry said, handing her the keys. "I don't quite trust myself."

Renay slid behind the wheel. In a moment, the car joined the downtown late night traffic. "Would you like the top down?" Renay asked, knowing how Terry liked to gaze at the sky and breathe the fresh raw air.

"Not tonight." She rested her head on the back of the seat, watching the flashing street lights cast shadows across Renay's face—oscillating streaks of light that quickly came and went in zebralike stripes. She closed her eyes, letting the smooth motion of the car sway her into lethargy as it sped onto the darkened highway toward home.

She was almost asleep when suddenly she was jarred awake by the piercing squeal of brakes as the car swerved toward the side of the road. She opened her eyes to see an old black Chevrolet crowd them off the road and stop abruptly in their path.

A man got out, swaying eerily in the beam of their headlights as he came toward the car. His sport shirt, wrinkled and open at the collar, hung out over rumpled, baggy trousers. He loomed grotesque and menacing before them—a giant puppet whose arms and legs jerked to movement without strings.

"My God! It's Jerome Lee!" Renay cried, stunned. She sat frozen in electrified astonishment as Terry reached hastily across to lock the door.

The form outside grabbed the door handle, not to get in, but to anchor his reeling stance. "Hey, baby. Aren't you going to speak to your husband?" His words were slurred and a tiny spray of spit came out with them. "Getting all high and mighty now with your honky friend. Intro—duce me—"

Somehow she found her voice. "You're drunk, Jerome Lee. Why don't you go home before something happens?" she pleaded, both pitying and fearing him.

"Oh-ho! So I'm not *good* 'nough to 'sociate with *your* friends?" The old belligerence and self-deprecation swelled the words.

His face pushed against the half-rolled-up window, and she could smell the strong, cheap whiskey. As he tried to peer over at Terry, Renay's mind worked rapidly, thinking of Terry beside her. Abruptly she put the car in reverse, almost knocking him to the ground as she shifted quickly, wheeling frantically out from behind and around his car, leaving him standing there looking after them, swaying in bewilderment.

She drove fast, turning off the main highway to seek the secondary roads to the house. She didn't want him following them again. The car responded to the pressure of her foot, gliding like a sleek animal through the night.

Terry took her hand from her side to open the pocket of the car. The hard cold metal brushed Renay's skin as Terry put the pistol back. She hadn't known that Terry had a pistol.

"I always keep one there—just in case—at night. Hadn't you noticed?"

Renay shook her head because she couldn't trust herself to speak. They said nothing all the way home.

The lights in the house cast a hard artificial glare upon them. Each could see the alarm and fear in the other.

"Want a nightcap?" Terry went into the kitchen and mixed bourbon and water.

Renay sat down at the table, her face strained, thinking about Jerome Lee. He was stalking her like a panther, his male ego tarnished by her disavowal of him. Men never think that women can leave; they can never believe a woman who has once been with them no longer wants them. This was what she had to fear.

She took a long sip from her drink. After a moment, it helped relieve the tension. "I don't think he suspects—about us."

No, she thought, Jerome Lee's mind wouldn't turn on that pivot unless an intimation had been made. Lesbianism was the last thing black males would think about when trying to determine why a woman had left them. They had too much black-stud vanity to believe that a woman could do what *they* couldn't do—another man, perhaps, yes—but not a woman.

Mechanically she took the cigarette Terry lighted for her, looking into Terry's worried eyes. "He would have said something if he had. He can get nasty."

"I don't think he fully comprehends that you've left him." Terry rattled the ice cubes in her glass.

"Why should he care? He hasn't cared about anything in the past."

"To a lot of men, a wife connotes vanity ownership. They hate to lose things acquired by choice. Then, too, some people just enjoy making other people miserable—if they can." Terry took the cigarette from Renay, who was not a habitual smoker, and began to smoke it herself. "Tell me," she said, looking steadily at her through the haze of smoke, "if he *had* guessed our relationship, would you have cared?"

Renay was silent, thinking of Terry and herself—how different it was with Terry than with Jerome Lee. Why should she care? The freckles on Terry's hands stood out, and a vein seemed to throb at her neck.

"No—no—I wouldn't have cared at all." Not now, not forever. It was a revelation to know that it could happen in such a beautiful way.

Terry's shoulders seemed to slacken from an invisible weight suddenly removed. "I'm glad," she said.

Renay moved her glass on the table top, watching the looping wet sliding marks left in its wake. Suddenly she laughed—a short, mirthless, hollow sound like joy swallowed up by a cave. All because of Jerome Lee.

"You know, it's a wonder all black women aren't in our world. They're the ones who can get the jobs, the ones left alone to bring up the children, the ones who head the families when the man isn't and often times *is* there. Black Amazons whose tallness and strength lie in their hearts and minds and wills. But strangely, they still love their men, work for them, pity them, bear the seed of their spawn, and take the outrage of those who can't be black warriors. I think it is this sympathy, understanding, tolerance and above all, hope that someday their males *will* rightfully become men in our society that helps them to cling to being women. And to the dream of becoming women in the way they would like to be."

The gray of Terry's eyes deepened. "If he didn't drink—if he changed. Do you—"

"No!" Renay said quickly, eyes steady upon her. "Don't you know people seldom change? Oh, for a day, week, years maybe, but not forever. What is basically there is still there. Besides, I have no feeling for him. There never was anything there except emptiness. It was never like that with you. I *love* you."

"Darling—" Terry closed the word between them. "We're going to have to be very careful," she said, crushing out the cigarette. "Until after the divorce. I wish you would stop playing at the club. He could follow you again and I wouldn't be with you."

Renay's hand lifted in a helpless flutter. "He could follow me anywhere." She wasn't going to let Jerome Lee frighten her. She had to prove to him that she was stronger than he knew.

"Yes, he could—" Terry murmured, running her fingers through her hair. The tinge of gray at the temples seemed more pronounced now. "Do what you must."

Renay looked at the thin line of Terry's eyebrows meeting, forming a tense bridge. "Everything is going to be all right."

Terry's face seemed to illuminate in a soft glow. "I don't want anything to happen to you—because of me."

"If it does," Renay said, trying to smile now to dispel the seriousness of Terry's words, "I wouldn't want it to happen because of anyone else."

CHAPTER 12

After a sleepless night, they got up early. Their Sunday breakfast, unlike the others, consisted only of coffee and orange juice. Neither was hungry. Both were still upset from the shattering remembrance of the night before. They did not talk about it, but the memory nagged them. Over their second cup of coffee, Renay thought of calling Denise.

"Go ahead," Terry urged her, "I'd like to talk to her myself."

Over the distance, Renay heard her mother answer the phone, bringing the past into perspective. A warm glow filled her as she thought of the times before. She could see her mother standing in the large, old-fashioned kitchen where the Sunday roast cooked slowly, creating an aroma throughout the house. Inevitably there would be someone to drop in after church to eat. Home on Sunday was family and friends and warm living.

"Mother?" A catch in her throat partially strangled the word. It was so long since she had said it.

"Renay?" The voice was the same, rich and low and full.
"Yes—Mother. How are you?"
"Fine, baby! It's sure good to hear your voice. Where are you?"
"It's good to hear you too, Mother. I'm home. I thought I'd call to see how you and Denise are. Is she behaving?"
"Now, child—after raising you and other people's children, you know I can take care of my own granddaughter. We're fine. The child's getting some meat on her bones now. Country air and country cooking." She laughed heartily. "Wait a minute. I'll go fetch her. She's getting ready for Sunday School."
Denise spoke excitedly over the phone. "Mommy!"
"Hello, darling. Are you enjoying yourself?"
"Oh, yes! I'm having lots of fun."
"Wonderful. I'm glad you are. Hold the phone. Here's Aunt Terry."
Terry took the phone, cradling it between her ear and shoulder as she poured more coffee into their cups. "Hi, honey—" She smiled as she listened to Denise's chatter about playmates on the block. Then she handed the receiver back to Renay.
"You be good. And don't worry grandmother too much." As she hung up, Renay laughed. "She doesn't seem to be homesick at all."
"It's a new experience for her."
Renay sipped her coffee, looking quietly at Terry, the long length of her face, the gray eyes that lightened with mirth and deepened with anger or thought. Then, in a half whisper, as if to herself, "I'm glad that she loves you too."
"She belongs to us," Terry said, getting up from the table to rinse out her cup. "Would you like to walk over to visit Mrs. Stilling with me? We promised—"
"Yes—if you want to—" she said quickly.

Mrs. Stilling's brown gingerbread house had an array of colorful potted plants in the window. Inside, the walls were covered with diagonally striped gold and lime wallpaper, antique furniture and braided rugs scattered over pine floors.
Mrs. Stilling was delighted to see them and immediately asked Renay to play for her. She sat down at the old spinet and played Mrs. Stilling's favorite Schubert, the allegro movement of the post-

humous A major piano sonata. Mrs. Stilling relaxed in her cherry rocker, head back, eyes closed, enjoying the music filling the room. Walden was stretched out on the floor by the piano, the music lulling him into a half-sleep.

"Lovely!" Mrs. Stilling breathed as the rich harmonies faded into silence. "What are you going to do with all that talent after you finish Waterview? You should go on for additional study."

"I don't know," Renay said, reaching down to pat Walden's head. She really hadn't thought that far ahead. Walden licked her with his rough tongue, inviting further spoiling by rolling on his back to have his stomach rubbed.

"Walden has certainly taken a liking to you," Mrs. Stilling commented, watching them. "Oh, dear!" she said, suddenly getting up. "I was so anxious to hear you play that I'm forgetting the social amenities. Would you like something to drink? Coffee, iced tea, brandy? Martha usually takes care of those things for me, but Sunday is her day off."

"Brandy will be fine," Terry replied. Renay said that she would also have brandy.

They sipped from large glasses that half hid their noses. "Miss Bluvard, would you like to see the library?" Mrs. Stilling invited, motioning for Terry to follow her.

"I'd love to."

The shelves of the paneled library were filled with rare and out-of-print books. A Chippendale desk stood by a glass door which opened onto a small flower garden outside. Mrs. Stilling apparently spent most of her time in the library with its television, stereo console and comfortable brown leather furniture.

Terry, poring over the books, saw Gide, Sartre, Freud, Dostoyevsky, Shelley, Keats, her own book which was now out of print, and a treatise on Thoreau by Dr. Stilling. There was a small collection of books by Chesnutt, McKay, Cullen, Hughes, Baldwin, Ellison and King.

Leaving Terry to browse through the library, Mrs. Stilling went back to tell Renay she would like to hear some Liszt and Bach. As Renay played, she sensed the improvement that the long hours of practice at the college and house had made in her playing.

Two hours later, they left to go home. As they unlocked the

door, the telephone's shrill peal greeted them, and Terry rushed to answer it. Renay heard the pitch of her voice drop and saw the frown that creased her forehead.

When she hung up, the frown still hovered questioningly. "That was Byron Ford, publisher of *Women's Flair*. He's driving out this evening to see me on business. It must be very important for him to come on Sunday. I suppose he'll want supper. What do we have?"

Renay began gathering her books to take upstairs to study for Monday morning's classes. "Nothing much. Leftover turkey. I could make a turkey-and-wild-rice casserole."

Terry took some of the books which were threatening to fall out of Renay's arms. "He may not even be hungry. I'll leave it to you."

Byron Ford was a large, affluent-looking man with a mane of heavy white hair which fell over a flabby face with pale eyes and commonplace features. He arrived late in the evening, dressed in a shimmering dark blue summer suit and a pale blue shirt set off by a red tie.

His slack face gave him a misleadingly nugatory appearance. Through the years, he had accentuated this and capitalized on it. His face was a stone-wall sounding board which no inner or outer reflections of words or feelings seemed to penetrate, but which were all taken in and locked up for future reference. Only when he smoked his expensive, strong-smelling cigars did he slip out of character, the eyes half-squinting perceptively through the smoke haze. As if aware of this frailty, he smoked only around his personal friends.

Renay prepared the turkey casserole, candied sweet potatoes with a dash of rum, and string beans floating in a savory cream sauce. The dinner was good, and Byron Ford ate heartily, carrying on desultory gossip about people Terry knew, and asking questions of Renay about her music and studies.

Byron Ford was aware that Terry knew him better than most people, and for her, he dropped his mask to match his shrewdness with her hardheaded insight. Each had admiration for the other's professional stature, but Terry had little respect for his tactics, he little respect for her personal life.

When dinner was over, Renay left them in the living room to go upstairs and study. Byron sat relaxed in a chair, cigar in one hand and drink in the other.

Smiling across the room at Terry, he said, "So you're writing a novel? Good. I remember the other book you wrote. It wasn't fiction. Let's see—what was it? Oh, yes! A slim philosophical book entitled *Reflections on Living*. It didn't do too well, did it?" His smile widened in mock condolence. "But everybody can't be Ayn Rand."

"No, and everybody can't be Henry Luce," she retorted, thinking Byron was never satisfied without a small war of words between them.

He narrowed his eyes over the soggy cigar. "I'm trying," he chuckled back at her, blowing the heavy smoke above her head. "Anyway, how can you write out here? Away from everybody and everything? A living graveyard. You need to feed on people and emotions." He put the cigar to a slow crushing death in the bronze stand by his chair. "Is it because of her?"

Terry stiffened. Now her relationship with Renay was being brought out into the open. "What do you mean?"

"You realize perfectly well what I mean. I'm liberal enough as to the race thing—colored people have a right to live, too. And, I'm broad-minded about the other, although personally, it never made sense to me when there're so many good men around. However, every person's sex life to himself," he grunted expansively, refilling his glass with scotch. "Phil told me about her. But, my dear, you're living together as if you were *married*."

"It may seem odd to you, Byron, but I *feel* married," she said evenly. Slim fingers curved around the glass she held.

"OK, only I'm worried about how it's affecting your writing."

"I've never written better before. It's like looking into a clear sea and seeing things buried that you hadn't known existed. I'm happy, Byron. Can you understand that?"

"Wonderful! I'm glad you're happy. It's doubly fine you're writing well. So fine that this brings me to the purpose of this visit. I want you to do an article for me."

"No article, Byron. I don't have time."

"Terry, baby, this one is very *important* to me. An interview with Mila Gaylord."

"The new sexpot actress?" Terry said in exasperation, recalling

the half-nude spreads in magazines boosting the actress's first movie role.
"The same, except she doesn't like being called a sexpot. She thinks that she has depth which male writers have overlooked in their interviews with her. She wants to make it known that she has brains also!"
"Does she?" Terry asked wryly.
"That's where you come in. She's become elusive with what she calls a male chauvinistic press. She says all they want is cheesecake. But she will let us do a feature story on her for *Women's Flair*—if *you* handle the interview. She likes your objective, truthful, honest approach," he quoted sarcastically.
"Byron, Christ! I've had enough of those kinds of interviews. Do one, you've done them all."
"But sweetie, as I told you, this woman is supposed to have more than looks—depth."
"By whose standards?"
"Who knows, the gal might have something. Besides, just think of all the magazines it will sell."
Terry did think of the magazines it would sell and thought too of Byron's wife who was probably pushing for a bigger house, and of his mistress, Marlene, who perhaps wanted a more fabulous apartment.
"Just do this one story for me, Terry. I'll pay you double the rate, and afterwards I won't trouble you anymore until you've finished the book. The story's made for you. You'd be surprised at the amount of mail we get from people asking about you." His voice became wheedling.
Now for his own selfish reasons he was buttering her up. The dissension between them showed in their conflicting glances. Anxiously waiting, Byron leaned forward. She did owe him something. He had bought her articles when others had rejected them. In the only way he knew, he had been her friend, helping her along, inspiring confidence in her work. But it would mean leaving Renay for a week or even longer.
As if surmising her thoughts, he said: "Mila's in New York City. You won't have to go halfway around the world to catch up with her."
Then there was the possibility Mila Gaylord might be another

one of those temperamental types she would have to run after, seek, follow, pin down. That would make the trip longer.

"*Please*, Terry—"

She was surprised. Byron never begged for anything. Rather than plead, he would always think of another way. It was this that made her say, "Let me think it over. I'll call you in the morning."

Lighting another one of his cigars, he got up slowly. The rich smooth odor soared with him, penetrating the room and her clothes. She would have to spray the room when he left.

"May I use your phone before I leave?" He grinned sheepishly. "Have to make a call and tell somebody I'm on the way over."

"Of course." She showed him to the telephone in the hallway and went back into the living room. By his subdued tone, she knew he was calling his mistress, Marlene—this man who boasted of the normalcy of marriage, who couldn't comprehend why she lived as she did.

"I'll look for that call first thing in the morning," he said, placing a fatherly arm around her shoulders. "We've known each other a long time, Terry."

"Yes, we have, Byron," she said. "Good night."

Upstairs, Renay had closed her books and was preparing for bed. Terry stood for a moment in the doorway, watching her quietly as she sat before the bureau mirror brushing her hair in long even strokes. A dryness seized her throat, and she swallowed.

"Darling, do you think you could do without me for a week or two?" Terry began in a half-serious, half-joking manner.

"You're going away?" The brush had paused in mid-air and Terry could see the questioning look reflected in the mirror.

"Byron wants me to interview Mila Gaylord—a new actress —for *Women's Flair*."

"Why you?"

Terry went over to her dresser to find a clean pair of pajamas. "She has some silly notion that she wants me to do it." Terry searched busily under the neat piles of slips, undies and brassieres. Renay kept the drawers so straight that it was hard for her to find things not in the jumble she had been used to.

"If she knows that you're the only one who can do it well,"

Renay said, winding her hair in a knot on her head, "go ahead, I'll be all right."

Terry was quiet, absently holding the pajamas she had finally found. "I keep thinking about last night. It all happened so quickly—unexpectedly."

"I can handle Jerome Lee," Renay said soothingly.

"I don't know—" Terry said slowly. "You never know what's really deep down inside people. You can be around them almost forever and never know until it comes out—precipitated by something or someone."

"Terry, don't worry—"

"All right. Anyway, just in case, keep the gun in the bedroom. You're not within yelling distance of Mrs. Stilling, you know. That's why I dislike leaving you alone out here."

"I've been by myself before in much worse places," Renay said. She remembered the dingy sleeping room where Jerome Lee had left her and Denise when they had first come to the city. He had stayed away for three days, supposedly looking for an apartment. She hadn't been afraid of the popping roaches and rats scampering through the thin walls, or of the drunken curses of men and women frustrated by the hopelessness of their existence as babies cried through the barrenness of their parents' anguish.

"I do owe this favor to Byron. If I do this, he knows better than to ask me for anything until the book is finished." Terry collected her robe and slippers to take to the bathroom. "You won't be lonely?"

"How will I have time with the work at the club and exams coming up?"

"You'd better have some good grades to show when I get back. I'll tell Vance to look after you."

"Terry, stop worrying. You just go and do a good story and hurry back."

"Hurry back I will, even if I have to strap Mila Gaylord to a chair to keep her still enough for the interview." She started out the door, then stopped to look back at Renay. "Love me?"

It was the first time Terry had asked her that, even in a light vein. "I simply hate you with love."

"I'll remember that," Terry smiled, "the whole time I'm away."

CHAPTER 13

To Renay, the house was lonely without Terry. The first few days she was busier than usual, staying in town late to study in the college library or to use the music practice rooms. The summer session had almost ended and the work became increasingly heavy as the instructors intensified their courses.

Sometimes, instead of going home for dinner, she ate the tasteless food and drank the tepid coffee served in the noisy school cafeteria. The place was infested with loud-talking students much younger than she, students who dressed in faded jeans and flaunted their beards and long hairdos. After her hastily eaten meals, she often returned to the music library to study for her theory exam, frequently finding herself the only student in the library. By the time she finally reached home, she could do nothing but fall wearily into bed, for the morning was always quick to come.

Terry telephoned her each night around midnight. Renay eagerly looked forward to talking with her, holding the receiver close to her ear so that not a word, sound or breath of Terry's could escape. These times, she told Terry how much she missed her, and Terry said that she was lonely and would try to get home as soon as she could. The conversation invariably ended in that way, with both trying to hurry time and bury loneliness.

Friday, tired from the Thursday supper club job and the morning classes, Renay decided to rest until time to go to work again. The afternoon was sultry and humid as only August could bring. Deciding to nap, Renay undressed and put on a thin shorty robe before falling into an exhausted sleep.

The insistent ring of the doorbell soon awakened her. She groaned, rubbing her eyes sleepily. Who could that be? Getting sluggishly out of bed, she went to the window and saw Lorraine looking questioningly up at the house.

"Hi!" Lorraine smiled, covering her eyes to shield them against the sun's glare.
"Just a minute," Renay yelled down to her. Quickly she threw off the robe and pulled on a pair of slacks and a shirt.
"Hot as hell, isn't it?" Lorraine complained, moving to stand in front of the air conditioner in the living room's side window. "Whee-e-e! That feels good."
The cool air blew lightly against Lorraine, lifting up the stray red tendrils of hair escaping the bun crowning her head. She wore snug-fitting polka-dot hot pants and a halter to match, and appeared far cooler than she claimed to be.
"Terry told us to keep an eye on you. So, here I am for guard watch!" she laughed, raising the palms of her hands to the air conditioner as if warming them before a stove.
"Fine. Where's Vance?"
"She's guarding the cash register. Today is her weekend money time."
"Oh."
"Do you have a cold beer? Beer tastes good in this kind of weather. Besides, the drive made me thirsty."
"I think so."
Renay went to the kitchen and took a can of beer from the refrigerator. The can made a sizzling sound as she peeled off the flip top. As she reached for a glass, Lorraine protested.
"No, no glass. It's better like this," she said, drinking thirstily from the can. "Mmmm, it's good and cold!" Going back to the living room, she slumped on the floor beneath the air conditioner. Lighting a cigarette, she blew playful smoke patterns into space while alternately sipping the beer.
Renay didn't particularly care for beer, but she had one with Lorraine. Watching her half-leaning on the hassock with one slim leg drawn up in an arch, she noticed Lorraine's suntan, a deep bronze except for the pale white ring around her wrist, exposed by a forgotten watch. Lorraine now was browner than she. She thought of the other whites who lolled on beaches all summer to get a tan. What would they do if they were brown all winter, too—when their brown was not a social symbol of expensive vacations and leisure time?

"Do you miss her?" Lorraine asked, scattering her thoughts.

"Yes—very much." What a foolish question. Certainly she missed Terry. Like missing the sun during a long rainy week.

Lorraine frowned, concentrating on the red-tipped toenails sprouting out between the straps of her Roman sandals. "It'd be fun to know whether I'd miss Vance or not. She's never been away from me." She placed the beer can on the floor. "Sometimes, it'd be nice to know that you'd miss a person."

Renay handed her an ashtray. "How long have you known Vance?"

"It seems all my life. I've lived with her for ten years. We met at a small private college in Ohio. Vance was an art instructor and I was a student. Things do get out somehow or other. Maybe by our being together too much—an unguarded look, too much attention, not getting involved with dating and engaging in meaningless female chatter about eligible males and marriage." She shrugged, resting her cheek on her knee. "And there was Vance—openly independent, aggressive with some of her so-called non-feminine qualities. Anyway, Vance had to resign. The president strongly suggested it.

"I often wonder about those days now that they seem so long ago. There were two very gay male faculty members who held wild parties and swished boldly around the campus and nothing was ever said or done about them except for a sly wink or a giggle or a limp wrist held up behind their backs. They were liked by everyone including the married professors' wives and even were invited to their staid dinners because, as one wife said: 'They are so amusing.' But Vance and I, we were lepers. I guess we caught it both ways: the males hating Lesbians because of the affront to their male egos, and the women feeling shaken by our independence from males and perhaps mostly because of their own fears of what might exist within themselves. After we left, we came here to Vance's home. She had some money saved up and decided to open an art-restaurant, as she likes to call it. *I* was to paint."

Lorraine sighed, balancing her cigarette precariously on the ashtray. "It was a fine idea. Only I had sense enough to know that Vance could paint rings around me and do everything better than I. She would be a success in anything she tried—even if she took up mountain climbing. She's self-sufficient. That's what ties me to her, and frightens me, too. I don't know if I can make it alone in the world. I haven't the guts. First my overprotective parents, and now Vance. I depend on her. She likes it, and it's easy for me. That's why I admire you—your independence even while living with Terry. You've got guts and show it—in your own quiet way." She smothered the cigarette and finished her beer. The can made a hollow sound as she tossed it in the wastebasket. "Now, may I have a real drink?"

Renay left to get a bottle of scotch and a bucket of ice cubes. Lorraine purposefully made her drink strong.

"Play something for me."

Renay ran her fingers over the keys and began *Tenderly*. "I like that." Lorraine said quietly, listening to the music. After a while, she said musingly, "You have a child. That must be nice. But isn't it rather hard now? I mean—"

"I know what you mean." Renay said. "Maybe it won't be as hard as trying to bring up a child in a house without love."

"You're right. If she loves the two of you, she should be able to understand—when the time comes." Lorraine mixed a second drink and went over to sit in the chair beside the piano. "You know, Renay, you're nice to look at. I don't blame Terry." Suddenly she gave a little laugh. "I wouldn't want to deliberately hurt Vance for the world, but sometimes I think I'd like to know what it's like with someone else—like does water taste the same in a different glass? Have you ever thought about it?"

Renay stopped playing to turn around. Lorraine was studying her, her eyes a dark inscrutable well. Incredulously she shook her head. The idea was so totally foreign that she couldn't speak. She didn't want anyone but Terry—a lover enshrined, a gift to cherish, a life forever.

"You're just too good to be true!" Lorraine laughed cynically, standing up to go to the bottle again. "It doesn't bother *me* drinking alone, but can't I fix you one?"

"No, thanks," Renay said, shaking her head. "I have to work tonight."

"Yes, I forgot." Lorraine started to strengthen her drink, then stopped. "May I go to the club with you? I don't think Vance will mind. I need a change of scenery."

"If you want to—" Renay remembered the beer which she hadn't finished. She drained the can. It was warm and flat.

"Great! I'll go home and change. I should be back soon. Wait for me?" Her hand rested briefly on Renay's arm, leaving a surprising coolness.

"Of course."

"Fine. See you later—" she called back happily, hurrying out the door.

Lorraine came back looking very lovely and cool in a thin strapless yellow sheath dress that molded her figure. Her red hair was loose this time, raining over her smooth shoulders. She left her car in the driveway and Renay drove. The sun had left the sky tinged with pink.

The club was crowded, catering as usual to the typical Friday night crowd launching the weekend merry-go-round. To be close to Renay, Lorraine chose a small table near the piano. Hovering over a dinner she hardly touched, she drank until intermission, when Renay noticed that her eyes were wide and shiny, and that she seemed overly animated.

"It's really nice getting out sometimes for a change. Vance doesn't like to go out too much. And God, when she does and gets more than two drinks under her belt, she has a terrible temper."

Renay looked away, not wanting to discuss Vance. She concentrated on the cup of coffee she had ordered, stirring it slowly. "Why don't you eat your dinner?" she asked, thinking Lorraine had wasted a beautiful steak. The mound of mashed potatoes had probing fork holes and the peas had not been touched. Only the tossed salad had been eaten.

"I'm not hungry. I'm *thirsty!*" Lorraine giggled, beckoning for the waiter. "Let me treat you to a drink."

"No, thanks. I'm kind of tired. A drink wouldn't help me much right now."

"Later—maybe."

When it was time for her to stop playing, Renay was relieved to be finished for the night. After this, there would be only one more work evening and then blessed Sunday. Thank God for Sunday.

As they got into the car, Lorraine said, "Let's go to Margo's Corner for a nightcap. I haven't been there for ages. Not since Vance practically tore up the place because I was talking to someone else for a long time." She giggled, remembering. "It was a perfectly harmless conversation, but she—"

Renay surmised the bar was evidently the kind Terry had told her she disliked: *I believe in some discretion—in not being a public spectacle.* "Some other time, Lorraine. I'm really *beat!*"

"Who knows if there'll be another time—alone with you?" Lorraine said softly.

Renay glanced at her sharply, starting the car with a jerk. Lorraine's restlessness reminded Renay of a colt eager to jump the corral fence and run with the wind. She drove home quickly and in silence while Lorraine drifted into sleep.

"We're home," Renay said, waking Lorraine. "Want to come in for a cup of coffee?" She thought the coffee might help sober her up for the drive home.

"Might as well, since you insist on making me behave," the girl taunted.

Clusters of stars made flecked patterns in the moonlit sky. Crickets shrilled their strident sounds in the lonely night, warning of tomorrow's heat to come.

"A million eyes around us and we see nothing," Lorraine said, face turned toward the sky as she waited for Renay to unlock the door.

Terry had given Renay instructions on safety precautions, and she had left a light on. Renay tiredly kicked off her shoes and moved to switch on more light.

"I think I'll have a coffee royal," Lorraine said in the kitchen.

"Whatever you like. It won't take long for the coffee to perk." Renay filled the basket of the electric percolator. "I think I'll just have a plain drink."

The rug felt soft to her stockinged feet as she walked back into the living room and collapsed on the couch. She closed her eyes and listed to Lorraine's movements in the kitchen. Soon she returned carrying a tray of ice, glasses and cups.

"See—I've made myself at home." She set the tray on the coffee table. The flavorful aroma of the coffee penetrated the room. Lorraine handed her an awesome-looking drink, then laced her coffee with scotch. "Why are you so distant toward me?" she asked, settling down on the couch beside Renay.

"I didn't know that I was," Renay replied cautiously, tasting her drink, which immediately started a little combustion in her stomach. It was approaching midnight, and the day's pressures weighed heavily upon her. The drink made her feel only more tired and worn. Soon Terry would call. The thought of talking to Terry made her feel a little less fatigued.

"There's something very striking about you, Renay. You're truly an artist's dream. I believe I could trace your features in the dark and draw you exactly as you are in the light."

The rare sound of a car engine droned slowly by the house, a low hum interrupting their talk. Renay could see the beams of light through the blind that was partially open. She had forgotten to close it. At this moment, she didn't feel like getting up to do it. They were probably straying lovers searching for a place to park.

"You're really tired, aren't you?" Lorraine moved closer to her on the couch.

The warm fragrance of Lorraine's perfume engulfed her. She shut her eyes and pictured a rose garden. "Yes—"

To her surprise, she felt the warmth of Lorraine's lips against hers, so light that she wondered if it had happened at all. Startled, she opened her eyes. Lorraine's face was near hers, the lips now brushing silk across her cheeks and eyes and hair.

"Please—please don't be angry," Lorraine whispered in the pit of her ear. "Don't you want to? I do—very much—with you."

Renay moved away from the words and the mouth trying to capture hers and the hands seeking to press her back into the diaphanous web. "No, no—Lorraine. Stop. You've had too much to drink. You don't know what you're saying."

"I *do*. I've been waiting to do this all day. To hold you—have you hold me—love you. No one will know. Je-sus! My teeth are on edge from wanting you. Please—don't you feel like this too?"

"I'm sorry, Lorraine—" Renay got up. "Home you go," she said, pulling Lorraine up and taking her firmly by the arm. "Vance is probably worried as hell about you."

"Oh, damn you and your loyal self. Do you think Terry's there just *interviewing* someone like Mila Gaylord? *Do you?*"

The question was like cold water thrown on her. She stiffened angrily. "I *know* Terry," she said confidently.

"You hope!" Lorraine snorted. "Away—anybody'll play —once."

"Goodnight, Lorraine," she said coolly. "Drive carefully."

She stood there in the light of the doorway watching Lorraine climb into her car and drive away. After locking the door, she began to straighten up the living room, putting her glass and Lorraine's cup on the tray. When she went into the kitchen, she saw him standing there, silently waiting for her.

CHAPTER 14

The scream that rose to her lips was silenced by fright. The sight of him paralyzed her, freezing her thoughts and feelings and movements. She gripped the tray as she stared unbelievingly at him. Maybe it wasn't he—an apparition—or maybe her imagination was so strong that it was making her see things that weren't really true. But when he spoke to her, it was clear that Jerome Lee was before her—a nightmare in reality.

"So! You're screwing around with bulldikers," he spat out contemptuously, lips moving in a sneer. "I saw you two through the blinds. Kissing!" he snorted, shaking his head incredulously. "That's real funny. You turning into a queer. Maybe that's what was wrong with you all along. And *you* getting a divorce from *me*. Wait until I tell the court about your he-she friends. You won't get Denise or a goddam motherfucking thing. *You hear me?*"

She was made alive again by the words slung like mud at her, alerting her to the moment and to him. Automatically she moved to put the tray on the table, trying to show composure, to let him know she didn't fear him or his threats. Her eyes focused unwaveringly on him, a hulking brown shadow illuminated under the kitchen's fluorescent light. He towered menacingly above her, a black giant whose Afro bush was too long and wildly matted. He was growing, by design or laziness, a beard which was ragged and hid most of his lower face like a mask. His once-white T-shirt was soiled and yellow under the armpits, and the rumpled brown slacks hung loosely on him. She could see that he had lost weight. He looked unkempt and not like the Jerome Lee who had once taken pride in his looks and clothes. The odor of cheap whiskey exuded from his pores; it was now embedded in his breath and skin and life.

Before trying to frame words, she struggled to contain herself, not to antagonize him further, to gain time to control her voice and thoughts. *Don't be afraid of him or of what he has just said.* She knew him in some ways better than he did himself. She had lived with him. She *knew* him. But how many people in the world had lived together without having really known each other? Some aspects were always hidden, for concealment is sometimes a basic necessity to life.

She found herself, her voice. "How did you get in, Jerome Lee?"

"Simple. Through a back window screen." He began to look around the kitchen and into the dining room, taking in the expensive furniture and deep pile rugs. "Nice setup. Real classy. The dike must have money. I guess it pays to fuck around with honky son-of-a-bitching queers. What happened—you couldn't get a man?" he scoffed. "I could have told you that. Who'd want *you*? Nobody. She's not the same one I been seeing you with all the time. Where's the other one? The tall, skinny scarecrow with no mouth?"

She decided not to answer him, to ignore his taunts and gibes, thinking that perhaps he would leave. Didn't it take two to make an argument? But she had forgotten: The sound of his own words were enough for him.

"The shitting-ass nerve of you, bringing my daughter up around bulldikers. Where is she?"

"Away—"

"With *her*?"

Let him think Denise was away with Terry. She wasn't going to tell him. "She's gone on a trip."

"Trip—*where*?"

"That's none of your business." She refused to have him going to Kentucky, and worrying her mother and Denise. That was what he would do.

Suddenly he reached out and grabbed her, shaking her viciously. "Goddammit—tell me where she is. I'm her *father!*"

"Are you *really* her father?" she shouted back in disdain, breaking away from his grasp.

"What do you mean by that?" he asked, eyes narrowing suspiciously, his mind speculating on what a male would conclude at such a denunciation.

"I mean, yes, you planted the seed, but what *else* have you done?"

"What the hell you talking about what else have I done? I *married* you, didn't I? I could have left you with a baby and gone on about my business."

There it was, out before them—what they had never talked about all the years. He had married her, but in the long run, wouldn't it have been better if he hadn't? Marriage isn't always the best solution. He would forever feel the arrogant black knight-errant who had done the right thing by a black maiden in distress—a noble deed performed in the name of honor.

Realizing his victory over her, he went on triumphantly: "I kept you. Provided the best way I could for my child—"

"The best way you could," she repeated derisively, thinking of his absences from home, the seething tenements they had inhabited, the hungry nights and mornings.

"So how can you say I haven't acted like no father?" he persisted, her irony escaping him.

"Have you *loved* her?" she asked in a whisper. He was now so close to her that she could see the red veins streaking jagged lines in the muddy yellow of his eyes. Her arms ached from the steel fingers that had clutched her.

"Have you loved *me?*" he breathed quietly, and for a brief illusory moment she saw his face soften in bitter despair. When he saw her look away without answering, he said: "I got me another woman now. She loves me. She told me to come and get my kid."

Yes, it would have to be another woman who had put the idea into his head, for alone the least thing he would want to be saddled with was a child—unless he knew it would hurt her. Always in the back of his mind like a gnawing growth was the desire to hurt her—make her suffer—for this was the only way he could feel like the conqueror, the master, the subduer. And because making her suffer was his prime concern, he did it ruthlessly, disregarding others who might fall in the wake of his vindictiveness. She could imagine the other woman, like those she had glimpsed time and again climbing boldly out of his car in front of their apartment.

Those bawdy phantoms who drank with him and had sex with him and who, too, were shadows of him, mirroring his audacity and self-destruction.

"I'm glad you have someone, Jerome Lee, to take care of you," she said placatingly, hoping he would see that she really was glad for him, and also hoping to divert his thoughts. His alcoholic's mind vacillated, quick to change, forget, for it was low in comprehension and retention.

Thinking that she was ridiculing him, he snapped back defensively. "This one is different. She loves me."

Different, perhaps, she contemplated, but not enough to change him. He looked worse than ever. The woman had to be either like him or stringing him along until she tired of him.

"You going to tell me where Denise is?"

"Are you interested in Denise, Jerome Lee, or is it just that you want to get back at me in the only way you know how—through her? You can't be outdone by someone who you thought was putty in your hands to do with as you pleased. A lamb who sat at home and waited in misery until you played out and came home to rest and were ready to leave again!" The anger and the outrage of the past brought tears to her eyes. The kitchen became a swimming blur, a room that would not keep still.

"You tell me where Denise is before I knock the hell out of you!" His fist curled up into a hard threatening knot as his arm bent at the elbow. Heavy veins stood out at his temples, straining as if ready to burst.

He looked like a wild black savage enmeshed in a tangle of conflicting emotions. For the first time, she was actually afraid of him. His anger, his belligerency and his hatred of her were more apparent than ever. He was capable of killing her and feeling totally justified.

She thought quickly of the pistol Terry had left with her, but it was upstairs in the bedroom. She needed something to protect herself—a knife. The knives were in the cabinet drawer behind him. She measured the distance to the cabinet, her eyes skirting the room. Then she saw the bottle of scotch on the table where she had placed it.

"Would you like a drink, Jerome Lee?" Perhaps she could relax him, then after a while persuade him to leave.

His gaze went to the bottle and lingered. "Oh, Jesus," she prayed silently, "just let him take one drink." She knew if he got the taste of it, one drink would compulsively lead to another until the bottle was gone.

"Ambassador—" he sneered at the expensive brand. "No, I don't want no bulldiker's booze. All I want is for you to hurry up and tell me, Miss High-'n'-Mighty, where Denise is—or your lady-lover won't know you when she gets back. I ought to stay right here and wait for her and then kill you both!"

Fear arose within her, and her first thought was of Terry. "She's out of town. You'd have a long wait."

"Yeah? Well, *you're* here, and I don't intend to wait all night to find out what I want to know. Maybelle told me I should have beat your ass long ago. *She* knows how to make a man happy."

"I'm sure she does," Renay said conciliatingly, pouring out a generous glass of liquor. "You sure you don't want a drink, Jerome Lee? You used to like scotch. Have one with me?"

Angrily he struck the glass from her hand. It hit the wall and splashed its contents over the floor and wall. The fumes filled the air like ether.

"I told you I didn't want no goddam scotch!"

She saw his muscles bulging as his arm flexed. A fierce, crazed look of meanness appeared on his face. To allay the panic spreading through her, without thought, she bent to pick up the broken pieces of glass and carry them to the trash can. Then, taking a cloth out of the drawer, she methodically began to wipe up the spilled liquid. Her pretense at calmness seemed to infuriate him more.

He watched her, his eyes mirroring hate. "You always did think you were better than me, Miss High-'n'-Mighty, Miss butter-won't-melt-in-your-mouth—" he stopped, recalling that this was what had attracted him to her in the first place—her proud queenly aloofness. She had carried this all through her life with him and this infuriated him to the point of despair. Because it was the only way he could imagine to make her submissive, he blurted out savagely: "I'm going to whip the pure black shit out of your yellow ass!"

"Yes," she said, turning to face him, "you want to beat me, to trample on me, see me grovel because you despise what you can't change. A man should be able to control his woman—especially a black man who can't control anything else. But do you really want to know why you hate me? Because I've survived your male deterioration. Do you understand? Survived! Through the muck and slime you've wallowed in and put me through, I've come out of it—our battle of wills. But you, you're in it and can't get out because you're stuck!

"You're too weak to struggle. It's easier to stay in. And you can't stand the idea that I've left the dirt and you, and you can't push me back into your quagmire again—to have me as the reason and scapegoat. So go back—go back to your bottles and your Maybelles and your self-pity—" She broke off, drained by her explosion and the presence of him. A sob escaped her throat. "God, Jerome Lee—please leave me alone. I don't bother you, do I?"

His eyes narrowed into slits as his chest heaved in angry gasps, devouring the air like a lion. "Bitch! You bother me just by living!"

The blow came swiftly, knocking her against the wall. She felt the others following like a rain of shocks, fists pounding, hitting her face, breasts, stomach. She fell to the floor, tasting the bile rising to her lips. His foot kicked her side and pain streaked white slivers of heat throughout her body.

His rage spilled over into obscenity, the words coming out in staccato rhythm with the blows: "Motherfucker—bitch—queer!"

She rolled onto her stomach, throwing her arms around her head to protect her face. She tried to scream over the pain, the horror, and in her numbness thought something had come out, but it was only the blood trickling down the corners of her mouth.

He's going to kill me, she thought, and in between the hell of the pain and agony and fear, the telephone rang, a nebulous jangling on the wall. The blows stopped. The phone rang on and on like a screaming rescuer. Then blackness overcame her with its benevolent wings.

CHAPTER 15

Edith Stilling found her early the next morning. The air was cool, the morning flavored with the fresh sweet smell of nature. Passing near the house with Walden at her side, she remembered that Terry was away. She noticed the outside night-light still burning, casting a pale artificial glare in the daylight. Pressing the doorbell, she squinted into the early morning sky. Walden moved restlessly in the grass, eyes and ears alerted for something to chase.

She pressed the doorbell again, holding her finger on the button, hearing the faint, beckoning ring. When no one answered, she concluded that Renay was probably still asleep. It was a trifle early, and Renay did work at night. She called to Walden, who was exploring around the side of the house.

As she went to find him, he bounded up to her, barking furiously. He ran in circles to the rear of the house and back again to her. His loud barks and agitated movements caused her to follow him to the back door. There the screen, almost torn from its hinges, hung open in a half arc. The kitchen door was partly open, and from within she heard a low moan. Frowning, she pushed the door open and peered into the kitchen to see the form in a crumpled heap on the floor.

"My God, Renay!" she gasped, moving quickly to the girl. She leaned down, recoiling at the pulpy discolored mass of the face. She stared in disbelief, and for a fixed moment she was unable to think or move. It was Walden who stirred her into motion, creeping beside her and whining at the still figure that did not reach out to greet him.

Renay seemed to be in a semi-comatose condition. Her eyes were glassy, pleading. Edith felt the slowness of her pulse. She had to get her off the floor. Mustering all her strength, she half dragged and half carried her to the living room. Somehow, through force of will and strength, she managed to get her onto the couch. She rested for a moment, breathing hard from the exertion. A doctor was needed.

She went to the telephone and with shaking hands dialed her personal physician, urging him to come immediately. It was an emergency. Then she went back to Renay. The girl's skin was clammy and ashen. She gathered pillows to prop Renay's feet up, placing her head lower than her waist as the doctor had advised. Then she covered her with a light quilt and sat down to wait.

Who could have done it? A burglar? But nothing seemed to have been touched. Perhaps she should call the police. The telephone's sudden ring startled her, sounding overly shrill in the early morning quiet of the house.

It was Terry. She was worried, for she had called and called last night, but no one had answered. Was anything wrong?

Mrs. Stilling tried to maintain her calmness. She spoke slowly, carefully, not wanting to alarm Terry. Someone had apparently broken into the house and attacked Renay. She had just called her doctor and now was going to call the police.

"No, no!" Terry shouted frantically. "Don't—don't call the police. I'll be there as soon as I can get a plane out."

"All right," Mrs. Stilling said quietly. "I'll stay right here with her until you come."

She got a pan of warm water and returned to Renay. Slowly she began to wipe away the dried blood caking her face. Walden stretched out on the floor, head between his paws, eyes following her movements.

"You're going to be all right, Renay," she said gently. "Thanks to Walden."

After what seemed much too long a time, she heard the sound of a car and looked out the window to see the doctor. Quickly she hurried to the door to let him in.

Renay regained consciousness on a day that was gray and murky. Occasionally the sun moved sluggishly from behind the clouds to scatter faint bright rays, only to disappear again behind a hazy veil.

Renay opened her eyes to Terry, who had taken up vigil beside her bed. Puffy blue rings encircled Terry's eyes, and her face looked drawn and haggard. She wanted to cry for Terry, but instead feigned a weak smile.

"Renay!" Terry breathed in relief. "How do you feel?"

She ached and was sore all over. She felt as if death had brushed her closely through fire and pain, and she knew that if it weren't for Terry, she wouldn't want to see or breathe life again. It *was* Terry, wasn't it, here beside her now?

"Terry—?" Her weak voice sounded strange to her.

"Yes, darling. How do you feel?" Terry asked again, hand on her forehead. The hand was cool and soft and comforting.

"I ache—all over."

"I know. It's going to take a while for you to heal. The doctor says that you were lucky. It could have been worse. He'll be here this evening to see you."

"What's today?" She had lost all concept of time.

"Wednesday." Terry's cheek brushed hers, cool on her burning face. "*He* did it, didn't he?" she whispered bitterly. "Jerome Lee—"

"Yes—" Terry's cheek moved away and she wished it back. A match flared as Terry lit a cigarette and blew a smoke canopy above the bed. Her white blouse was smudged and wrinkled, stretching over shoulders slumped in a weary arc. "He broke in and said all kinds of mean things. He wants Denise back—he's going to tell the court about us. He acted like a wild man."

"And he beat you terribly. God, I hate him," Terry said fiercely. "I detest him for everything he's done to you, for every damn miserable moment he's given you." Her face hardened. "Men can be awful sons-of-bitches."

"He can get Denise now, can't he, if he tells about us?" The thought spoken was so overwhelming that she tried to raise herself in the bed. Too weak, she fell back on the pillow, remembering that judges rarely rule against the norm.

"No, he's *not* going to get Denise. I figured it was Jerome Lee who did it. So I contacted my lawyer, and he went to find him at your old place. He was going to scare him, threaten him with the book—assault and battery, intent to kill, housebreaking, every damn thing he could. Only I think he must have thought he'd hurt you worse than he had, or gotten scared as hell. The landlord said that he and some woman packed up and left hurriedly." She drew heavily on the cigarette. "He won't bother you again. He'd better not."

Renay focused on the cool ivory of the ceiling and thought about Jerome Lee and his genie uncapped from a bottle, gelded by self-doubt, primed by weakness. Then she didn't want to think any more about him.

"I'm missing my exams."

"Don't worry. I'll call Dr. Larsons and explain that you're ill. We'll see if he can arrange for you to take them later. Rest now, darling. Try not to think about anything for a while."

"Not even about you?" Renay tried to smile. Her lips were sore from the stitches, and the smile didn't quite succeed.

"Just me—" Terry smiled, kissing her tenderly.

In a few days, when she could sit up without too much effort, she asked Terry to bring her books. During the day, she studied until tired; then she would drift off to sleep and awaken again to her work. Soon she began to regain her strength, and almost felt like herself.

Dr. Larsons granted her permission to take the exams when she was better, and two weeks later, Terry drove her into town, dropping her off at the college.

"You'll make out all right," Terry reassured her.

"I hope so," Renay said, feeling the usual apprehension experienced before examinations.

"Call me at Phil's when you're finished. I'm going to deliver this article on Mila Gaylord to Byron. Luckily I finished the interview the night I was trying to call you. Good luck!"

Renay waved back at Terry before she drove off. Then, taking a deep breath, she climbed the concrete steps to the rectangular stone music building.

"I think I did all right," Renay announced happily, sinking wearily into the car seat beside Terry.

"I knew you would. Dr. Larsons seems to be quite pleased with your work."

"He thinks I should be able to complete my year by January, providing I take a full course load next semester."

"You can do it. But you'll have to cut off the club. It'll be too much of a strain on you."

Renay watched the busy afternoon traffic weaving in and out around them, horns honking impatiently. The convertible's top was down, and through the dark sunglasses the sky looked shaded, clouded with a thin brown film.

"You win—" she said finally, a little slowly, a little sadly. "No more Ruzicka's." She would miss the club—the art of performing, knowing people were listening and enjoying what she had to offer and liked so much to do.

At home, sifting through the morning mail, Terry handed a letter to Renay. "This is for you."

The letter bore the Starling Music Publishing Company imprint in the return address corner. She opened it questioningly, reading the words with a mixture of surprise and disbelief. "Terry, you sent my song to them. They want to publish *Song for Souls!*"

Terry smiled, reading the letter over her shoulder. "Wonderful! I told you it had possibilities. Now if a noted band leader likes it—let's celebrate! I'll invite Vance and Lorraine over later. Would you like to go out for dinner?"

"No. Let's stay home."

"Home it is. *I'll* cook dinner. My one and only big forte is beef stroganoff. You'll have to take your chances on the rest," she laughed.

"I'm brave."

"There's no champagne in the house. Will scotch or bourbon do for the celebration?" Terry asked, reaching in the buffet for bottle and glasses.

"Scotch'll be fine."

Terry lit candles and set a festive table in the dining room. The beef stroganoff was delicious, and Terry served frozen peas with tiny pearl onions in them. Renay ate more than she had eaten in a long while. They had more scotch after dinner, and, feeling full and relaxed, Renay stretched out on the couch while Terry did the dishes.

The doorbell rang, and Renay went to let in Vance and Lorraine. "How's the sick gal?" Vance boomed. "At least you can recognize me now. A few weeks ago, you didn't know from nothing."

Lorraine smiled thinly. "Hello, Renay—"

"Is Terry in the kitchen? I think I hear her cussing out the dishes. I'll take this booze I brought along to her."

Lorraine sat down, eyes quizzically on Renay. "I wish I had stayed longer with you that night. Maybe then, it all wouldn't have happened. Do you feel like talking about it?"

Renay shook her head, looking away. No, she didn't want to talk about it or remember it.

Terry and Vance came back into the room, loaded with bottles, mixes and glasses. "Guess what, Lorraine," Vance began excitedly. "We have a celebrity among us. Terry tells me Renay's going to have one of her compositions published!"

"How nice."

Terry smiled proudly over the drinks she was helping Vance prepare. "I'll have to be careful now. She might start getting temperamental on me."

Lorraine raised her eyebrows. "Was Mila Gaylord temperamental?" She took the frosted glass garnished with the lemon slice and cherry, her eyes narrowing at Terry.

"No; surprisingly, she's a very nice person with a mind. She's getting married soon—to her director."

"Oh," Lorraine said, looking down at her glass.

"She's disappointed." Vance winked, sitting down and pulling up the creases in her slacks. "Lorraine has the stupid idea everybody's gay—or wants to be. A lot of people make terrible mistakes like that," she added, giving Lorraine a reproachful look. "Anyway, I'm certainly glad to see Renay on her feet again. Honey, you had us scared stiff for a while. I stayed here all night once nursing you *and* Terry."

Renay felt a sinking sensation in her stomach. Why did they have to keep bringing up that night? She excused herself, muttering that she needed more lemon for her drink.

"I'll have to get it for you," Terry said quickly, going with her. "Is something wrong?" she asked, reaching far back into the refrigerator for the lemons.

Renay leaned weakly against the sink. "They know about it."

"I *had* to get Vance to help me, darling. I was worried as hell about you. She and Mrs. Stilling were a tremendous help." Terry, still holding the lemon, watched her intently. "It could happen to anybody—to one of them. Nobody is immune to that kind of danger. People get attacked everywhere these days—on the streets—anywhere. You mustn't take it as a shameful personal embarrassment."

"It's about as bad as being raped."

"Please—try to forget it," Terry consoled gently.

Renay took the lemon from Terry, squeezing it absently into her glass. "I wish it were—easy to forget."

Terry gripped her shoulders, eyes strong upon her. "It'll take time. But painful memories, thankfully, have the astonishingly good habit of burying themselves quickly. Let's go back to our guests. OK?"

She nodded, holding the glass tightly. "All right."

After Lorraine and Vance had gone, Renay went to bed, leaving Terry, who felt the urge to write. Later, when Terry came into the room, the sharp glare of the light awakened her. She turned over to see Terry rummaging through the bureau drawer.

"I'm sorry. I didn't mean to awaken you."

"Terry—sleep with me tonight." Renay turned to face her, stretching her legs under the cool sheets. The bed was too large and lonely without Terry, who had considerately been sleeping in another room during Renay's convalescence.

"If you want me to—" Terry looked out the open window where the cool night air drifted into the room.

"I want you to—"

"I'll be back—soon."

She closed her eyes, hearing Terry in the bathroom and the spraying shower sounds. Then the faint click of the light and Terry was back. The side of the bed dipped as she got in.

"It's been a long day for you, hasn't it?" Terry said, drawing her near.

She opened her eyes, snuggling into the strong arms sheltering her, staying very still, a turtle in another's shell. She had been thinking, and her thoughts came alive. "I'd like to visit my mother and see Denise."

Terry's hand stroked her hair, softly entwining in its thickness. "When?"

"Soon. I won't stay long. I want to ask my mother to keep her until I finish my studies."

"It's up to you. I'll miss her."

"Me too—very much. But I must find myself again. I need time to think and plan. I don't feel I'll make a satisfactory mother until I've reckoned with this. Now, I'm bitter. I need time for it to wear off. I don't want my hatred for him to become a part of her too. She's a child—she'll know enough of hatred when she grows up. Can you understand?"

Terry's arms tightened around her. "I can understand."

Renay's head sank instinctively into the groove of Terry's shoulder. "Thank you. I knew you would." She could hear Terry's heart beating. "It seems like ages since we've been like this." The moonlight splayed over Terry's side of the pillow, making little lighted islands. "I don't want to go to sleep—not yet," she murmured, moving closer, meeting Terry's warmth and feeling the slight tremor of her body. "You haven't loved me for a long time, have you? Or does it just seem that way?"

In answer, Terry's arms locked around her as her lips caressed her eyes, her nose, and lingered like a sacrament on her mouth. They lay quietly, submerged in each other, softness sinking into its own.

"I love you—" Renay said. The words had a special meaning tonight. Her fingers traced a thin line down Terry's back—a line she had traced many times before but that always seemed an exciting new path. "It seems so long since we've done this. Now, it's like we've just found each other—you and me."

The light magic of Terry's hand sought and crept into the forest of her, covering the enclosure, imprisoning it, remaining—a butterfly without flight. "Mine—all mine."

The moon had disappeared, a silent meddler who had discreetly crept away, leaving them to a protective darkness veiling their love movements. Her mouth stayed against Terry's as her body pressed closer and closer—she couldn't seem to get close enough. And because it had been such a long time, the tactile motions were barely quickening before Renay cried out, clinging tightly to keep from drowning in a tossing, passionate sea. Her body trembled and convulsed in a volcanic shudder as the poignantly sweet pain moved through her.

"God, Terry, what your hands can do to me—" She was a little ashamed, a little amazed, and tremendously happy.

"We belong together." Terry stilled her with a stroke of her hand.

"I wasn't much help to you, was I?" Renay said softly.

"In loving, there's joy in giving happiness too."

"Let me make you happy like I was." Renay's hand closed around Terry's breast as she kissed her softly. "Let's—again."

CHAPTER 16

Home: Tilltown, Kentucky, a small town named after its one big industry, the Tilltown Tobacco Company. The town was insular, surrounded by fields of bright-leaf tobacco and farms, steeped in long-time black poverty and rigid white provincialism. To Renay, home was the one-story green frame house on dusty, unpaved Booker Street in that part of town whites called "colored town."

When she arrived late in the evening weary from the thirty-mile bus ride from the nearest airport, nostalgia overcame her as she got out of the cab in front of the house. Her daughter had apparently been watching for her from behind the stiff white flour-starched curtains criss-crossing the windows. She had hardly opened the gate of the new chain-link fence when Denise ran out to meet her.

"Mommy!"

"Hello, darling—" Denise's arms went about her waist as Renay stooped to hug her tightly. She had grown taller, and her young body was beginning to blossom.

"Grandmom's waiting!" Denise announced excitedly, hurrying her into the house.

"Renay—my baby's here!"

Now her mother was squeezing her and she could see the tears of happiness glistening on her cheeks. The three of them made a tight triangle in the living room.

Renay thought her mother looked older, the once youthful frame stouter, the dark hair graying, the clear light skin now brown-flecked. "Mother, it's so good to see you again."

"Renay—it's been so long." She stepped back to gaze at her. "Honey, you need to eat more. Stay here awhile and let me fatten you up. See what I done to Denise?"

"I sure do. She looks wonderful."

"I look wonderful—I look wonderful!" Denise chanted repetitiously, spinning in a pirouette.

"And the house—" Renay marveled, glancing around. "You've had work done to it." The living room had been repapered and a new gray rug covered the brown splintered wood floor. A television set with a sailboat nightlamp on top occupied the corner where her piano had once been. Everything was clean and neat and warmly comfortable. Her breath caught as memories of growing up in happiness and sadness and love confronted her.

"Come see your old room. I fixed it up for Denise."

The room was painted yellow and a modern mahogany bedroom suite had replaced Renay's old iron bed and rickety dresser. Bright green scatter rugs decorated the floor. "Mother, you've struck oil!" Renay teased, thinking how different it was from what it used to be.

"No oil, honey. I'm just not slaving for Miss Ann no more. I'm working five days a week now for the Community Day Care Center, and *not* seven. It's one of those new gov'ment-sponsored programs and Uncle Sam's paying my wages."

"You didn't tell me—"

"Lots of things I 'spect you don't tell me!" her mother retorted. "Now, why don't you rest until dinner? I cooked your favorite

Loving Her

baked ham, sweet potato pudding, and collard greens. All with homemade cornbread. Chocolate cake for dessert!"

"Hmmm. Sounds good and can I smell it!" Renay moved to unlock her suitcase, reaching in for a robe. "I think I'll rest awhile before dinner. It takes a lot of wringing and twisting to get here by plane."

"How's Aunt Terry?" Denise asked, perching at the foot of the bed to watch her mother unpack.

"She's fine and sent you a present." Renay handed her a square package tied with a pink bow.

"Oh, goody!" Excitedly she tore off the tissue. "A book! *God's Trombones* by James Weldon Johnson. She remembered the poem!"

"Yes. She read it and liked it very much and wanted you to have a copy of your very own."

"See the book, Grandmom?"

"Nice. Denise talks a lot about this Aunt Terry. Who is she?"

Renay saw the look of puzzlement on her mother's face. "She's a writer and a good friend of mine. I live with her." She looked down at the book and Terry's handwriting inside the cover. *For Denise, who introduced me to a fine poet.* Her mother's voice swept away the image of Terry.

"She's white, isn't she?" The words carried no inflection.

"Aunt Terry says it doesn't make any difference about color. People are people," Denise broke in, looking up from the book.

"Well, children, it's nice to know that there are some white people who think like that in this day and age. Thank the good Lord for not makin' ever'body alike. God only knows what this world's comin' to—wars and riots and killin's. White folks hatin' Negroes and Negroes hatin' white folks *and* their own people. Why only yesdiddy, a young boy I been knowin' since he was first borned, got mad at me 'cause I wouldn't call him black! I just can't git used to callin' ourselves black. Years ago, we'd want to chop off somebody's head—colored or white—for callin' us black. Anyway, if you and that white woman git along together—fine. But I don't think I could live with one. No siree!"

"White people work with you at that place, don't they, Grandmom?"

"Sure do. Maybe they figure that's a star in their crown—or

maybe in their pocketbooks," she chuckled. "Who knows? Now I'm goin' to finish dinner. I'll call you when it's ready."

Renay swooped up Denise with a you're-so-heavy grunt. "OK, sweetie, up from the bed! I want to take off the spread."

Outside the door, they could hear the muffled ringing of the telephone and footsteps hurrying to answer it.

"Renay—" her mother called to her. "That was Fran. She said to tell you she'll be by later on."

"All right, Mother," she replied, quickly tying her robe and slipping into her backless mules. "Now, honey, if you'll let your mommy get a little nap, we'll have a nice long chat afterwards. Wake me up when dinner's ready."

At the table, Renay filled her plate twice. The dinner was cooked just as she liked it. The ham had a sweet, savory, clove taste, and the large leafy garden collards were cooked with garlic and ham hocks. Renay and her mother lingered over strong black coffee while Denise went to watch television.

"Wish I had a piano so you could play something pretty for me." Her mother sighed. "Your father sure could sing. 'Specially after a meal like this. He had the prettiest tenor voice. Could hear him above all the church choir on Sundays. Too bad in those days, colored men with talent didn't have no chance like today. Albert could sing worlds 'round some of these white folks they got croakin' on television now. Gettin' all that money for hog callin'. That's all it 'mounts to."

"We'll find a piano before I leave."

"How long you stayin'?"

"Not long." She pushed back her cup, thinking now was the time to tell her. "Mother, I'm going back to school. I hope to get my degree by January."

"What? Lord be praised!"

Renay joined in her mother's happiness, remembering her mother's dreams of her finishing school so she wouldn't have to go through life as she had. Education, the black passkey for those not trying to open doors an easier and quicker way.

"You goin' to teach?"

"I don't know. I don't want to—"

"Well, there's so many other things colored people can do

nowadays. Things in me and your father's time we wouldn't never dreamed of. I see 'em on television doin' ever'thing. Even got their own shows. Makes me feel good when I sit here and see 'em and know all these white folks 'round here are seein' 'em too."

"Could you keep Denise for me until I finish? If you don't mind—"

"Mind? Why, child, she's comp'ny for me!"

"I can tell she likes being here," Renay said, scraping and stacking the dishes. Cake crumbs dotted the red-checkered tablecloth where Denise had sat. She brushed them up, dropping them in the plate on top of the pile.

"After you finish your college work, maybe then you'll find a nice husband this time. You and Jerome Lee were so young. Not knowin' what you were doin'. And he was always kind of stuck on hisself—" she stopped before saying more than she should.

"I'm not going to get married again, Mother."

"Oh, honey, you never know. You just got a bad apple that time. They're plenty good men 'round still—"

"You didn't get married again."

"Uh-huh, but not for the same reason *you're* not. Your father and I had a good life together. Short—but good."

She had been just a child when the tractor accident happened long ago. All she could remember was that he had been a tall, gentle man who laughed a lot and smelled of the outdoors and fields when he came home from work to lift her up to reach the sky. Sometimes, when the physical image became a blur, she would tiptoe into her mother's room to stare at the photograph of him—a handsome, Creole-looking man with a poetic face set off by dreamy eyes, dressed in the high stiff-necked collar and bold tie of the day. The picture was still there in its gold frame by the bed.

Renay carried the dishes to the sink, turning on the water and sprinkling in liquid soap. The television sounds of hoofbeats and Indian yells punctuated by sporadic gunshots floated back to the kitchen, filling the silence of their thoughts.

"I'll do the dishes," Renay's mother stopped her. "You had a long trip and Fran'll be here pretty soon."

Renay looked at the electric teapot above the stove. Seven o'clock. She had to call Terry. "At least let me put the food up for you." She covered the ham with foil and put it in the slightly yellowing refrigerator. It would be nice if she could surprise her with a new one for Christmas.

Fran came over with a bottle of White Horse and all the latest town gossip. They sat in the bedroom so Denise could watch television. Fran looked contented and relaxed as she talked animatedly and drank most of the scotch.

"Like old times, huh? The two of us together back in the old hometown. It's nice being here for a visit, but frankly, I prefer my own little pad back where there're brighter lights and more happ'nings. And too, my parents aren't around to bug me. No matter how old you get, they never think you grow up." Fran winked, taking a long drink from her glass. "When I get back, why don't you move in with me this fall?"

"No—but thanks for asking me."

"Still with her?"

"Yes—"

"She's white," Fran complained. "I don't trust white people. They use you."

"Not all of them—"

"But why do you want to live with her?" Fran persisted.

"I *like* her. We get along." Was there a way to explain to Fran about Terry—her lover—to make her understand? How do you tell your best friend that you are a Lesbian? One declaration would end their closeness, for Fran would always view her in the new light. She would secretly fear her, mistakenly looking upon herself as a sex object and fear being labeled the same because she was her friend. Renay couldn't take the gamble. Fran was the link to her home and her people.

"Hey—wake up! We got to kill this bottle!" Fran shouted gaily, freshening her drink. "You suddenly acting as if you're at a funeral."

"Sorry. You know I never was much of a funmaker."

"Yeah, you always did take things too damn seriously. I'm going to see that you get some new life into you. We'll do the town—such as it is. I'll get my new guy and we'll party one night."

She didn't want to party. All she wanted to do was stay home with her mother and Denise. "I don't—"

"Nope! We're going *out*. You ought to kick up your heels some.

Enjoy life, baby, for you never know when it's going to end. Anyhow, I want you to meet Lazarius. Some name for a nigger, huh?" she giggled. "He wants to marry me. But who's not ready to be tied down yet to no man is me! Unless I can find a black Onassis!" she laughed, elbowing Renay. "So far, I'm having too damn much fun being single."

Half listening to Fran, Renay smiled and thought of Terry. What was she doing now? When Renay had called earlier, Terry had been writing.

Fran was standing up, swaying a little. "I'll call Lazarius tomorrow and see if we can't go out the next night. I like to give him time to get it together—" she laughed. "One thing I can't stand is a cheap man."

As a concession, she told Fran she would go with them whenever they decided. But the most important thing on her agenda was to find a piano—her mother came first.

The next morning Renay called up Miss Sims. Delighted to hear from her star pupil after so long a time, Miss Sims wanted her to come over that very day. Renay told her that she would bring her mother, who wanted to hear her play.

They left Denise with a neighbor and in the twilight dusk walked to Miss Sims's house. Renay remembered the many times she had trudged to the Saturday music lessons. On the way, they passed hollow-eyed men and women sitting on sunken porches in shaky wooden chairs, trying to absorb the listless August air peppered with tobacco smells from the factory before going back into the humid dark shotgun shacks to bed. Children played untiringly around them, screaming like morning in the dusk as skinny long-eared rabbit dogs slumped under houses and chickens pecked aimlessly in grassless yards.

Her mother stopped to chat with those she knew, proudly making them remember Renay. She was Sunday-dressed in her blue nylon print dress, tiny white hat and gloves. She believed in dressing right when going to visit people like Miss Sims. While walking, she kept up a steady monologue.

"Funny, Miss Pearl never got married, even after her daddy died. Folks thought that since she didn't have him to look after no more, she'd start thinkin' 'bout herself. But no-o-o, her daddy done been dead and all she did was take in a boarder—one of the teachers at the school. Right nice lady—comes to church 'casionally with her sometimes. Kind of peculiar—standoffish."

When they reached the house, Renay was immediately struck by how different it looked. Flowers had been planted along the path leading to the house, making it appear warmer and less aloof from the street. The blinds were not closed as before, but were open wide, and a tall decorative lamp with a round basket shade glowed in the middle window.

Even Miss Sims looked different. She seemed less withdrawn, and her movements and speech were more alert. "Renay, my dear, how very nice to see you again!" she said, embracing her lightly. "She was my favorite student." Miss Sims smiled at Renay's mother, whose face shone with pride.

As in the past, the house was impeccably kept, and Renay saw that in the living room there was now a large television and phonograph combination with stacks of records beside it. She didn't know Miss Sims collected records. The living room even looked lived-in, with newspapers and magazines scattered about. The house seemed more cheerful and less like a well-kept mausoleum.

Miss Sims launched a series of excited questions about Renay's music, her studies and what she had been doing. She had heard of Dr. Larsons at Waterview. As she talked, it struck Renay as strange that Miss Sims had heard of and known people outside of Tilltown. But she had gone away to school, even to a private high school, and had traveled abroad one summer—the only black in the community who had ever traveled abroad. Why shouldn't she know people outside Tilltown?

Suddenly Miss Sims stopped in the middle of a sentence as her eyes focused on the woman descending the stairs so softly that no one else heard her.

"This is Miss Louise Tremaine. She came here to teach after you left. Louise, remember my telling you about Renay—my most promising piano student?"

"At last I'm meeting Renay! I've heard a lot of nice things about you—" Louise, short, round and barrel-shaped with a clear olive complexion, was slightly younger than Miss Sims. She had a warmly attractive smile and inscrutable dark eyes that held Renay's in a long searching stare.

"And you know her mother—"

"Yes—we've spoken at church. I know you're happy to have your daughter home, Mrs. Johnson. Is it just for a visit, Renay?"

"A short one. My little girl is here and I thought it would be nice for all of us to be together."

"Indeed!" Miss Tremaine agreed, reaching in the pocket of her black slacks for a pack of cigarettes. A match folder was attached to the pack with a rubber band.

"Let's all go into the music room and listen to Renay play," Miss Sims suggested, leading the way. "See, Renay—it's the same little room where you had your lessons."

It was the same little room with the Steinway and its bench of sheet music. Renay ran her fingers up and down the familiar keys. Then she began to play for them, and played until Miss Sims turned on the lights, washing away the long summer twilight which had dissolved into a deep slate gray.

"We—" Miss Sims began and quickly stopped as if somewhat stricken by the word "—should have asked earlier if you wanted some refreshments. I was just so anxious to hear Renay play again. She's certainly learned a lot since leaving me. I'm very proud of her."

"What would you like to drink?" Miss Tremaine asked. "Coffee, lemonade—something stronger?" At the last, she looked hopefully at Renay.

Miss Sims delivered a short laugh. "Louise likes a toddy now and then." She glanced half apologetically at Renay's mother.

Because Miss Tremaine wanted a drink, Renay said that she would have a scotch—with soda if she had it. The others chose lemonade. Louise handed Miss Sims her drink last and sat beside her.

As they talked, Miss Sims and Miss Tremaine sprinkled the conversation with asides of "Isn't that right, Louise?" and "Pearl, wasn't that the time we—"

Renay could sense the warmth between the two women, especially by the spontaneous way Miss Sims's face lighted up when Miss Tremaine looked at her or attended to her needs. Miss Tremaine saw that Miss Sims's glass of lemonade was kept filled and that she did not want for another of the assorted bakery cupcakes on the table. Miss Sims seemed happy and Renay knew why. Had

Miss Sims faced the real reason for her new-found happiness? She and Miss Tremaine might live together for years in a close but sterile companionship, never understanding just why they were satisfied with each other. Renay was glad for them, and sad, for in a way the relationship seemed somehow barren.

Before leaving, Renay told Miss Sims she would keep in touch with her. As she and her mother walked down the flower-edged path, Miss Sims and Miss Tremaine stood in the lighted doorway. Miss Tremaine's arm rested on the doorsill behind Miss Sims, and a look of contentment was on her face.

Halfway home in silence, she heard her mother say thoughtfully, "They seem to git along right nice together—don't they?"

"Yes—they do," Renay answered gravely, wondering if Miss Tremaine would take another drink before they went to bed and how they would say goodnight.

CHAPTER 17

The night Fran and Lazarius came to take her out, they brought along a friend, Bob—much to Renay's surprise and dismay. The four of them went to the Ebony Lounge, which Bob pointed out as the only decent black club in town. The Ebony Lounge had a black-and-gold glass front with a candy-striped canopy extending from the entrance to the curb. The lounge looked quiet from the outside because the manager was strict about loitering on the sidewalk in front of his premises. The club was kept up reasonably well, for the town was feebly attempting to keep pace with the plodding trend of southern racial progress. Whites from across town frequently dropped in for a drink and to slyly find out what the "colored people were up to." The younger ones, who cared less, stopped in on weekends to check out the homegrown musical talent.

The Ebony Lounge was situated in the exact center of the

ghetto's gaudy two-block business district. At night the strip flashed whorish neon signs hawking the sleazy Ritz Theater featuring black films, the Consolidated Finance Company, and the stale grocery stores whose windows were chalked with prices of pig's feet and pig's ears and whose doorways were cluttered with dried brown greens and rotting potatoes.

It was early and the club had not yet begun to fill up with the weekend goodtimers trying to relieve the monotony of their lives during the last two days of the week—to most of them, the only days really worth living. The club was life: friends, companionship, gaiety, forgetting troubles and making out. All this living took place against the backdrop of the blaring multicolored jukebox panting heatedly of lost love, new love, holding love and making love.

They made their way through the semi-darkened interior to a black leather booth near the front. An orange-skinned girl with red hair came briskly over to their table.

"Baby, what time does the band start?" Lazarius asked as the others tried to decide what they wanted to drink.

"Ten o'clock," the waitress said, pencil poised impatiently over her order pad. This was her best night and her only concern was to get as many tips out of it as she could by speed and hustle.

"Scotch and soda—" Fran finally said, and the others echoed her choice.

"Man, we sure fixed you up with a real fine chick, didn't we?" Lazarius smiled effusively at Bob, smoothing the wavy hair combed straight back on his head. A diamond ring flashed on the little finger of his right hand, its glitter vying with the colored bar lights.

"Real nice, Lazarius," Renay's escort grinned approvingly. Shifting in the booth, he spread his legs under the table, accidentally bumping Renay's thigh. Instinctively she moved away from him.

"And she's my pal," Fran added, looking pleased about the way the evening was going.

The waitress hurried back, quickly distributing their drinks. Bob mixed the scotch and soda for Renay, and she thanked him. The act made her mindful that she should at least try to be sociable.

"Where are you from?" she asked.

"Raleigh, originally. I've been here for about a year. I came to work for the Tilltown Tobacco Company in personnel."

"Yeah—" Fran sniggered, "they needed a spook to sit by the door!"

"Not really—" Bob countered, "it's just that management is now seeing the need for a closer liaison between employers at the top and employees. I take care of the black workers' grievances, complaints and whatever."

"Any special reason for your getting the position?" Renay asked.

He shrugged, taking a pipe from his coat pocket and carefully filling it with Tilltown Tobacco. "I majored in business administration at Duke. Afterwards, I worked for the Tilltown Company in Raleigh and they transferred me here."

"The job pays damn good," Fran interceded. "Keeping massa's black workers happy. Sort of like an educated overseer."

"Now just a minute!" Bob's teeth clamped down hard on the pipe stem.

"Don't get touchy, honey. Just my joke for the evening." Fran blew him a kiss across the table.

"You're kissing the wrong stud—" Lazarius said. "Here's your man. Right here, baby!"

"Lovie, that's for damn sure!" Fran laughed, cupping the hand holding the flare to her cigarette.

"I wish you were going to be here longer," Bob said, turning to see Renay better in the dim light.

His voice was deep and cultured, tinged with a slow southern drawl. He looked very clean and antiseptic in his white shirt and beige Botany suit. His nails were freshly manicured, the white moons prominent at the base. She wondered if he looked like this all the time.

She tasted the drink and listened to Fran, who was blowing her musical talents all out of proportion. As Fran talked, Bob's eyes fastened on Renay with renewed interest and admiration.

"What kind of music do you want to hear?" Lazarius asked them, peering at the chrome-plated selection box on the wall.

"Anything you want to hear, lovie—" Fran replied, bending her head close to his as he read the titles. He dropped several coins

into the slot, and Aretha belted out her blues hit, *Chain of Fools.*
 The place was beginning to fill now, becoming more alive with sounds and people. A slim twig of a young black man, wearing a blonde Beatle wig and dressed in tight red pants and matching shirt, backed into their table. When he turned around, his clown's face of light powder and eyes shadowed with purple mascara loomed garishly before them.
 "O-o-o-o, ex—cuse me!" he apologized in a high effeminate voice. "But it's so-o-o crowded in here!"
 "Fag!" Fran muttered in disgust.
 "Somebody ought to take him out in the alley and beat the shit out of him," Lazarius snarled contemptuously.
 Renay felt heat suffuse her body. She should say *something*. Yet what could she say in protection of someone like and yet unlike herself? In a way, she was a betrayer, for she had been repelled by him. Her head began to ache. She was a stranger among her own.
 "What's wrong, Renay? You don't look as if you're enjoying our company." Lazarius pushed aside the ashtray filled with Fran's red-ringed butts and Bob's ashes.
 "She's just the quiet type," Fran spoke up. "Order us another round so we can get happy. Doubles this time while we go to the little girl's room."
 The small restroom bulged with women repairing make-up and relieving alcohol-filled bladders. A line had formed outside the single cubicle where hissing sounds emanated from wavering legs as broken rivulets streamed under the door. Two women in elaborate wigs stood huddled in a corner, drinking from a pint bottle of Gordon's gin. One took a long swig, gagged loudly and upon seeing the stares said defensively, "Stuff in there's too damn high. 'Sides, ain't nothin' but watered-down piss anyhow."
 "Isn't Bob nice?" Fran said, jockeying for a position in line. "He's the town catch. But I guess he's not ready to be caught yet. He seems to like you. I just figured he would. That's why we brought him along. You two make a real cute couple," she hinted, inching ahead in the line.
 Renay contemplated the cracked walls inscribed with telephone numbers and names and obscenities dealing with who and what to fuck. Fran was trying hard to be a matchmaker. If only people would leave other people's private lives alone. It was as if no

one were satisfied unless assured that everybody had a somebody. Fran's turn finally came, and she entered the swinging door, tottering precariously on her thick square high heels.

Renay waited for her near the washbowl, slightly nauseated from the urine smells blended with perfume and powder and the inevitable cigarette smoke.

Fran was alongside her again, washing her hands at the yellow-stained white bowl. "What do you think of lovie?"

"He seems OK." A facsimile of the other slick, money-heeled men Fran was continuously attracted to.

Fran smiled complacently. Because the paper towels were all gone, she took a Kleenex from her pocketbook to dry her hands. "He'll do for this town."

They had to nudge and squeeze through the milling groups to their booth. A James Brown record was playing, and he was screaming and crying about being in a cold sweat. The wailing voice rose higher than the smoke pressing to the ceiling.

"What'd you two have to do in there, lay an egg?" Lazarius wisecracked.

"We don't have zippers on our pants," Fran flipped back.

Two men approached their table. The short, heavily muscled one, dressed in the people's attire of blue denim jeans and jacket, smiled at Lazarius. "Hey, daddy—what's happ'nin'? Long time no see."

"Nothing shaking, Alunkah." Lazarius slapped a brother's handshake between them.

"You ain't been by the hall lately. We need brothers like you with a *bizz–ness* mind," Alunkah laughed. "If you dig what I mean. How we goin' to git that power for the people without someone like you with the know-how and *con–tact* to beat the system? Ain't that right, Lububu?" He poked his elbow in his friend's side.

"Tha's right—" Lububu affirmed, standing like a pregnant pole in his loose dashiki. He sported a mighty, wiry Afro, and his small eyes were partially obscured behind tinted green glasses.

"And *who* are these f-i-i-ine lookin' sisters, brother Lazarius?" Alunkah smirked, tongue flicking wetly over his mushroom lips.

Lazarius quickly reeled off their first names. "You know Bob Stewart, of course."

Alunkah's broad ugly face tightened. "Of course—" he repeated mockingly. "We been tryin' to get Mista Stewart to come to our meetin's, but he just can't seem to tear himself 'way from that nice pretty air conditioned office." He shook his head in a slow exaggerated motion. "Maybe it's just too hot down where we are. Huh, Lububu?"

"Right on—" Lububu sanctioned without moving his lips.

"Well, brothers and sisters, have fun. Come see us now, Lazarius." Alunkah and Lububu gave the black power salute in parting as they disappeared into the crowd.

Bob concentrated on his drink as Lazarius noted cheerfully: "The band's on!"

Five musicians stepped onto the dime-sized stage behind the bar where a drum and amplifier were already set up. Young and lean, they gazed out into the well of their audience with half-sleepy pinpointed eyes. The leader came to the front and flexed his knees in the skin-tight plaid sharkskin pants. He welcomed the ladiee-e-s and gen-el-men and hoped they dug his group, the Youngbloods.

Without further ado, the drummer, guitarist, saxophone player and bassist struck one crushing dissonant sound and broke into their first ear-splitting number, the guitarist leading the herd.

They sipped their drinks and gave their full attention to the band. Before they had finished the round, the waitress was back again eyeing their not-yet-emptied glasses. "Y'all ready for another?"

"Sure," Bob said, reaching for his wallet.

The music rocked the room, bouncing off the walls and tables like huge hard marbles. The leader was screaming in the microphone, holding and twisting it like the neck of a poisonous snake:

> Babie babie babi-i-e-e
> Ah got what you ne-e-e-ed
> After you get this
> You ain't go'na ne-e-d
> No mor-r-r-re
> Ah-i-i-e-e-e!

The music was asphalt to Renay's trained ears, but the onlookers were apparently enjoying it, for they ad-libbed to the words, shouted "Yeah-h-h, work, work, work!" and gyrated as best they could on the small floor and at the tables.

The waitress brought the drinks, left the other glasses they hadn't finished, and waited. "Here you go, baby," Lazarius said, handing her a generous tip.

The waitress fluttered her false lashes at the bill, shoving it into the uniform pocket where loose change rattled like dice. She mumbled something indistinguishable and hurried off.

"Anybody hungry?" Bob asked.

"I am!" Fran said over her glass.

"After we finish these drinks, we'll go over to Ma's Stewpot," Lazarius said. "She's got the best soul food in town."

"Maybe they'd rather go to Kelley's." Bob looked uncertainly at the women.

"Nope. No white folks' restaurant tonight." Fran shook her head negatively. "Soul food'll straighten us right up!"

Inside the car, they had more drinks from a pint of Chivas Regal Lazarius kept in the glove compartment. The drinks were iceless, strong and served in paper cups. In the back seat, Bob put his arm casually around Renay. As they passed streetlights, Renay could see Fran's head furtively moving to catch the action in the mirror. The car's radio blared with an all-night rhythm and blues station featuring a jive-talking disk jockey constantly limelighting himself as Daddy Soul Motion.

With pride and ease Lazarius drove his big new white Roadmaster Buick with its red upholstery, bucket seats, push-button windows, stereo tape deck, FM radio, and air conditioning. He braked for a red light, then unexpectedly shot off in a proud show of horsepower, jutting ahead of a late model Ford in the left lane.

"Hah—hah! See me beat that white son-of-a-bitch back there!" he shouted triumphantly. "White bastard ought to get that trap off the road. Think I'll get a hog next time."

He swerved into a dimly lighted street in a deteriorating residential section and parked in front of a storefront restaurant hemmed by a crumbling brick apartment building and a garbage-strewn vacant lot. When Ma's Stewpot was crowded, the lot was used for parking. A white light burned faintly outside the door. Only the grubby window with Ma's Stewpot crudely painted on it made the restaurant's identity known.

The small room was dingy gray with cracked linoleum, a curved, scarred counter with sticky mustard and catsup shakers, and wooden tables that looked abandoned from various kitchens. The air was fetid with smells of leftover food, grease and coffee.

"Don't let the place fool you," Lazarius said, leading them to a table. "The food's great. Ma's just too cheap to fix the joint up."

"I still say if you'd rather go to Kelley's—" Bob said, looking at Renay.

"No, no, this is fine," she assured him, not wanting to interfere with their choice. It had been a long time since she had been to a place like this. It was like coming from one world to another where both were familiar.

A skinny, sullen waitress slouched to their table. The two top buttons of her off-white uniform were missing, exposing a faded pink slip. She was disgruntled because it was nearly midnight and the hungry drunks would soon be crowding in to feed their whiskey after the joints closed.

The waitress tossed a greasy handprinted menu which landed in front of Lazarius. "I don't need this," he said, handing the menu to Renay. "I know what I want. A mess of chit'lins, coleslaw and cornbread."

"Ribs for me," Fran ordered. "And hot!"

"I'll take the same," Bob said. "What would you like, Renay?"

She scanned the menu, not really wanting anything. The evening seemed too long for her, enmeshed in frivolous talk, bad music, too many drinks and not enough substance. Her head had begun to ache again, and she was missing Terry more and more.

"Can't make up your mind?" Bob smiled condescendingly.

"Oh, I'll have a hamburger, I guess." She didn't really care what she had.

"Hamburger!" Fran exclaimed, aghast. "You come to the best soul food place in town and order a *hamburger!*"

"Try the ribs," Bob suggested kindly. "They're usually good."

"All right," she said, looking at him and seeing Terry. "And coffee, please."

"*Now* she wants to put the fire out," Fran sighed, shaking her head.

The door swung open and a young tan boy sporting a black-power T-shirt came in with a stringy-haired blonde white girl in jeans. They sat down at the counter.

"Dig that—" Fran pointed openly. "Talk black—sleep white."

"What's wrong with that?" Lazarius parried in feigned indignation. "I wouldn't turn none of that stuff down if it was offered to me! Eh—Bob?"

"*Their men have little dicks!*" Fran's voice rose contemptuously.

"Fran—" Renay chastised softly, feeling compassion for the girl, whose face was reddening.

"You *would* take up for her. Renay lives with a white woman." Fran revealed witheringly, watching their faces to see their reaction.

Bob tried to contain his surprise, and Lazarius gave her a strange look. "And what's wrong with that?" Renay asked boldly. Lazarius smiled thinly.

Suddenly all broke into laughter—and the strained air was clear. None wanted the evening to end sourly. "Here comes the food!" Bob announced, happily changing the subject.

The waitress approached them, loaded down with a steaming tray of chitterlings, strips of red-brown barbecued ribs on thick white platters, round bowls of coleslaw and square pieces of cornbread.

A party of noisy half-drunk people surged into the restaurant. The waitress paused to glare at them before going to their table.

Renay tentatively tasted the ribs. They were hickory smoked and good, but she just wasn't hungry. She stirred the hot coffee that had suddenly become a mirage of Terry. Terry had told her to have a good time. Funny—she was here with her own, but she wanted to be with Terry, who was more than ever now a part of her. She lived in two worlds—neither black nor white but of their own making. She gazed reflectively at the girl talking earnestly to the boy. Even from where she sat, she could see the love in her eyes.

In the early morning hours, filled with the heavy food and sobered by the coffee, Lazarius wanted to take them to an after-hours place fifteen miles away, but Renay begged off. All she wanted to do was to go home.

Bob walked her to the door while Fran and Lazarius waited

discreetly in the car. "May I see you again before you leave?" he asked, taking her hand.

"I'm sorry, but I really don't have much time left. I have so many other things to do," she apologized. He was nice, but she had no reaction to him. She knew she would forget him as soon as she closed the door.

He was leaning close, and suddenly the thought jolted her that he was going to kiss her—the standard conclusion of a date. Before she could move away, he had her in his arms and his lips enveloped hers. She was repelled by him. He strained her more tightly to him, his hard male body strange against hers, not like the knowing softness of Terry.

She leaned against the door, breathing heavily, eyes closed for a blinding moment to shut out him and the act traitorous to Terry. Saliva formed in her mouth and she wanted to spit to cleanse it of him, to wipe her crushed, battered lips.

"Please—Renay—"

She turned quickly to unlock the door. Somehow she managed to say goodnight and thank him—for what? For the evening or for making her know that she could never go back to something like that life again?

Her mother had left the living room lamp on for her, and Renay knew that she was still awake by the line of light under her door. Now that she was home, the light would go out.

Suddenly the desire to see Terry engulfed her like a shattering storm. Her mother loved her and she loved her mother—but she loved someone else, too, in a different way. Love had many dimensions. Tomorrow, she would go home to Terry.

CHAPTER 18

When Renay alighted from the plane, she saw Terry's smiling face shining above all the others. The day was clear and slightly cool, and Terry looked well and happy in a white summer dress with a bright green scarf at the neck. "Renay—darling!"

People were brushing hurriedly about them, some glancing curiously, others indifferently, but all she knew was Terry's hair brushing the side of her face. Terry released her, and she suddenly felt lost with just the thin rays of the sun holding her.

"Come." Terry took her arm, excitement flushing her face. "We'll get your bags and go to the car. I collected the gang to meet you."

Vance was behind the wheel. Beside her, Lorraine was waving. Phil jumped out to take Renay's luggage from Terry. "Welcome home, stranger. We thought we'd leave you two alone for the first few minutes."

"Renay, that little yellow hat is just too *divine!*" Benjie reached out, touching her.

"Get in," Terry said. "We'll drop the boys off in town. They're coming out later for a little homecoming spread Vance is giving at her place."

"Chicken, you're looking as sweet as ever," Vance commented, offering a pack of cigarettes around. Only Lorraine took one.

"One thing, you sure travel light," Phil said, taking the key from Vance to put her suitcase and cosmetic kit in the trunk. "How's the dear old southland?" He squeezed into the back seat beside Benjie.

"Sunny and changing."

The car started with a roar, and Terry's fingers interlaced with Renay's. Vance drove fast, recklessly passing cars and going through caution lights at high speed. She looked shorter behind the wheel, squinting over the smoke curling from the cigarette dangling in the corner of her mouth.

"Here you are, fellows," she announced after an expert parallel-parking feat in front of their apartment house.

"Come in for a drink?" Phil invited, getting out with Benjie.

"No time." Vance raced the motor impatiently. "We'll look for you later."

Terry stayed close to Renay, fingers tightening around hers. "How's Denise?"

"Fine. She loved the book and reminded me to be sure and thank you for her."

"Did she want to come home?" Terry's eyes focused on the countryside flashing by.

"I explained to her. She seemed to understand." Probably because there was nothing to do but understand, especially when the decision had been made.

"Chicken," Vance said, her head half turning, "I've got a real good spread prepared in your honor."

"My God, Vance! Look out for that car!" Lorraine shouted, leaning forward. "If you don't slow down, none of us will be around to eat it."

"Never had an accident in my life," Vance snorted, slowing obediently.

"It's never too late," Lorraine retorted, throwing her cigarette out the window. "Renay, where is it down south they're having that freedom walk or something?"

"Mississippi."

"Has the south changed much to you?" Terry asked, resting her head back on the seat.

"Has it! In the stores at home now, they call you Mister and Miss, and even have the courtesy to thank you and say 'y'all come back,'" she laughed. "You don't realize, but to us, those things sure show a hell of an advancement!"

"The way they threw rocks and bottles here last week during that open housing demonstration, this city needs to start doing some advancing!" Vance pointed out sharply. "It was a near riot. All because people feel like they should live where they please.

Terry was marching and got caught in the middle of it. Luckily one of the bottles aimed at her missed the target."

"Terry?" Yes, she would do something like that. But, Christ, she didn't want Terry hurt. "I didn't know—"

"Oh, I had a personal score to settle with a landlord. Besides, I promised to do an article for the marchers."

"Humph! I suppose a lot of those people throwing rocks at the blacks would do the same thing to us, if a group of our kind decided to move next door. People are afraid of anything that upsets the status quo of their tight, comfortable little worlds," Vance deplored.

"I don't know," Renay said slowly. "At least it can be hidden. You can't hide a black face."

"What a morbid conversation for a day that's supposed to be happy," Lorraine interrupted.

"Morbid or not, those are the facts of life, honey," Vance told her. "We can't live happily by ignoring life's inequities, can we? Well, here we are!"

Renay and Terry climbed out, and Vance got the bags from the trunk. "We'll be over later. After Renay gets settled."

"Don't get too settled. You might not make it!" Vance laughed coarsely.

"You have a lewd mind," Terry shouted above the din of the motor.

"Home—" Terry was holding her and she knew warmth and happiness again.

"Terry, darling." Her arms rose up in an arc and formed a necklace around Terry's neck. "I missed you—I missed you—I missed you," she whispered again and again. The murmur was stopped by Terry's lips bringing a nectar of fire to hers. She closed her eyes, submerging herself in the sensations of Terry's hand making delicate little caresses on her neck, breasts and curve of her back.

The knowing weakness spread over her, flushing warmth and desire and excitement throughout her limbs. She didn't know if she was still standing or if Terry was holding her up there in the middle of the floor in broad daylight. But when Terry began to stroke and

Loving Her

knead the intimate hidden places, she knew that she couldn't stand here much longer like this with her desire aching for release.

"Terry—"

"Yes, darling—" The tip of her tongue was a petal inside the sensitive dip of her ear.

"I—I—can't stand it."

Terry's lips made dewdrops of kisses all over her face, and Renay's head fell back while heat as warm as the sun scorched her neck. Then, through the labyrinth, she felt the softness of the bed where Terry made her remember and feel and glow in how it was between them.

They arrived at Sherwood Forest Inn before Phil and Benjie, and Vance led them up to the apartment. The place reflected an artist's dream—or nightmare. The walls were a riot of colors—rainbows of blue, gold, purple and pink. Pillows of all descriptions were scattered carelessly about the living room and soft music stemmed from somewhere in the wall. The apartment resembled a stretched Pollack painting delineated with mod furniture.

"Who designed this?" Terry asked, surveying the room.

"We both did," Vance answered proudly. "If you look closely, the subdued colors are Lorraine's and the brash ones are mine. Put them together and this is what you get."

"Only the two of you could have thought of it," Terry said, laughing.

"It's very—well, odd, but pretty," Renay quickly added, touching a triangular white leather chair that spun around and around like a child's top.

"Well, who wants to be like everybody else? Come on in the kitchen and get a drink. Smell my spaghetti sauce." Vance lifted the lid off a huge pot where red sauce simmered and a pungent spicy odor escaped. "I have a conglomeration of stuff here. Look, Sicilian meatballs made with beef, Italian sausage, piñon nuts, raisins, cheese—"

Renay saw meatballs the size and shape of eggs. "They look good."

"Also to show off my culinary talents, I have some Jewish appetizers." She reached for bowls of chopped liver and pickled herring mixed with sour cream. "Work up a hearty appetite, girls. The food's here!"

"What, no soul food?" Renay quipped. "You should have consulted me."

"Damn, that's right!" Vance exclaimed. "Tell you what, chicken, next time, we'll get together and have soul night."

Lorraine walked into the kitchen, swaying a little in the doorway. She wore a pair of gold slacks and a matching headband almost concealed by her rumpled hair. An empty glass was in her hand. The smeared pink lipstick made her smile lopsided. "So you're here. Just woke up," she explained self-consciously, reaching shakily for a bottle. "Nobody poured one yet? Vance, dear, where're your manners?"

"I was just getting ready to mix them a drink. One of my expert ones."

"Oh, yes! She's an expert at everything," Lorraine muttered sarcastically.

"What'll you have? Pabst Blue Ribbon?" Vance imitated the commercial. "The stuff's all here. Bourbon, scotch, gin, wine—"

Terry chose bourbon and Renay scotch.

In the living room, Renay sank into the large curved white sofa until she felt like Alice falling into the rabbit's hole.

"Vance did all the cooking?" Terry said incredulously, passing the chopped liver on thin slices of rye bread. "Delicious—"

"Sure. Vance is like Duz—does everything," Lorraine scoffed, merging into a clutch of prismatically colored cushions on the floor.

"She's just jealous of my multi-faceted talents." Vance set a large tray of bottles and glasses and ice on the coffee table. "But there's one thing *she's* damn good at, too!" Vance leered facetiously.

Terry gazed at the array of bottles. "From the looks of all that Canadian whiskey, Jewish wine, French brandy, Japanese beer and what haven't you, you must be preparing for the United Nations."

The doorbell rang and Vance grinned. "Here's the UN now. Must be the boys."

Phil and Benjie came in a flutter of excited talk and kisses for everyone. "My God! I smelled the food clear down the highway. What *is* all this stuff?" Phil asked, spreading his arms in delight.

"Just look at all that liquor! Terry, you should have gotten us acquainted long ago."

"A simply *striking* place," Benjie observed, settling on the floor near Lorraine.

"Glad you like it." Lorraine moved a short distance away from him, lifting her glass to her mouth.

"Come on out to the kitchen a minute, fellows," Vance beckoned. "I'll show you some good eating."

As Benjie paraded ostentatiously out of the room, Lorraine's eyes narrowed at his yellow silk shirt and close-fitting egg-shell pants. "I don't know—" she mused, filling her glass. "If I have to be around men, I prefer real ones."

Vance came back at that moment with a bowl of pickled herring. "If you had a real one, honey, you wouldn't know what to do with him."

"How do you know?" Lorraine flung back, eyes flashing. "What do you know about me before—"

"For heaven's sake," Phil said laughingly, returning with Benjie and a handful of napkins. "What's all the shouting about?"

"She's a little off-key tonight. Now! Try some of this—" Vance handed Terry the pickled herring.

"And have your Alka-Seltzer handy when you go home. I usually do after these parties of Vance's." Lorraine smiled sweetly around the room.

"I say-y-y! She's in a bitchy mood tonight. Wrong time of the month or haven't you been taking care of business regularly, Vance, dear?" Phil smirked.

"Why can't you boys learn to be sedate like Terry and Renay? *They* don't go around making off-color remarks." Vance swigged from a bottle of Japanese beer.

"Oh-o-o, Phil! These chicken livers are out of this *world!*"

"Old Jewish recipe," Vance said, pleased. "Help yourselves."

"What's that salad I just saw?" Phil inquired.

"Insalata di crescione. Watercress to you."

They drank and talked and finally sat at the circular dining room table, where Vance served them. After eating, they slumped in the chairs and on the floor, full and slightly high from the continuous rounds of drinks Vance had urged upon them. The music piped about them was dreamy, and Renay wondered whether it was the food or Jackie Gleason's dulcet trumpet sounds making them sleepy. Benjie cradled his boyish head on Phil's lap, drink balanced on his chest, eyes half closed. Lorraine was the only one wide awake as she drank steadily from her glass.

Terry glanced anxiously at Renay, noticing the tired lines under her eyes. "It's been a wonderful evening, but I guess we'd better go. Renay's had a long day."

"Aw, not yet," Vance protested, opening another bottle of beer.

"She's beat, Vance. After all, she just got home."

"We have to go too," Phil said, yawning. "Got to work tomorrow. Work—the poor man's dilemma."

"Everybody's got to go and do something." Lorraine stood up, wavering a little, words slightly thick. *"Me*, I've got nothing to do. Nothing at all."

"Except take care of me, honey." Vance put her arm around her. "Isn't that enough?"

"You're perfectly capable of taking care of yourself," Lorraine snapped petulantly, shrugging off the embrace.

"Vance, sweetie, you *must* give me that terrific meatball secret so I can fix it for Phil."

"Everything was beautiful," Phil praised. "I can't remember when I've eaten so much."

"Not even in bed?" Lorraine sniffed obscenely.

A shocked silence permeated the room, silencing them for a chilled moment. "Goodnight," Terry said warmly, injecting life again. "Thanks for everything." She pressed Vance's hand tightly and smiled faintly at Lorraine.

"I'm going to buy a piano, chicken," Vance said to Renay. "Just so you can entertain us."

"She'll probably learn to play it before you get back. To prove how *expert* she is," Lorraine smarted.

"Come on, Benjie," Phil called. "Let's go."

In the car, Renay huddled sleepily on Terry's shoulder. "Home to bed," she murmured, burying her head deeper. "There's absolutely no place like home."

"I'm glad you feel like that," Terry said softly, rubbing her face against Renay's. "Go to sleep. We'll be there in a few minutes."

Renay was in bed before Terry, luxuriating between the cool sheets and basking in the familiar scenes again. The night air blowing through the window was chilly, and Terry had thrown a light blanket over her.

"I've almost finished the first draft of my book," Terry said.

"Good. Are you pleased with it?" Renay watched her as she put out her cigarette, squinting at it as if thinking hard.

"Yes. Mrs. Stilling is reading the first part of it. She used to teach literature at the university. Sometimes what I think is good, isn't. Like the first one. It only sold eight hundred copies."

"Well, you had eight hundred readers," Renay smiled.

The squeal of tires sounded suddenly outside as a car slammed to an abrupt stop. Downstairs, they heard a loud banging at the door.

"Terry—let me in!"

Moving quickly, Terry looked out the window. "It's Vance. Just a minute," she called down.

Renay quickly pulled on a robe and followed Terry to the door.

"She's gone!" Vance cried, wild-eyed, nervously running her fingers through her short hair. Her shirt had worked half out of her slacks, giving her a bedraggled tragic-comic appearance.

"Who's gone?" Terry turned on more lights to see Vance better.

"Lorraine!" Vance shouted irritably, as if the question were absurd. "Have you seen her?"

"Why, no—she isn't here. Where could she go this time of night?"

"Dammit, Terry, anyplace. She's drunk and in a nasty mood. She could have sneaked off with another woman or maybe a man—just for sheer bitchy meanness. God, I hope it's not with a man. I couldn't take that!"

"Sit down, Vance. Try to calm yourself. Renay, how about making some coffee?"

"All right." Renay left them to go to the kitchen.

Vance began to cry low, muted animal sounds, face hidden

behind the shield of her hands. "She must have hitchhiked into town with somebody—one of the customers downstairs."

"Don't worry. She's probably all right. Lorraine can take care of herself," Terry consoled her.

Vance took out a handkerchief to blow her nose. Renay brought the hot coffee in heavy, steaming mugs. Terry strengthened Vance's and her own coffee with brandy.

"Maybe she went to that place again," Vance theorized, holding her cup with both hands. "She used to like to hang out there until I made her stop. Hell, what's the name of that joint?"

"Margo's Corner," Renay supplied, remembering. And at Terry's questioning gaze, "She wanted to stop off there the night she went to the club with me."

"Jesus, that's right. Margo's Corner." Vance's fingers made a loud popping sound. "What a dump! Go with me, Terry, please. I've *got* to find her."

Terry looked helplessly at Renay. "I'll go with you, but finish your coffee first."

"Why does she do things like this to me? I give her everything she wants. She doesn't have to do anything in the world."

"Perhaps that's the reason," Terry said quietly. "She doesn't have to do anything. She's got too much time on her hands. Why don't you persuade her to get an interest again? She doesn't even try to paint anymore, does she?"

Vance was crying unabashedly again, her face streaked with tears. She looked like a middle-aged soft-faced man, her legs spread wide on the edge of the couch. "Think she'd like to do another show? That'd keep her mind occupied." Her eyes questioned hopefully.

"If she does, please don't criticize this one too harshly like you did the other. After all, she's no longer one of your students. And she's not a kid anymore either." With a sigh, Terry finished her coffee. "Let's go. Renay, are you coming with us?"

"You don't need me. I'll wait here. She may call if she returns and doesn't find Vance."

"You're right. Come on, Vance. I'll drive."

It was dawn when Terry finally returned, looking weary and

dejected. Falling heavily on the couch, she groaned tiredly. "Got any of that coffee left?"

"I drank it all waiting for you. It won't take long to make some more." Renay went to rinse out the percolator, measuring the coffee and sprinkling a tiny bit of salt over the grounds to bring out the flavor. Soon, the fresh perking aroma began to scent the kitchen.

Stretched out on the couch, arm flung like a child's across her face, Terry appeared to be asleep. She half sat up when she heard Renay. "Lorraine's left Vance," she began quietly, eyes fixed on her cup. "She must have guessed that Margo's would be the first place Vance would look for her. She left a note for Vance with that swishing bartender who subsists on intrigues, a cryptic little quotation from Nietzsche. 'Is not life a hundred times too short for us to bore ourselves?' The bartender said that she left with a stomping butch in a leather jacket on a motorcycle headed for Florida."

"How awful for Vance."

"Maybe good riddance for Vance; good riddance for Lorraine."

Renay picked up the brandy bottle. "I think I'll have a drink." She tasted the brandy, feeling it course down and start a tiny flame. "How's Vance taking it?"

"Hard."

"Perhaps you shouldn't have left her alone."

"She's in bed. I gave her some sleeping pills. She should sleep late. I'll check back later. I took her key to make certain I could get in."

A sparrow fluttered lightly across the windowpane like a quick moving shadow that could or could not have been.

"Whew—I'm tired!" Terry breathed, setting her cup on the floor.

"Go to bed."

"Don't think I can make it up there. Lie down here with me."

Renay glanced skeptically at the couch. "Is there room?"

"Darling, there's always room if you want to make it."

Renay slipped down, curling into and around Terry, burrowing deep into the soft cocoon submerging her. She could smell the strong smoke from the bar still clinging to Terry's clothes and hair.

"Have you ever had anyone leave you?" she asked shyly, not wanting to know but needing to know.

"Uh-huh. But in the long run, they didn't matter. Only one—"

Renay felt a sharp pain tug at her. There was another who had been important in Terry's life. "What did you do?"

"Oh, I stayed drunk for two weeks. Cruised. The usual things. Then, time mercifully helped. I snapped out of it. You have to keep on living until it's time to die."

And because she had to know: "Did you really care for her?"

Terry smiled slightly, understanding. "It wasn't like with us, not at all."

Renay's arm was across Terry's body, thinner since she had been away. Her head was under Terry's chin, and Terry's breath lifted her hair like a gentle wisp of wind.

"Lorraine may come back," Terry said. "Vance has been pretty protective toward her. She's still young and curious about life—" her voice softened. "The young are restless and fickle—like you will become someday."

"No, not like me." Renay pressed her mouth to Terry's to stop the accusingly harsh words. "There's a difference. I love you."

Terry gave a stifled cry. Then she squeezed Renay tightly, arms enclosing her in an exquisite pain. "Hmmm, just for that, I think I can make it to bed after all."

"I don't—"

"Why not?" Terry asked as her mouth touched Renay's forehead, nose and lips in short flashing kisses, lightning striking here and there.

"I don't want to lose it on the way up. Not any of it. Keep still."

"Renay, oh Renay—I couldn't get up now if I wanted to. You're making it too good—" Terry murmured to the form above her now.

"Keep still. Let me love you."

The sparrow flew to the top of the highest branch where he sang and sang to the morning sky.

CHAPTER 19

The days went swiftly, coalescing one into the other, and soon, the season began to change. Shoal clouds of birds made huddled masses in the sky, migrating away to another haven where warmth could harbor them again. The leaves were beginning to change from bright red, gold, and orange to a crisp dry toast-brown that fell faster as the cold winds chilled the bare thin bones of the trees. Fall had come, and the icy sheath of winter was near.

While Terry worked painstakingly on her book, Renay's days were occupied traveling back and forth to the college for the fall term. A letter came from Terry's lawyer, asking Renay to meet with him to prepare for the divorce hearing which had been slated for November. The attorney, David Howell, was a colorless business-like man whose watery blue eyes faded behind thick glasses. He had counseled and known Terry for years, and Terry thought highly of him.

In his spacious book-lined office, he and Renay went meticulously over the questions he and the judge would probably ask, and he advised her to get two witnesses to testify. She thought first of Terry, and then, Fran.

"I don't foresee any problems," David Howell said confidently, leaning back in his swivel chair. "Your husband isn't contesting it—we can't even locate him." He gave her a professional, reassuring smile. "The hearing will be closed. Just get a good rest the night before."

The morning of the court hearing was cold and dreary, a desolate backdrop for the day she awaited. She was slightly nervous, dressed as her lawyer had suggested in a conservative blue suit, white blouse and gloves. While they were waiting in stiff-backed chairs for the case to be called, Renay introduced Terry to Fran. The two women stared long at each other until Terry finally smiled and extended a hand. Fran barely touched it.

"I'm delighted to meet you, Miss Brown. Renay often talks about you."

"I've heard a lot about you too, Miss Bluvard," Fran said coolly, deliberately turning away to Renay. "Nervous, honey?"

"No. I just want to hurry and get it over with."

"We're next," David Howell said, gathering his sheaf of papers. Taking Renay's arm, he walked with her into the closed court chambers.

The hearing was brief. The divorce and custody of Denise were granted, and before Renay could even think about it, they were outside on the courthouse steps. The bitter air blew through their clothes and smarted their faces.

"Anyone feel like a drink?" Terry asked, hiking the collar of her leather jacket closer to her ears. "This is a cause célèbre."

"I could stand one now," Renay replied in relief, looking encouragingly at Fran. *Please say you will; I want you two to like each other.*

"Thanks, but I have some impatient sixth graders I must get back to. I only asked for half a day. Some other time, maybe." She kissed Renay's cheek. "The worst is over now. Good luck. Call me sometime." She glanced briefly at Terry before walking briskly away.

Terry's eyes followed her down the street until she disappeared into the throng of pedestrians. "I don't think she approves of me."

"Nonsense. She just has to get back to school," Renay said assuagingly. "It was real nice of her to take time off to do this for me. We've been friends for a long time."

"Let's go get that drink," Terry said. "I need it."

The November days were cold, but the chilled air was warmed by expectant holiday sounds that charged the air with anticipation.

As she sat before Edith Stilling's fireplace, Terry was buoyed with high spirits—the exhilaration of relief upon completing her book.

"Your novel, *A Forest in the Heart*, is based upon you and Renay, isn't it?" Mrs. Stilling said, sipping a glass of sherry.

Terry took the bulky manuscript Mrs. Stilling handed to her. "Are you shocked?" she asked gently, looking into the bright, snapping flames.

"When you reach my age, you don't shock easily. By this time, if you're worldly wise at all, you've either heard of or seen almost everything, and what you haven't seen comes as no surprise. I halfway surmised it. Your relationship today isn't unique, not with gay liberation challenging society. I think, however, that only the strong, unselfish and flexible can survive so-called unconventional unions. They have to think above and beyond." She reached for her glass again, thoughtfully regarding the dark-amber-hued liquid before putting it to her lips. "The reason some give against it is that such a love is abortively barren. It cannot produce the fruits of a heterosexual relationship. Remember Stephen pondering in *The Well of Loneliness*: What could a man give her Mary that she could not—a child?"

"I remember. But didn't Stephen conclude that such a love as she had for Mary would be complete enough in itself? Children don't necessarily have to be the only fruits of a marriage. Happiness together, just loving one another, can be enough. I've seen childless marriages in which people are completely fulfilled. I also know of marriages which have disintegrated because of the arrival of children. Sometimes with children the love becomes divided, and there is no time for discovery or for treasuring aloneness for its own sake.

"Have you considered the race factor too? I know you have. Living in this country, it is a monstrosity that cannot be ignored even by the totally deaf, dumb and blind. It is just one of the tragic facts of life."

"I don't *think* of race in our relationship—"

Mrs. Stilling nodded slowly. "That's understandable. Perhaps it's because you're both oppressed members of our society, and as such, you experience many of the same ostracisms, hurts and pains which make you compassionate toward each other. But one day, since neither life nor love is forever idyllic, she may become angry at you for something trivial, or at the whole white race for something done to the blacks. You too could become angry and, as the angry do, want to strike back. Ugly racial slurs could be wildly exchanged—nigger—honky. These words would mean more than mere flashes of temper in a homogeneous interracial marriage."

Terry watched a burning log collapse and flames shoot higher. "No, I really don't think so. I look upon her as just Renay. I've never uttered a racial profanity in my life. People to me have always been just people. Besides," she smiled, "didn't you say one had to be strong?"

Mrs. Stilling smiled back, pulling the knitted shawl closer around her shoulders. "Yes—strong. 'I would be strong, for there is much to suffer; I would be brave, for there is much to dare.' Harold Arnold Walter's creed." She finished her sherry, setting the glass down with a sigh. "I enjoyed your book."

"Thank you." Terry rose, the manuscript tucked under her arm. Walden got up on lazy legs, stretched and slumped back down again by the fire. "It was something I had to write. To say." She had mixed emotions about it. She liked it, but wondered if it, too, would end up like the other one.

"Of course you did."

"Goodnight, Mrs. Stilling. And thank you."

She returned home to find Renay, tense and drawn, talking on the telephone. She didn't seem to recognize Terry when she entered, nor did she move or say a word until Terry was beside her. Then she broke into a frenzied flood of tears as anguished sobs shook her body.

"Terry—Terry!"

"Renay, what is it? What's happened?" She reached out, drawing her into the protective circle of her arms in an attempt to stem the cries long enough for coherence to break through.

"Denise—it's Denise—" Renay's body trembled with the deep sobs tearing through it.

"Shhh. Now, what's wrong with Denise?" When Renay's cries became louder and more hysterical, she shook her. *"Renay!"*

The word was sharp as a slap. The cries subsided into low mournful moans as she burrowed into Terry's shoulder like a frightened rabbit scurrying into a strong tree. "My mother just called. Jerome Lee was in Tilltown. He found Denise was home and went to see her. He—he asked mother if he could take her for a drive. He was drunk, but mother didn't know. He—he had an accident. *Denise is dead!"*

"Oh, Christ!" Terry said, suddenly feeling Renay's pain lacerating her. She turned her head quickly away so Renay couldn't see her face. "How awful!"

Renay's tears now flowed like an ominous sea. Terry's arms tightened about her. "Renay, please try to get control of yourself. We'll go to Tilltown tomorrow," she whispered softly.

The next morning, Renay packed to go alone. She told Terry this was the way it had to be—something she had to do by herself. It was a part of her life that she had to close alone.

Despite the sedative Terry had given her the night before, Renay's eyes were puffed and ringed with blue circles of sleeplessness. Terry sat tensely on the bed watching her pack, nervously smoking cigarettes, only half finishing one before lighting another. "Are you sure you don't want me to go with you? I want to—very much."

Renay shook her head, not looking up from the clothes she was folding. "It's better that I go alone." She wanted to avoid explanations, embarrassment to Terry and small-town speculation which might affect her mother.

Then softly, like a whisper, "Please—let me go. If only to be with you—"

"I have to do this alone, Terry," Renay said tonelessly. "Can't you understand?"

"All right," Terry conceded grudgingly. "It's just that I don't want you to do it alone. You have me now. But if you feel you must—"

Renay kissed the top of Terry's head. "Thanks. We'd better hurry, or I'll miss the plane."

CHAPTER 20

When Renay came back, there was a strange aloofness about her. She appeared to be sealed in an impenetrable vacuum of her own, making no attempt to communicate with anyone. She remained taciturn, her face set in hardness. Terry was both puzzled and afraid for her.

For several days Renay stayed alone in her room, shades drawn to simulate twilight. She barely touched the food Terry carefully prepared and brought up to her. Most of the time, she wrapped herself in a deliberately self-induced sleep. When she was awake, she did nothing but stare at the wall.

She appeared oblivious to the downstairs movements. She could hear Terry moving about the house, her sounds in the kitchen, her answering the intermittent peal of the doorbell. She recognized Vance's heavy voice, Walden's bark, and murmuring hushed words of others. But she did not get up, and they did not climb the stairs to her. They deplored but respected the solitude that pressed her into the murky, dark unreal world of her own, where nothing existed but her thoughts.

Suddenly, after a week of isolation, she was struck with a grim determination as firm as death itself. Goaded with her fixed impulse, she went downstairs to get a bottle of whiskey, and was back again without Terry's hearing her. Then she began to act out the solitary pantomime alcoholics follow in their natural pattern of drinking. In an old bathrobe, she sat in a chair and began the unvarying act of pouring, drinking and pouring again.

In the beginning, the whiskey burned her throat, making her cough as the fire of it glided down to the bottom of her. After a long while and more drinks, every sinew of her body seemed needled by devil's claws warming her body with false solace. With each drink, her thoughts seemed to loosen from the tautness gripping them, unhinging a door that had been closed too long. Then, as if a bright beacon had instantly flooded her mind, illuminating her thoughts in sharp clarity, she knew what had to be done. For the first time in a long while, she wanted to open her mouth, hear her voice and speak words that needed to struggle free.

She got up shakily, a little appalled to discover her body lacked the firmness motivating her mind. Unsteadily she made her way to the door, where she mouthed the first words she had spoken for an undeterminable time, the word that was the most natural to utter.

"Terry!"

In a moment, Terry was there, tall and lean—like the tower of strength she had been missing. The gray eyes looking at her were clouded with worry that would not go away and that Terry could not hide.

"What's wrong, Renay?" she asked, taking in the bottle and the girl holding tightly to the doorsill.

"What's wrong?" Renay repeated, swaying with the burden of the whiskey weighing heavily down upon her. "Funny, you asked me that a long time ago. Remember? The first time you took me to your apartment, you asked 'what's wrong'?"

She backed away from Terry's worried eyes. "Everything's wrong again. I've lost my little girl. A sweet, intelligent little girl with bright eyes and dimples. She had a world of exciting days before her—the wonder of growing up, the discovery of love—each day a new jewel within itself. Why—why?"

"Renay—come—lie down."

"I don't want to lie down!" Her eyes filmed glassily with tears. Turning, she lifted the bottle to her mouth. Some of the brown liquid spilled down her chin. "She's dead—gone! A part of me. He must have done it on purpose, that goddam son-of-a-bitch, Jerome Lee!"

"No—no, I don't think that," Terry protested quickly, moving toward her. "Not to his own child."

"If he got drunk and mad-assed mean, he'd do anything. *He's alive, isn't he?* That bastard. That *black* man who can only fight his personal battles and frustrations with black women. Oh, goddam, goddam!" She fell across the bed, her body racked with heaving sobs.

"That's good," Terry said, caressing her gently. "Cry. I'm glad to see you can cry again."

"I thought I'd get drunk to see how it feels. How it made *him* feel. Me, I just feel sick and tired of the world. I'm not happy at all."

"You're not in the mood to be happy, that's why." Terry's eyes were anxious upon her, pleading. "Don't drink anymore. You're not used to it. You'll be sick."

Renay's voice was muffled against the pillow. "Do you think God's punishing us for this? The way we feel about each other? It's supposed to be unnatural, isn't it? Isn't that what people and books and doctors say?"

"They're changing—the world's changing toward us—" Terry looked long at her, the aged pain of suffering but not hopelessness in her eyes. "Do you feel good or bad about it?"

Renay moved to face her, trust yielding through the tear-brimmed eyes. "I just know I love you," she said softly.

Terry bent over her. "Then it's all right. It's only wrong to hate, not wrong to love." Her body warmed Renay, a reed pressed against her breasts and stomach. "Accidents happen. Every minute somebody's loved one dies. Life is full of tragedies; minutes and seconds ticking away misfortunes. I don't think certain people are ferreted out for tragedy although sometimes it seems so. I believe all sadness has a meaning, too—a significance that makes it not just a hallowed grave for grief, but a meaning somewhere for someone."

Renay's words were low, a droning monotone in an echoless room. "You should have seen her in the casket. Tiny, pretty in a pink dress with white lace. She in a casket and Jerome Lee in a hospital bed!" She laughed shortly. "Mother took it hard, blaming herself for letting Denise go with him." She rolled over and away from Terry, reaching again for the bottle. She turned it up, drinking deeply, feeling it reach her throat, gagging her, not staying down this time but trying to come up and out. She swallowed hard, forcing back the acrid liquid.

"Jerome Lee—Jerome Lee—bitter fruit upon my tree—" she sang and laughed. "New song—like it?"

Anxiety darkened Terry's face. "Why don't you go back to school next week? Get occupied. Stop wasting yourself."

Renay looked at the smooth wall where the strange things had appeared to her. "I wonder what he said while they were riding? 'I'm going to kill you, Denise, to get back at your damn bitch of a mother.' He could say things like that, you know. Or, 'Look at the great big tree, Denise. We're going to crash!' "

She screamed, a subdued eerie wail that made Terry know she had been in the car and seen the tree and felt the crash. "Talk, darling, talk. Scream it out. I'm here—" Terry cradled her in her arms, rocking her back and forth.

The sobs convulsed her body, a catharsis releasing an upheaval of emotions. Suddenly with a strangling, retching sound, she raised her body. She tried to rush to the bathroom as nausea filled her mouth. The floor came up, but Terry's arms kept her from meeting it, holding her, guiding her to the bathroom where the sickness gushed out.

Her mouth felt dirty, and she could smell the rancidness of her breath. "Terry—Terry—I'm sorry—"

"That happens. You'll feel better in the morning." She helped Renay to bed, pulling the covers over her.

"Stay here with me, Terry. I'm afraid to go to sleep. I'm afraid to stay awake."

Terry kissed her, lips touching to still the fear. "I'll be right here. Go to sleep."

When Renay's breathing became more regular, Terry slipped into the next room, not wanting her restlessness to disturb Renay. Exhausted from the long days of too much thought and worry, she fell into a deep, tired sleep without dreams.

She was surprised to awaken to a fully grown morning. It was raining, and for a treasured lazy time, she stayed quietly in bed, listening to the steady drumming on the roof.

Getting up, she tied her robe around her to go in and check on Renay. The door was open, and before she was inside the room, she could see the neatly made bed, and was as certain as spring following winter that a note would be propped against the bedlamp.

An unnatural calmness was about her as she went to pick up the piece of paper with the message in Renay's neat hand. She read the words without surprise, a nagging knowingness emerging from the dregs of her thoughts:

Dearest Terry,

I'm going away because it's best for both of us. If I continued to stay with you the way I am now, I would only make you unhappy. Eventually you would start feeling guilty too.

I have a check from the music publishers and some money saved up. I'm going back to school. Please don't try to see me. I could never forgive you if you did. And please don't think too harshly of me.

Renay

She squeezed the note, then slowly tore it into fragments. This should have seemed unreal to her, a scene from a fantasy play.

Her hands crept to her forehead, pressing the temples, acknowledging the winglike gray skirting each side. At her age, there was no need for hysteria, accusations, or self-pity. Renay had left as others had in her past—some with a word, others without—drifting sand through her heart. Only this she had wanted to keep and cherish, for it had what the others did not—fulfillment, love.

Despite the pragmatic thinking which cooled her at a moment that should have invited recriminations, anger, even tears, she felt an emptiness within as sadness made a tiny sepulcher in her stomach to catch the unshed tears.

She stared out the window. The rain was coming down harder, a cold freakish winter rain that ought to be snow. The day Renay had come to her had been like this.

She looked out the window for a long while, watching and listening to the sky's tumbling of tears. Her head tilted back, her eyes closed, and the corners of her mouth settled in hopeless defeat. She knew it would rain all day.

CHAPTER 21

Soon it was Christmastime and the downtown streets were strung with decorative colorful lights, tinseled trees, flush-faced Santa Clauses, harassed shoppers, and starry-eyed children with noses pressed into storefront windows, staring hopefully at the array of toys that performed miracles. Each year it was the same, and yet somehow it always seemed new.

Terry did not merge with the holiday spirit. Instead she stayed home, writing and taking occasional strolls in the brisk morning cold. Paying homage to the season, she had dutifully placed a small artificial silver tree on the table near the fireplace, garnishing it with red balls and a star. But she found this to be a wearisome task. Christmas was a time to be around loved ones, to share in the delights and fervor of the holiday.

The day before Christmas it snowed—a soft, fresh, clean snow which was especially beautiful because it was the first snow of the season, and too, because Christmas just wouldn't seem the same without it. The snow fell slowly in lazy drifting flakes from a pale gray sky, and from her window she could see it settling on the trees and grounds, as light and downy as frozen clouds of breath.

Her radio was on and the clear, strident young voices of a high school chorus singing *Joy to the World* filled the room. Hearing the music, she felt lonely and nostalgic as she remembered Christmases of other times and places. She reached for a half-empty whiskey bottle on the coffee table. She had been drinking more since Renay left, brooding and thinking too much. She *should* feel relieved and happy; her publisher was enthusiastic about her book, but not even that could banish the deep feeling of emptiness within her.

She sipped her drink, which did nothing for her mood. Even now with the radio on, the silence was heavy about her, thick with lurking memories. Perhaps she should get out—do something. She was reacting almost as Renay after the funeral, closing herself away from life. But wasn't hers a kind of funeral, too?

Her thoughts lingered on Renay—fragile musings that skirted lightly so as not to probe too deeply and open the wound. She had seen Renay once since she went away, not face-to-face, but on a noon television program that featured local talent. Renay had been interviewed by a smoothly groomed male emcee about her recently published song. Upon seeing her, Terry felt a mixture of pride, happiness and sadness, watching her give perfunctory answers to the stock questions. She had looked older, with lines circling her eyes and face, which was much too thin. Not once did she smile during the show, her actions mechanical and remote as if she would rather be somewhere else. Terry had wanted to reach out, hold and comfort her as she had done so many times in the past.

She shrugged off the memory, setting her glass down sharply. The chorus was jubilantly singing *Jingle Bells* in high-spirited unison. This was the time of year for joy, not sadness. She should get out and see her friends.

The snow stopped that evening, leaving the roads icy and treacherous. She drove cautiously to Vance's place, surprised to find so many cars parked outside the inn. The sounds of gaiety struck her like a sudden warm embrace as she entered. It had been a long time since she had been around people.

Vance's flat face smiled broadly as she moved quickly from

behind the bar. "Welcome, stranger! God, it's good to see you. I got a mob here tonight. Want to come upstairs where it's quieter?"

Terry shook her head. "No. I need to stay here with the noise and people."

"Be my guest. I'm damn glad you've finally come out of hiding. What do you want to drink? Bourbon?" Terry nodded and Vance patted her hand. "I'll join you. Got a new face I want you to meet." She winked.

Terry sat down at a small corner table. A large Christmas tree with the smell of the forest was at the front of the room. The jukebox played Christmas music rendered by a guitar-grinding rock group whose only words she could understand were "Santa Claus" and "town." The hard music and twanging voices were loud and bad, but somehow that seemed to help.

"Here we are!" Vance placed two tall glasses on the table. "Heard from Renay?"

Terry's head jerked up, a sudden cloud of anger and displeasure darkening her face. Why did Vance have to bring up Renay when that was the reason she was here—to forget? "No," she replied coolly, picking up her glass. The drink was strong and tightened like a fist inside her stomach.

"Well, they're all alike," Vance philosophized, sitting down heavily. "Drain you, get tired and leave. My motto now is the four f's. Find 'em, fool 'em, fuck 'em, and flee 'em. Pretty good, huh?" Vance laughed uproariously, slapping her trousered thigh. "Here comes my latest f now. Met her in town at the art museum, looking at Picasso. Want me to find you one? That's the best way to forget. She's got a friend—" Vance eyed her expectantly.

Terry saw a small, pretty girl with long golden hair approaching their table. She looked quite young—a Goldilocks without her three bears.

"Nancy, honey, meet my best friend, Terry Bluvard."

Terry spoke and Nancy said "Hi" in a tiny, girlish voice. As she joined them, her eyes settled and stayed entranced on Vance.

"Go get yourself a drink, honey, and then come back," Vance ordered.

The girl got up obediently and Vance's gaze lingered on the round firm buttocks outlined in the close-fitting dress. "Cute, huh?

She's got a friend who looks as good as she. All I've got to do is have her make a phone call," Vance proposed.

"Thanks, but I'd rather be alone."

"Who can have fun alone? Besides, what the hell do you do for sex? Everybody has to have some kind of sex life!"

"Do they?" Terry said coldly, frowning. "I hadn't thought about it. You know, Vance, actually, if you don't think about it, you really don't need sex. Anyway, what's sex without love? Simply a mechanical physical release that doesn't touch the heart or mind." She sighed, twisting her glass between her fingers. "It doesn't even lift the spirit."

"Crap! The trouble with you is you're too idealistic. You've got to be realistic to make it in this world. Renay was a nice kid. I liked her, but Christ, don't bury yourself because it went sour. Eventually, they all do. I don't know what happened—why she left—but I got over mine, didn't I? And when the smokes dies, you wonder what the hell all the shouting was about in the first place."

"We're two different people, Vance," Terry tried to explain patiently. "Maybe what you had wasn't like what we had."

"Bullshit! If it was all that great, why aren't you together now?"

Nancy came back with a whiskey sour. A group of merrymakers had formed a ring around the jukebox, trying to harmonize with Bing Crosby's *White Christmas.*

A tall, stunning girl in a low-cut black dress stopped by the table and smiled down at Vance. "Hello, Vance. Aren't you going to introduce me to Terry Bluvard?"

"Sure thing! Terry, this is Connie Hayes."

Terry smiled at the girl, whose purple-shadowed eyes were a deep fathomless blue. Connie Hayes pulled out a chair, her eyes holding Terry's.

"Connie's a singer," Vance began, going on to acclaim Connie's talent.

"Isn't anyone going to buy me a drink?" Connie asked, her gaze still heavy upon Terry.

"Of course. What would you like?" Noticing Vance's smug grin, Terry offered her a cigarette.

"She likes gin. Come on, Nancy, let's go get some more drinks," Vance said, pulling the girl away from the table.

Connie leaned back languidly, blowing smoke in Terry's direction. She had a model's face—features flawless, makeup perfect. Her voice was low and musical, and she smoldered with sex. "I'm an admirer of your writing. I read, among other things."

"Oh? That's nice to know," Terry commented, flicking ashes into the tray. She was beginning to feel weary already, bored with a scene she had played many times before. She could perceive how the conversation would proceed—the nuances, gestures, long-drink looks and the finality.

"You have lovely hands—your fingers are so long and slim."

Terry looked down at her hands, remembering. Renay had often remarked about them. *God, Terry, what they do to me.* White hands probing a golden sphere of which she could never seek enough. An ache curled up in her and died. "What?"

"I was saying that I've wanted to meet you for a long time."

Terry looked across at the perfectly curved red lips and back at her drink. Her cigarette had burned to a forgotten ember in the ashtray, and she reached to put it out. "Vance said that you sing."

"Clubs, mostly. You must come to hear me sometime." Her eyes narrowed over the curling smoke hazing her face. "Are you here alone?"

"Yes."

The voice became huskier: "I can't imagine Terry Bluvard being alone. We'll have to remedy that."

Terry felt the girl's hand brush hers and linger before she crushed out her cigarette. She stared at the twisted dead butt with the ringed lipstick crowning it like a small mouth. The girl's thigh was now warm against hers. She felt nothing.

"We're back!" Vance said cheerfully, unloading a tray of fresh drinks. "Christmas Eve, folks. Let's all drink up and be merry!"

Nancy giggled, snuggling worshipfully against Vance, unmindful of the curious glances around them.

Connie's leg shifted as her hand lightly grazed Terry's knee. Vance stared at them for a long moment before saying: "Want to go upstairs now, Terry? We can finish the party up there. The four of us."

Connie's eyes half-closed on Terry. Her perfume swept Terry's senses as she leaned closer, wanting another light for a cigarette.

Her perfume smelled like a bed of too-strong gardenias—Renay's scent had been as light as the breath of a rose. The lighter made a sharp clicking sound between them, breaking the mood into a lost moment.

Terry quickly finished her drink. "Thanks, Vance, but I think I'll go home." She stood up, smiling a stiff, polite smile at them, ignoring the surprise on Connie's face. "It was nice meeting both of you. I'll call you sometime, Vance."

In the car, she rolled the window halfway down, and the cold air swept in beside her like an icy stranger. She thought fleetingly of Connie who was like Jean who was like Lorraine who was like all the rest she could lump into one basket.

The car radio was saturated with Christmas music. Sighing, she turned it off, hearing only the low drone of the car's engine. The night was clear and star-stretched, the snow a bright white sheet beneath the glittering canopy of the sky. The snowplows had cleared the road, and she drove home quickly along the ribbon of night.

As soon as she unlocked the door, she saw her curled up asleep in the big leather chair by the fireplace. Renay had built a fire, and flickers of reddish-orange flames made tongued images over her face. For an interminable moment, she stood there staring down at her, rooted to the rug that held her feet imprisoned like weights on an island of caution.

"Renay?" The name came out as a question—she couldn't believe that the person on the couch was real and not a figment of her mind. "Renay—" This time louder, but not loud enough to startle her. She watched the eyes open slowly as a smile lighted her face.

"Hello, Terry. I let myself in. See, I still have the key." She held out her palm to show the key nestled there. "It's Christmas Eve, and I was so lonely without you. It didn't seem right, so I got a cab with a surly driver who hated bringing me all the way out here. But he did."

She looked very small and tired, and the shadows still darkened her eyes. She had cut her hair which now made only a flip above her neck, close to the tops of her ears.

"How are you, Renay? Are you all right?"

"Terry—darling—you always ask me that. I am now. It was a long, hard struggle with myself, but I'm all right."

Had she moved or was it Renay who came to her? Before she touched her, she had to know, for the knowledge would make all the difference in the world. "Have you come back?" She closed her eyes to hear the answer, not trusting that which might bring back the fear, suffering and need.

"Yes, Terry. I've come back, if you'll have me."

Now Terry reached out, drawing her close, folding her arms around the warmth of the body thin as a needle in her embrace. "I've missed you so much."

Renay's arms were strong around Terry's neck. "Merry Christmas—"

"I don't even have a present for you," Terry said, laughing a little shakily, voice not sounding like her own, too filled with the desire to cry. She hadn't cried in years.

"We're together again. Isn't that gift enough?"

"Oh darling," Terry murmured happily, drawing Renay nearer as if she couldn't believe she was actually there beside her. Outside the far-off church bells tolled their clear resonant sounds, proclaiming the midnight Christmas service. "You know what?"

Renay stirred, nestling into the contour of Terry beside her. "Hmmm?"

"I've been thinking. After you finish school, let's go to Europe. I want you to see Paris with me." Her hand found the dent between Renay's shoulder blades. "I want to show you all the exciting things—the Louvre, the Arch of Triumph. We can see the snow-capped Alps together, the French fishing villages and the old chateaus—people and cafes and streets that with you would become gloriously new again!" She brushed her cheek against Renay's. "I think it would help us both to get away for a while."

Renay's lips seared two warm petals in Terry's neck. "I'd love to go anywhere with you, Terry." Then softly, almost shyly, "Love me again."

Again. That which was stronger than words: touches, kisses, movements. Teeth clamped to stifle the cries that escaped when passion heated and blackness descended, shot through with flashes of red and gold lights—heaven and hell too, when the piercing ache swept through the groin like a knife.

Renay's body moved in a gentle, fluid surge beneath Terry. Rhythms of love, giving, sharing, mixed with the rising volcanic heat of desire as her body answered, called and held. Her arms hugged Terry tightly, then her hands slid down to cup the hips and lay as two veiled wings buoyed by a moving cadence. Suddenly she made a gasping sound as the wings became tightly locked arms once more. For an unendurable moment of frightening ecstasy, her body heaved to Terry's, fastened, quivered as a windswept leaf, and fluttered to earth again.

They remained silent in each other's arms for a span of time in which thought was enough. Two as one, one as two, waiting for the morning, which promised to be even better than the night.